THE LUCKY POLICEMAN

THE LUCKY POLICEMAN

by

Rupert Penny

RAMBLE HOUSE

ISBN 13: 978-1-60543-057-7

ISBN 10: 1-60543-057-9

Published : Great Britain 1938
Reprinted: Ramble House 2008

Cover Art: Gavin L. O'Keefe
Preparation: Fender Tucker

THE LUCKY POLICEMAN

I

HILARY PEAKE stared at the lunatic dispassionately for a moment, and then permitted himself to smile.

"How are you feeling, Simon? he asked kindly. "Is there anything you would like to tell me?"

Simon Selby did not answer for perhaps half a minute. He sat huddled up in a chair, one hand fingering his mop of flaxen hair and the other his foot-long beard. Only his eyes and nose were visible: mouth and chin and ears and cheek-bones could only be guessed at, since he had used neither scissors nor razor for three years.

"I feel well, Professor," he replied at last, speaking in a low deliberate tone. "Yes, very well. It's kind of you to ask."

Peake nodded, and repeated his former question.

"Is there anything you'd like to tell me?"

Selby shrugged his shoulders.

"I've been reading, and thinking, and drawing a little," he said.

"What did you read?"

"A book by an American—Rascoe, I think his name is. About Villon and Homer and Dante and people like that. He's very good on Milton—very good indeed. I'll ask Lavinia if I may lend it to you when I've finished."

"Thank you. And what did you think?" asked Peake; but Selby ignored the question, turning his head towards the window and the setting sun.

The room was small, and its only furniture a chair and table securely clamped to the felt-covered floor. The walls too were lined with felt, and the high window barred; from this the dying sun beyond caused shadows to radiate like spokes across the lunatic's body, so that for a moment to Peake's fancy he looked like some striped shaggy beast in a cage.

"Rascoe is very good on Milton," he repeated. "He says all the things I always felt at school, but didn't know I was feeling. I learnt a little bit off by heart—would you listen to it? '*Paradise Lost* and *Paradise Regained* are horrible examples of what may occur when a man with a displeasing type of mind happens to be an expert versifying technician in what is loosely called the biblical style.' Don't you think that's fine? Doesn't it make you feel lighter, somehow?"

"It might if I thought about it," agreed Peake gravely. He knew that Selby liked to be commended on his literary judgements, and he knew also that today it was as well to humour him, since the end of the month was approaching, and the lunatic soon due for one of his periodical attacks. Although in many ways a highly educated man, and an expert in his own line, the study of obscure mental diseases, Peake was almost totally ignorant of literature. He had heard of Milton, he knew, of *Paradise Lost,* he believed, and without realizing the dimensions of the task he was setting himself he made a mental note to read the book.

"And what did you think?" he asked once more.

"Oh, about a lot of things. When I was small, and my sister tried to stop me catching spiders. But I've told you about that before."

Peake nodded. It was unlike Selby to be so reticent, but consistent of him to mention the spiders: it was his way of saying that he did not wish to be questioned about his thoughts.

"And what did you draw?"

The other drew in his breath sharply.

"Nothing," he said decisively—"nothing at all I can't show you—I burnt them. They were not nice pictures at all."

Immediately Peake's glance went to the grate, normally unused because the room was heated by a steam radiator, and in it he saw a little pile of ashes. He frowned, staring at Selby with some surprise.

"You *burnt* them?" he queried; and at once the lunatic's eyes shifted, and his hand went instinctively to his coat pocket.

"Please let me keep them," he begged, in a strangely humble voice. "I haven't many left—only three, and they're so hard to get. You can't imagine how hard."

But Peake shook his head sternly.

"You must give them back," he declared. "Otherwise you'll get me into serious trouble, and I can't think that you would like that. At least, I hope not."

"Oh no, of course not, Professor. But I did so want to keep them. Oh dear, I suppose I must give them to you."

By now his hand was in his pocket, fingering something. Then he took it out, and peered slyly at what lay concealed in his palm.

"Please," said Hilary Peake.

"If you're sure you'd get into trouble if I didn't—"

"Quite sure, unfortunately."

"Oh dear, very well then, there they are, and now please go away."

Averting his head he held out a packet of book matches, which Peake took.

"Thank you," he said. "I'll remember your kindness."

And then, after a thoughtful glance at the lunatic's bowed head, he opened the door silently with his key and went out.

Esther Spence opened her eyes very wide.

"But of course not, Professor," she said emphatically. "Give Mr. Selby matches! I hope I should be the last to do such a wicked thing. Not that he doesn't ask for them often enough, though, to be sure. Never a day goes by but he doesn't try to get round me one way or another. 'Oh, Nurse' he'll say, as friendly as you please, which he isn't always, 'Oh Nurse, I thought I'd like a candle this evening for later, when it gets dark. Perhaps you could let me have one, and some matches, so I can light it when the dusk comes.' But as true as I'm standing here, Professor, never a match have I given him all the years he's been here, and how—"

"Very well, Nurse," Peake broke in. "I only asked, just in case: somebody must have let him have them, you know. When you look at him last thing, see what you think, and if necessary perhaps you'll sleep in the next room. I fancy he's got one of his bad turns coming on soon. How's Miss Vining? I haven't been along to see her yet."

"Just the same as ever, poor soul, full of slaughter and dead bodies and swords."

"That would be Ezekiel," murmured Peake. "Where's Bellamy?"

"I don't know for sure, sir. He was due off at half past seven, but I haven't seen him go out yet."

At that moment footsteps were heard outside the door, and the subject of his question entered: a tall dour-looking man, a head higher than Peake, and towering as much again above the dumpy figure of Nurse Spence.

"Ah, Bellamy," said Peake. "I just wanted to ask if you've been giving matches to Mr. Selby?"

"No sir, I have not."

The answer was quiet but positive, and the simple denial, Peake reflected, carried quite as much weight as the Nurse's volubility.

"Then that's all right: but somebody has, all the same. He had this in his pocket."

As he spoke he held out the almost empty packet, and Bellamy moved forward to look. Then his bushy eyebrows went up, and he gave one of his rare smiles.

"Have you asked the doctor?" he suggested. "He might know."

There was no particular animation about the words, but nevertheless Peake frowned. From Bellamy that was a pretty broad hint.

"Thank you," was all he said. "Shall you be late tonight?"

"No sir—are you expecting trouble?"

"Possibly—he seems a little restless. Let me know at once if you *should* happen to hear anything—but I'd be there first, I dare say."

"Yes sir," agreed the male nurse gravely, but with the suspicion of another smile: his habit of sleeping heavily was the subject of frequent comment.

Professor Peake, as he liked to be called in due recognition of his many American degrees, had at present only two patients in his charge: Simon Selby and Mary Vining, a young girl suffering from religious melancholia. That she would recover in time he had little doubt, but at the moment she was far from normal. Not once in the six months she had been there, however, had she shown any suicidal tendencies, and that was something to be thankful for, though of course there was no question of relaxing precautions. With melancholies there is always that danger: they imagine themselves to be too depraved to live, meriting only the basest tortures of hell; or they believe they hear a voice which tells them their time is come.

Yes, he knew the nature of Mary Vining's affliction, as a medical man can recognize measles, though her case had certain features which interested him; and scarcely a day passed when he did not wish that Simon Selby's trouble was as simple. The man was definitely neither an idiot nor an imbecile: he was not a cretin, nor a melancholic. He did not suffer from hallucinations, he was afflicted with remarkably few illusions, even fewer delusions, and he was not an epileptic. One eminent English alienist, invited by Peake to study the case, had declared himself still baffled at the end of three months. "He's a sane person who behaves like a maniac at peculiarly regular intervals," was his final word: "yet he isn't a maniac in the accepted sense of the term." "An intermittent maniac," Peake had murmured, and smiled a trifle bitterly, for after four years of watchful study he was still disappointed. He could not classify Simon Selby's complaint with reference to the known varieties of insanity, and he could not explicitly state in what respects it differed from them.

And yet, he consoled himself at times, it would be untrue to say that he had been able to do nothing for Selby: on the contrary, he had done a lot. After only a year's patient investigation he had discovered that his charge's periodic attacks could be considerably lessened in force if his hair were allowed to grow unrestricted; and, a little later, that a haircut had a more deleterious effect than a shave. By denying Selby the attentions of a barber he had succeeded in giving him longer intervals of comparative sanity; sometimes as long as two months. In general, however, at the end of every five weeks or so there came a day when his patient was restless and irritable; and a second day when he sobbed bitterly like a hurt child; and two more days when he behaved quite abnormally, at one moment stalking his shadow, and the next biting and scratching and tearing at the wall in a frenzy of uncontrolled energy. Sometimes, though, the symptoms varied: for twenty-four hours on end he would hammer on the floor with his fist, gently but incessantly, until he fainted from the pain of his blistered hand. If he were asked what he was doing he would momentarily look up and say 'Not long now—he's nearly deaf'. Once, too, he had done nothing but draw interlocking triangles on endless sheets of paper, beginning with small ones very carefully done in the top left-hand corner, and ending with a hurried scrawl of the pencil that approximated to a circle; but usually he was violent. During the rest of his existence Selby seemed almost sane. Meeting him at a friend's house, without his unnatural growth of hair, you might have thought him perhaps a little odd, but only if you were observant. At all times, however, he was sure to be collecting something. Occasionally the objects of his searching were harmless—labels from potted-meat containers, orange papers, photographs of Cabinet ministers born between 1850 and 1893; and occasionally, as now, they were a probable source of danger, which meant that his desires had to be discouraged. For three months it had been matches: or more strictly, Peake believed, match flames. Whenever he got the chance Selby would obtain a box—once from Peake's own pocket unperceived and once from his sister's hand-bag. He would conceal it until he felt free from observation, and then strike the contents one by one, blowing the flame out after a second or two and placing a dot in a note-book against the particular make of match. Peake, looking one evening through the secret spyhole in the door, had been horrified to see him striking and extinguishing and noting down, until the lunatic became impatient with a match that remained alight, and threw it down on the felt-covered floor. After that the strictest precautions were taken.

Peake paused outside another door, listened a moment, and then knocked.

"Come in," said a girl's voice, and a moment later he faced Mary Vining. As always, her appearance surprised him, accustomed to it as he was: she looked so utterly normal. It was not till she opened her mouth that she gave her state of mind away: up to then she might have been, to the ignorant eye, a smart young private secretary coming obviously from a well-bred family, her interests perhaps dancing and skating and golf at the week-end, and her soul, so far as she was concerned, no more than something she audibly blessed when mildly put out.

"Good evening," she greeted him. "It's nice to see you again, Professor—I was hoping you'd come before it was too late."

"Too late, Miss Vining?" he queried gently.

"Yes," she answered, her face suddenly tense and serious, and her voice taking on a sombre tone: the voice of someone who spoke truly of doom and desolation to unbelieving ears.

"The time is come, the day draweth near: let not the buyer rejoice, nor the seller mourn: for wrath is upon the multitude thereof. Yes, Professor, you had best be prepared. It's my duty to warn you, because you've been kind to me—very kind. I don't know what I should have done without you. Behold the day, behold, it is come; the morning is gone forth; the rod hath blossomed, pride hath budded. Make a chain: for the land is full of bloody crimes, and the city is full of violence.

"Professor, I must make a chain at once, and when I have made it I must go to the city. You never know—I might be able to do something, and I have had most definite instructions to try. It must be a long chain, and then I will go about looking for righteous people, and I will chain them together for their protection. Yes, that's what I'll do—but woe to the women that sew pillows to all armholes! Professor, that puzzles me a little. That's what it says, clearly—see, verse eighteen. 'Woe to the women that sew pillows to all armholes, and make kerchiefs upon the head of every stature to hunt souls!' Oh dear, I do hope there aren't many of them. You'll help me, won't you?"

Peake nodded sadly: she was so very earnest and bewildered.

"Oh, thank you: and you'll remember about the chain? I don't expect I'll be able to do it all by myself, because I'm wicked too. Often I simply can't think why somebody better wasn't chosen; but I suppose the responsibility is a kind of punishment. Do you think that's likely? I believe it must be. You will help, won't you?"

"I'll always do everything I can for you, Miss Vining,," he promised; and as he walked back along the corridor, and slowly up the stairs towards his study, he sighed deeply several times, wishing that he could do more. Long years of experience had not hardened him to the pitifulness of mental derangement: sometimes he felt that it troubled him more acutely now than when he had been young. Compared with others he might have done much, it was true, but compared with what still remained to be done, and with his own anticipatory hopes, he seemed to have accomplished nothing, and there was in fact but little time left. Supposing he died before he had discovered the secret of Simon Selby's abnormality? It might well happen, for he was sixty-five, and he knew that his heart was none too strong. For a moment he stopped on the landing, considering the matter. Would it not be better almost that Selby himself should die, rather than be delivered into the hands of some narrow-minded know-all who would cut his hair and shave his beard and tie him up in a strait waistcoat every time he became restless, as likely as not?

He sighed again, shook his head at himself, and went on his way. Perhaps after all it would be better if he, Peake, were to die first: at least, then, he could dream no more of Thomas Jefferson Jay.

II

EVERY WEEK-DAY evening, at eight o'clock or thereabouts, wet or fine, Hilary Peake shut himself up alone in his book-lined study and did at least two hours of steady work. He varied this self-imposed rule only on Sundays, when he began at 7.00, and in a whole year he would miss perhaps half a dozen evenings—no more. Mostly he busied himself arranging and tabulating the results of his day's discoveries; but sometimes, when he seemed to have found out nothing that he had not noted a hundred times before, he would sit motionless over his desk, thinking, his hands cupped over his ears and his fingers in contact with his scant grey hair. On other days he would read, digesting the latest theories, studying all the systems of psychology yet invented, re-reading treatises published fifty or a hundred years ago, and long since out of print, seeking always to enlarge his knowledge and clarify his vision. His only relaxation was to sip red wine at intervals—acrid *vin ordinaire* which sharpened his palate and—he believed—his wits.

Tonight, before settling down, he paid a visit to his assistant, Dr. Charles Wrench, and at once broached the subject he had in mind.

"What kind of matches do you use, Charles?" he asked, and the younger man looked faintly surprised. He was tall and dark, and would have been more handsome without the scar which ran from his temple to his left nostril. He was in his own private den, and Peake noted without disapproval that work was evidently over for the day: Wrench was busy with his stamp collection.

"Swans," answered the doctor, pointing to the box on the table in front of him. "Why do you want to know, Professor?"

Hilary Peake smiled meaningly.

"Can't you guess?" he suggested.

"Good lord, you don't mean Simon?"

"But I do. He gave me these tonight."

Wrench regarded the packet of book matches briefly, and suddenly coloured.

"I was wondering where they'd got to," he said. "He must have picked my pocket, I suppose. They're some I was given at Mrs. Montgomery's last night. I'm very sorry, Professor—I ought to have known better than to go in there with matches on me. As a matter of fact, when I said just now that I was wondering where they were, I meant I was wondering last night, when I got back. I couldn't find them anywhere, and I still don't see quite how I came to overlook them."

He frowned to himself, oblivious of how Peake was taking his explanation.

"They must have got mixed up with my wallet," he said at last. "That's all I can think of. Yes, and that would be how Simon got hold of them, too. I remember now I took it out to get at my pen, and I probably put it down on his table for a moment. I'll take care it doesn't happen again."

"Please see it doesn't," agreed Peake, without reproach. "You know my feelings about fire. I'm afraid Simon may be giving trouble soon," he added.

"Really? He seemed all right at tea-time. But I suppose he didn't have my matches then—not to himself, I mean. It probably excited him. Will it mean sitting up?"

"Oh no, I don't think so. I've asked Nurse to sleep in the next room if she thinks it's necessary—there's no need for you to bother. By the way, did I hear you say you were at Mrs. Montgomery's last night?"

Again Wrench coloured a little.

"Yes," he admitted.

"But I thought you couldn't stand the woman."

"I can't, but Nurse asked me to deliver a message, and somehow we just stayed on."

"And how is Miss Selby?"

Peake grinned suddenly as he spoke, looking for the moment years younger, and Wrench smiled.

"Very well, thanks," he answered. "She'll be coming up to see you some time—something to do with her brother's clothes. She thinks he could do with a new suit."

"Whenever she likes—she's always welcome. By the way"—looking round the room at the doctor's book-shelves: "have you got something about Paradise by a man called Milton?"

Wrench made no effort to conceal his surprise.

"I may have a copy somewhere," he said. "Shall I hunt it out for you?"

"If you wouldn't mind. Is it interesting?"

"Well, I suppose it might be if you like that sort of thing. Personally, I don't."

Peake hesitated, wondering whether to confess the depths of his ignorance. Sometimes he had an idea that Wrench found his cultural attainments inadequate.

"Would it take long to run through?" he hazarded.

"About a month," replied the other, with a perfectly straight face. "I'd as soon eat a cubic mile of batter pudding myself—aren't you sleeping well?"

"I see," said Peake. "Forget I asked you—it sounds as if Rascoe was right."

At a few minutes short of four o'clock that night the Professor's bedroom door was subjected to a furious banging.

"What on earth's the matter? he called out irritably, switching on his bedside lamp. And then, as the thought struck him: "Is it a fire?" he asked.

A voice shouted indistinctly in answer, and then Wrench came running in, his dressing-gown but half on and his dark hair tousled.

"Wake up!" he exclaimed, ignoring the fact that Peake was not asleep. "He's gone—Nurse just told me. Not a sign of him anywhere, she says—heaven knows what's happened."

"You mean Selby?" queried Peake sharply. "Get along down and look round—I'll be with you in a minute. Hey, wait a bit!" he added, to the doctor's disappearing back. "Is Miss Vining all right?"

"Yes—she's awake and thinks it's the end of the world or something."

"Let her have a light if she wants one—and tell them to make less noise."

His order was justified, for from below came a confusion of sounds: the growl and squeak of voices, the banging of doors, and the hurrying of footsteps that echoed on wooden floors.

Downstairs he listened to Nurse Spence's story, while Bellamy and Wrench searched every possible hiding-place, and the maids clustered together nervously in the kitchens. She had not after all slept in the room adjoining Selby's, since he had seemed quiet enough at half past ten. She reminded Peake that he had given her permission to use her own judgement, and to this he agreed. Well, she said, about quarter to four something woke her. What it could have been she didn't know, but wide awake she was in a trice, and out of bed listening. Her first thought, as was only natural, was for her patients, especially Mr. Selby, and she came downstairs on tip-toe. She went along first to Miss Vining's room, it being on her way, and looked through the sliding grille in the door, but the girl was fast asleep. She then continued down the long corridor to Mr. Selby, and she gave him her word that if she had been less observant she might easily have been taken in by the dummy on the bed, considering the poor light from that Woolworth's slow-burning bulb. But she was never one to let her eyes deceive her, and she was in that room like a flash. The first thing that attracted her attention, once she was satisfied that the bed indeed lacked a human occupant, was the window: wide open it was, and two of the outside bars ripped away. She looked out, but could see nothing, and had not wasted a moment in running upstairs again to tell Dr. Wrench.

"Thank you," said Peake, frowning still more heavily, and went immediately to Selby's room, switching on the central light from outside. Before entering, however, he tried the glass-panelled door at the end of the corridor a few yards away, but found it locked and bolted. This led into the courtyard from which the house took its name, and round it ran a high wall previously considered unclimbable.

Next he examined the bars guarding the window of Selby's bedroom, and shook his head in a puzzled way: two of them were certainly missing. Then he heard footsteps behind him.

"Well?" he asked: but Dr. Wrench shrugged.

"Not a sign. I'd better put some clothes on and have a search outside. Good lord!"—as his eye moved from the ill-made dummy in the bed to the window. "I didn't see that properly before—how on earth did it happen?"

"I don't know. Either he was ten times stronger than I ever thought, or things aren't what they seem. We'll be able to tell better in daylight. Have you looked in the courtyard?"

"Yes—couldn't see a thing. How he got away beats me—that's why I've been searching the house."

"But how would he get in again? The glass door was locked, and he couldn't get through here without a key."

"Obviously not," agreed Wrench, rather shortly. "Else he wouldn't have gone for the window, though I'm shot if I know how he did all that. But there *is* another way in, if you remember: through the cellar, and up into the pantry."

Peake stared at him in surprise.

"What made you remember that?" he asked, with apparently irrelevant curiosity.

"Because I used the cellar as a dark-room last winter. The door's open, what's more—both doors were, outer and inner."

The Professor frowned again.

"You've searched the place thoroughly?"

"Very—I'm certain he's not in the house. He must have got over the wall somehow—that's why I think I'd better shove my things on. What are you going to do?"

"I don't know, quite: telephone the police, I suppose."

"The police? But surely you needn't do that yet. It'd be much better to find him ourselves if we can—not much fun letting a lunatic escape in England, you know."

Peake nodded.

"That's why I don't want to get wrong with them," he explained. "Incidentally, I hope you won't go telling them so airily that I 'let him escape'?"

Wrench grunted.

"You know I didn't mean it that way," he muttered. "But it's no good standing here—if he's legging it across country we ought to be after him."

"And have you got the slightest idea what you're going to do if he isn't in the gardens?" asked the older man. "Just stand outside the gate and whistle, or what? No, I'm sorry—I guess I shouldn't have said that. I'm worried, Charles."

Wrench smiled unexpectedly.

"So am I," he confessed. "I can't help feeling that if I hadn't been so beastly careless about those matches, maybe this wouldn't have happened."

"Oh, nonsense—you've nothing to blame yourself for. I don't understand about that window, though, and I shall want to know who left the cellar door open. Where's Bellamy?"

"Gone to dress. Will you be coming too?"

"No—somebody ought to stay here, just in case he turns up."

III

DICKIE DONOVAN, crime correspondent for the *Evening Sentinel,* stretched his long legs over one of Chief-Inspector Beale's arm-chairs, and sighed contentedly.

"You've got nice habits for a policeman," he said: "free beer, free cigarettes, and a touching faith in human nature."

Beale's grey eyes twinkled. He was in his own rooms, with work finished for the day, and he was glad to see Dickie, who was often useful and always good company.

"The beer I grudge," he remarked, "the cigarettes were a present from a misguided aunt, and the faith is imaginary. What gave you that idea all of a sudden?"

Dickie waved his hand towards the mantel-piece.

"That ivory ornament is worth at least forty pounds," he declared. "You know I'm keen on ivories, you can rest assured I'm human, whatever you'd like to think, and for all you know I mightn't be as honest as I look."

"You could hardly help it," demurred Beale. "And anyway, it's insured: the fellow who gave it to me enclosed a policy. Thoughtful, don't you think?"

"Very. For forty pounds?"

"No, for seventy-five," was the almost apologetic answer. "A present from old Reiner, if you must know."

"The American meat king?"

"The American bully-beef manufacturer."

"But how and why? Are policemen allowed to receive presents?"

"Certainly, so long as they aren't bribes. This wasn't—I happened to find his wallet in Hyde Park. Quite like a fairy-story, isn't it?"

"But not quite like you, surely? I mean, to accept a very glorified tip for doing nothing but stoop down to pick something up."

"Oh, everybody stoops at times," said Beale. "Problem: when does the honourable man allow himself to be tipped, as you put it? Would you draw the line at Christmas and birthdays?"

"There's no comparison."

"But why not? All you're grumbling at is that I didn't do anything to deserve that ivory. What do I do on my birthday, then?"

"Same thing—nothing. But there's still no comparison—unless you'd accept a birthday present from a stranger."

"And what would be the grounds for refusing one?"

"Darned if I know," said Dickie, after thought. "It just doesn't seem natural, that's all."

"You mean there's no apparent reason why any stranger should dream of giving you anything, and consequently you'd suspect a trick? But in this case there was a reason. Reiner was grateful because I'd found his wallet: he *wanted* to make me a present. Maybe you wouldn't understand that, though."

"Now now, nasty! But how do you know he wanted to?"

"Simply because he did. He needn't have done, you know, even if only because I'm a policeman, and paid good money—not much of it, but good—to keep my eyes open, on duty or off. Yet he went to all the trouble of finding out my name, buying that ivory, getting it insured, and duly sending it to me with a very friendly little note saying how hurt he'd be if I didn't accept it. Why should I hurt him? Why shouldn't I bow three times to the goddess of luck, and let everybody feel pleased? What you're upset about is that I found the wallet and you didn't."

Dickie acknowledged the truth of this readily.

"I must spend more time in the Park," he said. "There ought to be a lot of rich Americans over here for the Coronation. And talking of Americans, did you see that Hilary Peake's in the news again?"

Beale shook his head.

"Man or woman?" he asked simply; and Dickie stared.

"You never heard of Hilary Peake?" he suggested incredulously.

"I may have done, but I can't remember everything."

"Well, don't go letting your betters hear you don't know who he is—they'll think you're getting withered."

"Then I really ought to know?"

"You really ought. Shall I tell you?"

"If it's interesting.

Dickie asserted that it was.

"And I shall spread myself," he warned Beale. "It isn't often I get the chance of picking you up."

"Well, I said everybody stooped at times. Be as long-winded as you like—if you're dull I shall doze."

"Right. The story begins in New York early in 1029 with the Jay family. You can picture them as terrifically rich, long established, and big people in the social world—very big people. Their only handicap was the youngest son, Thomas Jefferson Jay, by all accounts rather a limp sort of creature—not much brains, hardly any character, and a sight too much ever-ready cash. But for some reason or other he was always a favourite with old Mrs. Jay, the leader of the clan. She was his grandmother, and didn't keep quite the same careful eye on him that she did on the rest of them. The result, not surprisingly, was that he got into the wrong company, learnt a lot of damn-fool tricks which he thought were smart, and finished up, three years out of college, by running amok at a race meeting in Long Island. Before the Jays could intervene he was arrested, and within a week the whole world knew the truth about him. There'd been rumours—all sorts of queer happenings which seemed to have only one explanation when lumped together: and now here it was borne out by medical opinion."

"He was a black man in disguise," said Beale drowsily. "You can't fool American doctors."

"No, a confirmed drug addict."

"Really? Who confirmed him?"

Dickie sighed.

"You obviously don't want to hear the rest of the story," he decided. "And there was lots more, too."

"Oh, but I do. The next shot's a close-up of Grandma Jay receiving the news. Am I right?"

"For once. She didn't think much of it, either. In fact, she started moving heaven and earth to have it hushed up, but without success. You see, for all their wealth and position—probably because of them—the Jays had enemies. I don't mean thugs in slouch hats waiting round the back end of a hedge with a sub-machine gun, but sleeker thugs in evening dress, armed with intense aspirations towards the top of the Social Register. People who'd be more than glad to see the Jays come down a peg, so that they could get the chance of going up one. That's the way of high life in the States, so they tell me: it takes a comparatively long time to reach real altitudes, a couple of generations anyway, and about ten minutes to get to the bottom again. Several people considered that it was more than due for the Jays to go down lower: they'd been somebodies too long, and were dangerously well on the way to becoming the lord high somebodies. Interested yet?"

"A little, certainly. What did the rivals do—cash in on the publicity? I mean, exploit it?"

"Better than that: by devious hidden means they caused an enquiry to be started into the question of Thomas Jefferson's sanity."

Beale nodded appreciatively.

"Clever," he said. "Lunacy's certainly harder to live down than cocaine."

"Exactly. Anyone can have a weak character without damning the rest of his family, but even a loony's second cousin's grand-niece is looked at attentively if she giggles more than once in an evening. Yes, it was very clever: and chiefly so because it was more or less justified."

"He really was a lunatic?"

"I don't know about that, but he was certified as one all right—eventually. Forgive the inartistic anticipation. First, though, as you can probably guess, there was a battle royal over what still remained of Thomas Jefferson. On the one hand stood his family solid behind him, led by old Mrs. Jay and backed up by a small picked army of so-called mental experts all ready to depose that Jay's condition was due solely to over-indulgence in drugs, and that with due care he'd be as fit as they were themselves in pretty nearly next to no time. The only fishy thing was that none of them would specify a precise date for aforesaid recovery, or even an approximate one. The method of treatment was everything, they said, and of course each would be only too delighted to undertake the case.

"On the other hand, opposing, was an equally strong army of equally competent experts prepared to depose with equal emphasis that Thomas Jefferson's mental capacities, such as they had ever been, were now irretrievably ruined. Suitable nursing might possibly allay the symptoms to some slight extent, but that was the maximum to be hoped for. He was, and he would almost certainly remain, so mentally deficient that he was fit neither to vote, to marry, nor to be trusted with his own liberty. In other words, he ought to be labelled and incarcerated.

"Each side had its axe to grind—up or down with the Jays: but all the experts were cautious enough to give themselves a loop-hole. One lot said 'Of course he's curable, though it may take some considerable proportion of our skill . . .': the other lot declared 'Of course he's mad, though a miracle might conceivably happen . . .'

"Anyway, the upshot was that somebody started formal proceedings for Thomas Jefferson's certification, or whatever its American equivalent is, all the experts duly said their little pieces, and the astounding result was a draw—fourteen experts all!"

Beale grinned, and reached for his pipe.

"Be plausible," he reproved, "even if you can't be truthful."

"But I am being truthful," Dickie assured him. "Fourteen all it was, and stalemate, except for one thing—or one person, rather:

Hilary Peake. You say you've never heard of him, but over there he was as well known as, say, Sir Oliver Lodge here. He was known in England too, of course, but not so widely: with us it takes longer for a man like that to reach the surface of public recognition."

Beale sighed heavily.

"Why can't you put the thing into plain words?" he grumbled. "Peake is obviously *the* mental specialist of specialists—he simply couldn't be anything else now. If you want your white rabbit to be a surprise, you shouldn't spend so much time in brushing its coat."

"Who, me? I'm above such vulgar things as surprises," said Dickie airily.

"Nonsense—you were spreading yourself, as threatened. Kindly do it a little thinner."

"All right: Peake was *the* gold-star alienist, with an international reputation and all the rest of it, and during the whole business both sides had been trying their hardest to get him to play for their team."

"And he wouldn't?"

"No. He put his attitude towards the affair quite clearly at the beginning, and he stuck to it. 'If I'm asked by a competent legal authority,' he said, or different words same meaning 'to examine Thomas Jefferson Jay or any other person, and to give my unbiased opinion about his sanity, I'll do so, but I won't accept prejudiced instructions. In short, I'll examine him on behalf of justice, but not on behalf of either his family or their opponents.' "

"So everybody knew it was really a private fight, with Jay as the football?"

"Yes, though only the spectators said so openly. His relations were saving their beloved T.J.J., from a cruel and undeserved fate, and the other lot, represented by the correct officials, were safeguarding the liberty of the people, or the sanctity of American womanhood, or something equally high-sounding and irrelevant. Even the gutter urchins in the Bowery, though, knew that the real issue was the consolidation or downfall of the Jay family as social leaders."

"And the score was fourteen all," murmured Beale. "What did they do—agree to extra time and go out looking for seven other devils as ignorant as the first lot?"

"No: they chorused that if it pleased the court, both sides to the dispute desired the examination of the prisoner—that's virtually what he was—by Professor Hilary Peake, and by his decision they'd be content for the court to abide.

"In brief, Peake said the man was screwy."

"And that's the end of the story? Very nice too."

"On the contrary, I've scarcely begun. An offer of beer would come timely."

"Help yourself within limits—average ones, not your own."

"Thanks. Well, I now have to show how Victory left a Bitter Taste. The chief reason for this was a miscalculation on the part of the winners. You see, Peake made it plain that in his opinion Thomas Jefferson's insanity was due solely to his indulgence in drugs, and not to any family taint. That had the effect, public opinion being the queer shifty thing it is, of making the Jays out as martyrs to the dissolute habits of the wretched Thomas, and so far from sitting back with a smirk and watching them tumble from the high places quick sharp, their enemies were horrified to find themselves with a much smaller following after the case was over than while it was going on. Like that business in Galsworthy's *Modern Comedy*. 'Shall a noble and upright family be disgraced because of the sins of the least of its members?' people asked. 'Are we the sort of cheap nasties to punish A, B, C, and the rest of 'em for the errors and non-inherited infirmities of T.J.J.? No blooming fear. Stick by them, chaps—better the autocrats we know, and can always howl out now if they get too uppish, than them as would dearly like to take their place.'

"So the Jays stayed where they were, though on slightly less secure terms than formerly, while their enemies swore a bit and made the best they could of it. All the same, things weren't by any means satisfactory. The Jays were still burdened with a lunatic son to live down, and the others of course were quite determined that he shouldn't be forgotten. I don't suppose any other lunatic ever had so many kindly-worded enquiries made about him, or was so frequently referred to as 'Your trouble'.

"Coming from some people, that sort of thing amounted almost to open rebellion according to the Jay standards. They must have squirmed a bit, I guess, but they had to pass it by—they simply couldn't afford to do anything else. They knew well enough that their position was shaky, and what they said about Thomas Jefferson to one another in the security of their own opulent drawing-rooms, doesn't bear thinking on. Probably the asylum was the safest place for him.

"It hardly needs to be repeated that all this wasn't a state of affairs that could be tolerated a moment longer than was necessary, and the Jays tried their hardest to remedy it. You see, from now on they were fighting not only against their enemies, but against time.

If Thomas went and died on them, that would mean defeat. They'd never be able to clear themselves then, because a dead lunatic is even more damning than a live one: he just can't recover.

"They're a hot-tempered lot, so people say, with white smooth skins and dark smooth hair. The men inclined to be handsome in a rather unpleasant way and the women plain but striking. The characteristics persist too, strangely enough: lots of Jays of both sexes have married blondes, but the children always take after the important side of the family. With very few exceptions—Thomas Jefferson was one of course—they're quietly bossy in their manner when they're being nice, and bitingly rude when they're not. To all appearances, none of 'em cares a rap for anybody in the world except old Mrs. Jay. Mrs. Cornelius Jay, she is to mere acquaintances, and ignorant persons have been known to suppose that originally she came from another stock. They were wrong, though: she only changed her position when she married, not her name.

"How she set about assuming the leadership of the family I can't say, and I expect they've all forgotten, if they ever knew, but by the time her husband died, when she was fifty, she was practically dictator. Managing director, anyway."

"And how old is she now?" interposed Beale. "Don't tell me she's a hundred and four, because I've been imagining her as eighty-five exactly. You've already disappointed me once."

"How?"

"By saying she had black hair."

"Oh, I wasn't talking about her in particular—just the Jays as a whole. She's probably gone white ages ago, though she isn't quite as ancient as you're hoping. Today she must be about seventy-five or six, very small and active. People call her highly concentrated."

"In fact, she's much like the average matriarch in the average family novel. There nearly always is one."

"Yes, I know it's a standard pattern, but I believe there really are some in real life—the ones who get themselves recognized as matriarchs, I mean. The rest are just old women—somebody's grandmother and somebody else's great-aunt Lou, and a bit of a nuisance to everybody because she can't see to read and never learnt to knit and insists on answering the wireless back.

"Well, the moment Thomas Jefferson was whisked away to his padded cell the Jays began systematically to agitate for his release, and they went on doing it literally for years. Every possible method of approach to the problem was explored—same like our Government does—and all their resources of wealth and position and personal influence thrown into the armoury. Among other things, they set to work steadily to win over such of their enemies as weren't wholly irreclaimable, and to find some effective way of discrediting the rest. If one's to believe everything that people say, there was simply no limit to the pains they'd take over that last, either. I've heard it stated quite solemnly that they had a big part in the rounding up of the Porterville gang—hold-up men and so on, you remember. Nine of them were trapped in a barn and died fighting, and to everybody's surprise one of the dead bodies turned out to be the son of a rival family. His relations have never been able to stop proving he wasn't anything to do with the gang at all: corpses are known by the company they keep."

"Killed elsewhere and dumped?" suggested Beale professionally. "Chesterton's leaf that had to have a forest specially made to hide it in?"

"That's the idea, though there mayn't be much truth in it. The important thing is to remember that the Jays fought too, and fought hard."

"And one of the first victims was Hilary Peake."

At this Dickie Donovan stared for a moment.

"Not bad," he conceded. "Yes, he was in a way, though even the Jays couldn't do much with a man like that. He came out of the judicial part of the business better than anybody, and the only reason they wanted to get at him, of course, was because he'd decided against them: just revenge. At first they tried saying that in fact he hadn't been unprejudiced at all, but really playing ball for the other side. They didn't go far with that idea, though: it was so obviously untrue that they damaged themselves more than him by suggesting it. Even now it's not clear what they eventually did do, but the fact remains that about eighteen months later, in 1931, Peake suddenly threw up a first-class job as principal of some research department, and emigrated to England. He didn't say much about his reasons, but there was a general feeling that his decision was in some way connected with the Jay case.

"No"—as Beale frowned, "I can't produce any evidence, so it's no good glaring. All I can say is that Peake's never publicly contradicted the rumour that he was driven out. The suggestion was certainly made—by the Jays' enemies, of course, in an attempt to show up the nature of their activities.

"Well, I mustn't drag the thing out. When a rich and influential family goes all stiff with concentration for a particular object, they're apt to get somewhere in a few years. In 1934 they succeeded in starting a second official enquiry into the state of Thomas Jefferson's mind. There was none of the previous buffoonery, however. The court didn't fancy another draw: it merely nominated three eminent alienists to examine Jay, and report their findings, and on the basis of those reports a decision would be reached.

"Now that was fair enough, in the circumstances, and nobody knows what would have happened if the idea could have been carried out as planned. None of the three experts had previously testified, and as a matter of fact they were all foreigners, so nobody could accuse the court of bias. All seemed set for a just decision—and then an unfortunate thing befell, and threw the whole affair into a turmoil: one of the three appointed examiners died in a car smash.

"At once there were those who professed to see the hand of the Jays behind this latest development. They'd obviously pushed him through the narrow gate, people said, because they'd some good reason to know his report would be unfavourable, and unless somebody did something they'd doubtless go on polishing off mental experts until they got their way. Catty, that, to put things mildly, but there's almost no limit to what you can say about people if you do it the right way. One clumsy old New York dowager didn't, though. She'd got no use for knowing nods and meaning smiles and triple-edged remarks, but burst out with it in such a piercing whisper that somebody heard her who shouldn't have done. That probably saved the Jays from any real danger that these wild stories would start being believed. They at once took the matter up, and very soon the old dowager found herself landed with a peach of a slander case against her. She was thundering glad to settle for two hundred and fifty thousand dollars in cash and a broadcast apology.

"Again I speak literally: the terms of settlement included the stipulation that she should buy ten minutes' time on one of the principal radio circuits, announce full details to the press a week beforehand, and then in her own reverberating voice apologize from shoe to shoulder-strap. The Jays made quite a bit of play with the whole thing, especially when they gave every cent of the money away to charity.

"Well, getting back to the proposed examination of Thomas Jefferson: they weren't the only ones who'd been busy. Somehow or other their enemies had been pulling wires behind the scenes too: different wires, of course, and not in the general opinion quite such reliable ones, so that when the result be-known it was rather like a home-made firework that really goes off.

"One morning it was curtly announced that in consequence of the unfortunate death of Herr Professor Otto Baumer, his place on the committee of three would be taken by Professor Hilary Peake. It was further stated that Peake, although now resident in England, had consented to re-examine Thomas Jefferson Jay without fear or favour.

"Naturally, the family were dumbfounded: this was something they hadn't been even remotely prepared for. They made the most frantic protests, but all were over-ruled, and in consequence the betting changed from two to one on to three to one against.

"Now, Ted, what strikes you most about the position to date?"

Beale rubbed his pipe against his cheek.

"I know what I'm expected to answer, anyway—the uncomfortable position, to say the least of it, of Hilary Peake. If he now declares Jay sane, he'll be greeted on one side by screams of 'Turncoat!', and on the other by 'Sane? Of course he's sane—he's never been anything else, and it's taken you five years to find it out!'. Added to which, of course, he'll be accused of having been bribed or threatened into cooking his verdict, whichever way he decides. Also, if he says that Thomas Jefferson's still mad, he'll be snarled at as somebody who's made his mind up tight beforehand, either because he's too conceited to change it or because he wants to get his own back on the Jay family for driving him out of America.

"Still, you know, for all it isn't a nice position, I don't quite see what else he could have done but accept, once he was invited. Just think of what people would have said about him if he'd refused! Go on—what happened?"

"The two foreigners disagreed, and Peake again declared Jay to be insane. The court passed his decision after exhaustive questioning, which he came through well, and that was that."

"Stout fellow!" said Beale. "It must have taken a bit of doing. I don't suppose he'd be very popular with the Jays after that?"

"I don't suppose so: but it didn't matter, because he was away back to England by the next boat, and anyway they didn't have much time to waste on him. They were too busy looking after their own affairs, because for some reason this second reverse had exactly the opposite effect of the first one: it sent them down from the high places at last. Not toppling down in utter disgrace, mind you, but slithering helplessly, like a man trying to stay at the top of a greasy pole, and people hanging on to his coat tails from below and pulling."

"Did they slither right down to the bottom?"

"Oh no: the Jays are still somebodies, but now they're only one family group out of many. They've no longer any pretensions to being a cut above *all* the rest of the world."

" 'Sic thingummy gloria whatnot'," said Beale heavily. "Once translated, I believe, as 'Gloria was sick in the train on Monday'. It was a near thing, though."

"It was that. The general opinion—sorry to keep harping on one string, but after all I am a reporter, and one must pay homage to one's gods sometimes—the general opinion supported the view that if Peake had reversed his decision, Thomas Jefferson would now be a free man, instead of cooped up in some four-by-two asylum. Similarly, the Jays wouldn't have had to share their exclusiveness—they'd still be Supreme Court instead of just Congress."

"And similarly again, there wouldn't have been any future developments to look forward to. Or have there been any? When did you say all this was 1934? Then lots could have happened since. Did the Jays reorganize their ranks and start the good work all over again?"

Dickie expressed ignorance.

"They still make the usual periodic protests, of course, but there's been no tension in the thing for a long while. It's old and stale and out of date, and nobody believes they'll ever get Thomas Jefferson out of the loony-bin alive, and once he's dead they'll have his skeleton with them forever. In the end the family'll probably disintegrate and be forgotten too."

"And so that *is* the end of your story?"

"The end of that story, certainly: but it wasn't the one I set out to tell you—merely to explain just who Hilary Peake is. You said you didn't know, you know."

IV

BEALE looked at his wrist watch.

"The time is just quarter to tomorrow," he observed. "You've got fifteen minutes to finish the entertainment. Another mouthful of beer?"

"Thanks—and imagine I'm a hippopotamus, please. Well, what I started by saying was that Hilary Peake's in the news again. When he came to England in 1931 he bought a large house in the New Forest, and turned it into a sort of private asylum, where he could take a few interesting cases and study them at his leisure. He hasn't been doing the thing on at all a big scale, though. I think he had four or five patients at one time, but lately he's had only two, a religious maniac named Vining, and a man called Simon Selby. Mind if I look at my notebook a moment? I'd like to get names and things clear."

For a minute or so he studied several pages of his incredibly bad handwriting, and then looked up with a nod.

"Everything apple pie," he said. "Peake's household consisted a week ago of ten souls, as they say: the man himself, the two lunatics, four servants, a male nurse called Bellamy, a female one called Spence, and Peake's assistant, Dr. Charles Wrench. For some reason or other Peake's never bothered to take a medical degree, and anyway Wrench is chiefly interested in the mental side of the business. He's a youngish fellow, about thirty, and I believe he acts as secretary as well: types out reports of observations and so on. The nurses are quite ordinary, the Spence woman fully qualified, but Bellamy more of a handyman than anything else.

"The main trouble with Simon Selby is that nobody quite knows what is wrong with him. Part of the time—the majority, in fact—he seems sane enough, but every five or six weeks he breaks out into mental eruptions, as it were, and leads them a fine old dance. At least, he did until last week. The reason why Peake's in the news again is that last Thursday evening, in a manner as yet undiscovered, Selby escaped, and since then nothing's been seen of him."

Beale nodded.

"I remember hearing about it vaguely," he said. "Fellow's all hair or something, isn't he?"

"His face is—rather like Shock-headed Peter gone to seed, by all accounts. The reason was to do with some treatment that Peake was giving him, apparently—found he was better when they let his hair grow wild. I shouldn't think he'd be a pleasant sight to meet in the New Forest at night, and I hear the local inhabitants are getting a bit restive.

"Not much of a story, is it?"

Chief-Inspector Beale regarded his friend's innocent glance severely.

"What did you just swot up your notes for?" he asked. "To be able to say it isn't much of a story? Get on with it, and hang the time. Simple Simon escaped five days ago: all right, how? Who saw him go?"

"Nobody. His escape was discovered by the nurse—the female one—about four o'clock in the morning. It appears that he'd been a bit restless the evening before—he'd got hold of some matches from the doctor's pocket, and matches always excited him. Early in the evening Peake told Nurse Spence to keep a look-out, and sleep in the next room if she thought it necessary. She went along last thing, and decided he'd keep till next day; but in the middle of the night something woke her up, she immediately thought of her patients, and found his room empty."

"Why?" interrupted Beale.

"Because he'd escaped, dear man."

"No: why did she immediately think of her patients?"

"Oh, I don't know. She said it was just natural, but I dare say it was really a guilty conscience for not having done her job properly. He'd gone through his bedroom window, which looks out on to a sort of courtyard. There's a high wall round, and the idea is that he climbed over it and vanished into the silence of the night."

"With the help of what?"

"Nobody knows. He's supposed to have just climbed."

"I see; presumably knotting his beard into a rope-ladder first, though."

"Maybe. Apart from his bedroom, there's no entrance to the house from the courtyard except one locked and bolted door and another semi-underground one that leads into the cellars. This was later found to be open, or at any rate unfastened, but Wrench and the male nurse say they satisfied themselves he hadn't used it, and there's no real reason to suppose he ever did get back into the house."

"Nor much reason to suppose he'd want to, I should have thought. They were on the safe side in looking, though. How did they know he'd got out of his bedroom window?"

"Because normally it was barred on the outside, but two of the bars had been wrenched out of the surrounding stonework. That's another mystery: experiments have proved that he isn't likely to have been able to move them himself from the inside."

"But all Samson's strength was in his hair, wasn't it? And if he didn't pull them out, who did—Dr. Wrench?"

"Vulgar," said Dickie sadly. "You're not treating this thing seriously."

"I am: who pulled out the bars?"

"Don't know—nobody does. The police theory is that he took the opportunity beforehand to have a go at them from the outside, when he was at exercise, and no one watching."

"Is that feasible?"

"Provided you make him abnormally strong. There's no means of proving that he wasn't, though Peake apparently doesn't think much of the idea. It seems the only sensible one, though, especially as he often had the courtyard to himself for an hour."

"Press praises police: police collapse in dead faint. What's Peake's alternative?"

Dickie's face assumed a comparatively serious expression.

"I can only tell you if you promise not to pass it on," he said. "He's certainly got one, but it's inclined to be libellous."

"Oh, you needn't bother about me. How do you come to know so much about things, by the way?"

"A fellow I know told me—he was down there writing it up for a news agency. You see, the position's this. Selby's only surviving relative is his sister, and for the last year or so she's been living in the neighbourhood: cottage and housekeeper and all that. She moved there after the death of her mother, partly to be near Selby and partly to be near Dr. Wrench. There's quite a sort of friendship."

"Sure it isn't a romance?"

"It would be if it weren't for her brother."

"Who fights shy of him—the doctor?"

"No, she does—won't hear of marriage at any price. The handicap of having a lunatic in the family again."

"Yes: and Peake thinks she helped her brother get away, with or without Dr. Wrench's knowledge and connivance."

"Yes: press praises police again. Faint please, and then I can fill up."

"Likely to be anything in it?"

"Not a drop," said Dickie in a disappointed tone, holding the last bottle upside down.

"I meant Peake's idea."

"Oh. Well, I can't say, not knowing the persons concerned. I shouldn't expect so, really."

"Do they know what he suspects?"

"Oh no."

"Do the police?"

"Not from him—that's why you mustn't pass it on. Peake naturally can't do anything till he's got some sort of evidence, and at present he hasn't."

"Then kindly explain who says he thinks the sister had anything to do with it."

"Oh, there's not much doubt: a word here and another one there, so the fellow who told me all this says. You can take it that Peake does think that."

"And you're sure the only ways out of the courtyard are over the wall, through the cellar door, which was open, through another one which wasn't, or back through the bedroom?"

"Certain, so Wilson says: no drain-pipes to get in an upstairs window by, and all other downstairs ones on that side still barred. The cellar door ought to have been locked too, only it wasn't. Nobody's offered to explain why not."

"How high is this wall?"

"Twelve feet, about."

"And made of what?"

"Bricks."

"*Could* it be climbed?"

"Wilson says not without some sort of help."

"Anything else of interest about the courtyard? Any sheds or overhanging trees?"

"Nothing at all. The garage backs on to it on the outside, but the wall doesn't get any lower."

"Were the missing bars ever found?"

"No, not a trace of them, which is yet another mystery. They're about a foot long, and as thick as a walking-stick."

"What was Selby dressed in when he made his escape—night-clothes?"

"Must have been, judging by what he left behind: all his stuff made up into a sort of dummy and stuck in the bed. Apparently a lot of the doors in Balmer's Court—that's the name of Peake's place, and very nearly appropriate—had sliding panels in so that the doctor and nurse can see what's going on from outside. At night there was always a light of some kind on, too, which was how the Spence woman found he was gone."

"The dummy presumably not working?"

"No."

"Did Selby take any of his personal possessions with him? Or don't lunatics have any?"

"He doesn't seem to have had a lot. I think his watch was the only thing missing."

"What did Peake do when he'd satisfied himself that Selby was gone?"

"Telephoned for the police within an hour of the discovery, after it was certain that he wasn't in the house or grounds, and Wrench and Bellamy had gone off to look for him."

"To look where? In the New Forest?"

"More or less. They don't seem to have followed any special plan—just cruised about hopefully in Wrench's car. Of course they didn't see anything."

"And nobody else has either?"

"That's not quite so definite. Extensive enquiries have been made in the district, naturally, and the police have had half a dozen reports from motorists who think they saw or heard something that might have been a man lumbering about among the trees. It was always at night, though, and ten to one it was a wild pony or a wild imagination every time. But there is something else. The owner of a small house on the edge of the Forest, about three miles away, complained of being burgled, and the nature of the missing articles is interesting. The only things taken, apart from some loose money that was lying about, were food, a suit of clothes, a pair of shoes, a pair of woollen gloves, a cricket shirt, and complete shaving kit: brush, razor and soap."

At this Beale grinned.

"How very touching!" he remarked. "Portrait of a hairy escaped lunatic sitting quietly down by a forest pool in the moonlight and shaving off several years' growth with stolen implements. I hope the razor wasn't a safety?"

"As a matter of fact, I believe it was—why?"

"Oh, nothing, if you can't see for yourself. What did the suit of clothes have in the pockets?"

"Nothing—it was just back from the cleaners. About Selby's size, too."

Beale grunted, and Dickie eyed him curiously. Some train of thought had obviously been started, but the Inspector only grunted again when asked to explain.

"I never do other people's jobs for them," he said: "anyway, not when I'm miles away in an arm-chair—it's too easy to be totally wrong. Go and ask the coppers down in the New Forest why I sniffed slightly, if you really want to know. They'll be able to tell you if they're any good—it's obvious enough to me here, in my ignorance. Comparative ignorance," he added, to soothe Dickie's feelings. "Did he leave any fingerprints anywhere?"

"Apparently not."

"And tell me something else: couldn't he have got out through his bedroom door?"

"Not unless somebody deliberately let him. The door's got no handle, only a patent lock, and from either side can only be opened with a key. There are only four in existence—one each for the Professor, the doctor, and the two nurses."

"I see. Anything else of importance?"

"No. They've been searching for five days now, and they're no nearer laying hands on the man than when they started. His sister swears she's just as mystified as everybody else, and Wilson couldn't see any reason to suppose she wasn't telling the truth. Maybe I ought to say wouldn't, though, because that's Wilson's great failing. He always believes what a pretty girl tells him, and Lavinia Selby's extremely pretty—so he says."

V

MRS. MAYDEW re-read the short paragraph in the local paper, and pondered, her thin mouth tightly pursed. The date was Friday, May 7th, and the paper had only just been delivered; the paragraph stated that the lunatic who escaped from Balmer's Court on the night of April 29th had not yet been recaptured, although the police were actively following up clues in co-operation with Professor Hilary Peake, the American mental expert in whose care the escaped man had been at the time of his disappearance.

'Drat him!' she thought waspishly. 'I wonder if I ought to let Prudence go?'

Mrs. Maydew was housekeeper at Yewhurst Hall, a large country house just outside Brockenhurst, and in the absence of the owner abroad she was sole guardian of the female domestic staff. In her hands, temporarily, lay their safety and well-being, and it was a responsibility in which she delighted. She had never had daughters of her own to manage, and she had always been of a managing disposition. With Lady Cynthia at home there was not over-much opportunity to exercise her capabilities, her ladyship being a person of independent views and a strict disciplinarian; it was only in her absence, as now, that Mrs. Maydew could assume what she felt to be her rightful role in life. She looked forward for months beforehand to these opportunities, wished they were more frequent and of longer duration, and made the utmost of them when they did occur.

Her present problem was concerned with Prudence Hill's half day; called half by courtesy, though in fact extending only from three o'clock in the after noon till half past nine at night. Prudence was young, and good material for Mrs. Maydew to work on, except for a displeasing degree of self-assertiveness at times. She was inclined to be cheeky; she did not seem to realize that Mrs. Maydew deserved not only her respect, as being both her elder and her better, but also her obedience, and Mrs. Maydew was determined to teach her these truths. The girl had been there just three months as second housemaid—her fourth situation, though she was only nineteen. If she were not looked after she would never settle down to her proper station in life, the housekeeper had decided, but begin to put on airs and graces with the worst of them: so that it was an entirely altruistic action on her part to do the looking-after.

Mrs. Maydew's dilemma was whether or not to let Prudence Hill have her half day, and she weighed the points for and against with the delicacy of an honest butcher weighing meat.

There was no doubt that she would be well within her rights to refuse: Balmer's Court was only five miles away by road, and nearer if you went through the woods, and escaped lunatics were dangerous. It was said that he had almost certainly not come this way, but you could never be sure. Common sense, a quality of which Mrs. Medway believed she possessed an unusually large share, suggested that since he had not been found, after a week, nobody could possibly know which way he had gone. The road between Yewhurst Hall and the village of Minchley, where lived Prudence Hill's grandmother, was lonely in stretches, nothing but a dusty white ribbon winding between gloomy enclosures, and common sense—again—suggested that it would be safer not to let a young girl ride along it unattended in the dusk, with possible danger behind every trunk and branch, a hairy madman waiting to spring out with a wild shriek from every patch of shadow.

If Mrs. Maydew could have had her way, of course, Prudence would never have been allowed to cycle the seven miles to Minchley alone, lunatic or no lunatic, daylight or dark: but Lady Cynthia had laughed to scorn her hint that it was a somewhat improper proceeding.

"Any girl of nineteen who can't look after herself on her half day isn't much use to me," she had said. "And you know as well as I do, Maydew," she had added, "that if she wants to get into trouble—the sort you mean—she will, whether it's in the middle of the Minchley Road or out in the orchard when you're in bed and asleep. Don't be so disgustingly pre-war."

Nevertheless, Mrs. Maydew always regarded Prudence with suspicion on her return from her grandmother's, checking eye and cheek and shoe with a possible departure from virtue; and now, she reflected, it would be a gesture towards her own strict principles if she were to refuse the girl her holiday. Neither Prudence herself, nor even Lady Cynthia, if she ever got to know, could surely say anything in view of the particular circumstances.

And yet, there was another side to the question. Also at Minchley lived Mrs. Maydew's sister Laura, with whom she had never been very friendly, but from whom she hoped and expected, in due course, to receive money enough to enable her to retire from active work. She had continually in her mind's eye a picture of just the sort of cottage she looked forward to, with a little garden and a cat and all the day long to investigate her neighbours' affairs. She herself was sixty, but her sister was ten years older, and in the nature of things could not hold out much longer, especially as she had been almost an invalid since her last attack of rheumatism.

Often Mrs. Maydew had assured herself that she was genuinely sorry for Laura, and as often she regretted consciously that they had never got on well enough together for her to enjoy visiting her sister. But there it was; it took all sorts to make a world, and the fact remained, despite regrets and would-be kindly feelings, that she much preferred giving Prudence Hill a small parcel to deliver by hand on Fridays to making the journey herself by bus at the week-end. She saved not only the fare that way, but any possibility of unpleasantness. A small pot of home-made jam, a few scones, the week before last's illustrated papers: such little attentions would please the invalid far more than a two-hour visit from herself, and she could not very well stay less because of the bus service. It would be no more trouble to do up a parcel this week than it had been last, and it would do the girl good to feel that she was being useful.

All the same, there was still that lunatic's escape pricking the back of her mind. Could it be reasonably held that she had failed in her duty if the girl were to go as usual, and—the chance was so remote as to be barely worth considering—something did happen to her? (What the something might be Mrs. Maydew would not speculate upon with any thoroughness: a bad fright was as far as she cared to go. Once an obscene vision of Prudence battling desperately not for her chastity but for her very life had tried to force itself upon her, but she had resolutely turned from it in disgust.)

Surely no one could blame her. Nothing had happened last Friday, though the lunatic had been just as much at large then as now, and far more likely to be near at hand, since he had only just escaped. Today he was probably half-way across England. (It was the fact of his escaping on a Thursday night which had delayed the delivery of the local paper the next day until after Prudence had gone: otherwise Mrs. Maydew would have had the same problem to face, at much shorter notice. As it was, she had allowed the matter to revolve in her head for a week, though with no very satisfactory result.)

'No' she decided, 'I won't let her go.' But, even as she delivered her verdict, the private part of her mind seemed to smile at her saucily: it knew well enough that she was up to her old trick, trying to find out how she would feel if she were finally to settle things that way, by pretending she had done so. Admitting the truth of its unspoken charge, she again poised her attention upon her thoughts: and the second footman, passing the pantry door, noticed her standing motionless by the window, tall and thin and a little bent, her hair white, her dress black, the paper clutched in her left hand and her right fingering the band of velvet round her 'scrawny neck, and her dull eyes staring sightlessly.

'Old cat looks as if she's paralysed' he thought. 'Wish she were, too.'

Prudence Hill was a small smiling girl; her hands were small, her figure dainty, and her feet, as her grandmother never tired of telling her with pride, were truly admirable and obviously inherited from herself. She made short work of the journey to Minchley on the scullery-maid's bicycle, duly delivered Mrs. Maydew's parcel to Laura Clerk, and accepted a sticky-looking toffee which proved to be unpleasantly full of coconut. Her grandmother's cottage was only a few yards away, and she was soon greeting the old woman affectionately, telling her such news as there was, and making tea.

About half past eight, as they were finishing supper, there came a knock at the door, and Tom Jenkins appeared. He was tall and ungainly, very red in the face and shy, but at the same time obstinately determined: with or without her encouragement he intended to court Prudence Hill.

The girl pouted a little as she saw who it was, and for a moment glanced despairingly at her grandmother: Tom's persistence was becoming rather a threadbare joke. Had she not told him bluntly last week that he could take himself and his red face and his earth-grained hands as far away as he pleased, since he was not to her liking? She had not put it quite that way, not wanting to hurt him more than was necessary: but she believed that she had made herself clear.

"What, you again?" she queried outspokenly.

"Prue!" exclaimed old Mrs. Hill reprovingly: she disliked bad manners.

"Oh well—I suppose you're wanting to ride home with me?"

Tom made an affirmative noise, cleared his throat, nodded belatedly to Prudence's grandmother, and shifted his cap to his other hand.

"Not very safe at night, like, on them lonely roads," he suggested. "Specially now that daft chap's loose. Might need someone with you, that you might."

"And quite right too," agreed Mrs. Hill, who had nothing against

Tom. "Such a time they be catching him, too, don't they? You be a good girl now, Prue."

But Prudence still looked cross: not so much because she actively disliked Tom Jenkins as because, at the moment, she was far more interested in the second footman at Yewhurst Hall. Right under Mrs. Maydew's nose had he dared to kiss her in the servants' hall—Mrs. Maydew being at the time asleep after a favourite lunch; and again in the dining-room while she was dusting, and yet again in the camphor-scented cupboard under the back stairs. Secretly she half suspected that on his part it was only a lark: he had taken scarcely any notice of her at all for the first two months; but she was not so sure about her own feelings. There could be no possible doubt that he was very handsome, anyway, whereas she had never thought Tom Jenkins worth looking at twice. Besides, his hands were so dirty. She knew he couldn't help that, of course, working out in the fields all day, but she still preferred Arthur's, smooth and hairless and well kept. Arthur intended to be a butler one day, and cherished his personal appearance.

"I'm sick and tired of hearing about that blessed lunatic," she said suddenly. "Old Maybug nearly stopped me coming today 'cos of him, only she wanted her parcel delivered, and it was too much fag to do it herself. I bet he's miles away by now. All right, you can come part of the way back with me, only you'll have to push my bike up Longman's Hill. That's only fair, isn't it, Grannie?"

The old woman smiled slowly, not at Prudence but at Tom.

"I reckon he won't mind," she said simply.

Tom did not: it was little enough to have to do for the pleasure of riding home with Prudence, he thought dimly, looking at her. Pretty she was, even though so tiny—a sight prettier than any of the girls his friends had got: Fanny Orme with her rabbit's-teeth, and Mabel Strong who was all elbows and nose. He would willingly push her bike up Longman's Hill, and all the way to Yewhurst Hall if need be, and perhaps she might kiss him good-night. He believed she had nearly done so three weeks ago, only she hadn't quite. He realized, however, from her manner towards him, that he would need a great deal of luck.

Unfortunately for him, his hopes were never to be fulfilled.

The first part of the journey passed without incident. Occasionally he ventured a remark to the figure darkly gliding at his side, now an inch or two in front, and now behind, but mostly they proceeded in a silence broken only by the faint rattle of their bicycle chains revolving, the impact of their tyres on the hard road, and the distant noise of an owl. Prudence was not feeling talkative, her attention being concentrated upon the best means of dismissing Tom before they reached the entrance gates of Yewhurst Hall. She would certainly not let him accompany her up the drive, and she hoped that she would be able to get rid of him before the game-keeper's lodge. Old Benkin might be prowling about with his dog, and she did not want him gossiping to Mrs. Maydew, nor—more particularly—to Arthur.

Riding now through the gloom—not by any means a complete darkness, since it was only nine o'clock, and the declining moon barely hidden by clouds—she resented Tom's presence even more than she had expected to. He was so heavy, so in earnest with his aimless interruptions and boring questions. Did she like her post still? (Though only a week had gone by since he had haltingly asked her the same thing!) Had she ever been to Balmer's Court, where the lunatic had escaped from? It was a fine mild night for the time of year, wasn't it?

She resented him more strongly than ever before: for being the person he was, for being where he was, and also—though not herself fully aware of this—for mentioning the lunatic, and so reminding her that at the bottom of her heart she really was a little afraid. It was nothing in particular that she feared: just the fact that somewhere near perhaps, even possibly within a mile, was an unguarded madman with hair all over his face, probably starving hungry and apt to be desperate, so the newspapers hinted. His potential proximity seemed to give the air an appreciable keenness, in spite of Tom's remark, a subtle significance to the clouds veiling the moon, and a menacing quality to the darkness of the trees on either side. It made the road seem longer and the pedals of her bicycle harder to force round; and every minute or so it made her want to glance suddenly over her shoulder, in case there should be three of them.

It was due to this desire that Prudence unexpectedly succeeded in getting rid of her companion. For quite five minutes she had fought against the temptation to look backwards just once more, to make absolutely sure; but at last it grew too strong for her, and she turned her head. Tom also looked round, their front wheels swayed inwards, and their machines collided.

The immediate result was that Prudence uttered a sharp cry of surprise and fell off, catching her left knee on a flint and tearing her stocking. For a moment she stayed where she was, her breath seeming inexplicably to have left her. Then she picked herself up with Tom's clumsy assistance, stared at her bicycle lying on its side, and then at him. It was too dark for her to tell what his expression was, but in her imagination she could see him smiling—though in fact he was gravely solicitous. Why she should then have turned on him without warning she could not have explained clearly, but turn she did, calling him an awkward lout and demanding to know why he couldn't look where he was going, where the money was to come from for a new pair of stockings, and how she possibly could account for all the dents and scratches her borrowed bicycle had undoubtedly received. All this poured out in practically one breath, not to be stopped by the feeling that she was behaving quite unjustly, the certainty that she too was becoming red in the face, and a hazy realization that she spoke so because she had been badly frightened.

Tom said nothing, but picked up her bicycle in a dazed silence. This was not the Prudence with whom he believed himself in love, not the smiling quiet-spoken girl he desired so ardently to court, even though she said little enough to him, and gave him few enough smiles. This was a strange shadowy spitfire, blaming him tempestuously for what was at worst a pure accident.

For some seconds they stood trying to stare at one another, the girl out of breath again and very near tears. Then she put out her hand for the machine he was holding, and the touch of the cold handlebar on her bare fingers steadied her. She had taken off her gloves to examine her torn stocking while she was sitting in the road.

"I'll go on by myself," she said, more quietly, mounted the bicycle, and pedalled away without another word, while Tom gazed stupidly, a riot of thoughts assaulting his slow mind. Should he cycle after her? How much did a pair of stockings cost? Did this mean she would have nothing more to do with him? Could she really be the kind of girl he had imagined, after saying all that, or had he made some terrible mistake?

In the end he decided that he had had enough for one night, and prepared to turn homewards disconsolately. Was it his fault that she had fallen off? He could not remember now, but if so it might make a difference: there would then be some excuse for her loss of temper. She could not have been badly hurt, anyway, since she was still able to ride. As he was about to move off a thought struck him, and he laboriously lit a match, but was unsuccessful in discovering any blood on the road.

For two miles Prudence cycled steadily, until she came to the bottom of Longman's Hill. It began sharply, and there was no sense in trying to ride up it: she knew from experience that she would not get even a quarter of the way. Accordingly she dismounted, her knee by now becoming sore, and for the first time she wished vaguely that she had not so suddenly dismissed Tom Jenkins. After all, as she knew very well, the collision had been more her fault than his.

She was no longer frightened of the night, however: unaccountably, she now felt quite safe. The air had become warmer, the moon more real, the shade less threatening. It might still hold danger, but she did not find the possibility disturbing. All the same, Tom would have been very welcome at the moment: pushing a bicycle uphill was hard work. 'It's making my vest stick to me' was the way she thought about it.

Two thirds of the distance up she paused, remembering suddenly that she ought to be on the other side of the road when walking, so the butler had told her one day. No cars had passed her in either direction for some minutes, but it was as well to be careful, so she crossed over, leant her bicycle against the bank, and took off her gloves: she must find out whether the damage to her stocking was serious. Stupidly she had put on her best pair, and there was a dance at the village hall in a few days' time. If she got on the right side of the Maybug she would be allowed to go, provided she were back early, and she had no other stockings fit to wear there. She would want to look her best for Arthur's benefit—then he might walk home with her. Quite what she expected that to lead to she was not sure, but she would certainly let him kiss her again if he wanted to.

Should her stockings be badly torn it would mean borrowing from the kitchen-maid, she reflected, as she moved forward to catch the light of her bicycle lamp. On both sides of the road were solid groves of tall oak trees, and the night was very silent. Before her the way home stretched upwards, seeming to lead straight into the star-specked sky, but she was too concerned about her stocking to notice.

She put her left foot on the bank, pulled back her mackintosh and skirt, and fumbled expertly with her suspenders; and as she began to peel her stocking off there came a sudden rush of feet behind her. Before she had time to realize what was happening, or do more than give a little gasp of horror, something dealt her a heavy blow on the back of the head. She fell down, half stunned, and her last sensation was the touch of a human hand on the back of her neck, pressing her face down into the soft earth at the foot of the bank. She felt nothing more.

VI

THAT night for Mrs. Maydew was one of the most uncomfortable that she ever remembered passing; for she found, to her dismay, that she simply did not know what to do; responsibility proved to have its unpleasant side. When Prudence had not returned by quarter to ten she was mildly surprised; when not by quarter past she was angry; but by eleven o'clock she was definitely alarmed. 'What *can* have happened to her?' she demanded silently of the kitchen clock; but did not supply an answer, nor try to.

She took the butler into consultation—against her better judgment, because she profoundly distrusted his opinion in all things. She approached him indeed, for the sole reason that at that time of night there was nobody else in the house still up, and she felt the need to consult someone. But she got little help from him, beyond advice not to treat the event with disproportionate gravity. He was a slow matter-of-fact man, and he had a sensible matter-of-fact explanation for the second housemaid's non-appearance. "She's had a puncture," he told Mrs. Maydew. "She'll be in directly." And when there was no sign of Prudence by midnight, and the housekeeper tapped at his bedroom door to inform him of this, he grunted rather bad-temperedly. "Stopped at her grandmother's," he said. "Old lady's ill, I dare say."

"Then she ought to have let me know," declared Mrs. Maydew even more bad-temperedly, and retired to bed. Once alone in her room she tried her hardest to reassure herself: nothing was really wrong, and it was stupid to go on worrying. All the same, she did go on; she was infuriatingly ill at ease, and passed the long hours till daylight in intermittent dozes. When she was awake she set all her energy upon not thinking about what might have befallen Prudence Hill; but when she dozed she had no such control over her mind, and could not prevent its being peopled with screaming terrified figures beset by hairy agile monsters.

When the second footman, sent over post-haste to Minchley the next morning, returned with word that Prudence had left for Yewhurst Hall at twenty minutes to nine the previous evening, accompanied by Tom Jenkins, Mrs. Maydew contracted her mouth into a thin tight line and telephoned the police. Thereafter the matter was out of her hands, though she could not foresee that later it would rarely be out of her mind.

Tom Jenkins told his story to the enquiring sergeant slowly, but with apparent straightforwardness.

Subsequently he repeated it to the local inspector, and then to the district superintendent, and all three agreed that he seemed too ingenuous to be lying. His account would be checked where possible, of course, but the truth must be faced, as far as it was known. Prudence Hill, nineteen years old, four foot eleven inches in height, slight build, fair hair, second housemaid at Yewhurst Hall, the property of Lady Cynthia Verney, at present abroad, had disappeared somewhere between Minchley and Brockenhurst on the evening of May 7th. According to available information, when last seen the missing girl was riding a bicycle, and wore a brown mackintosh, a navy-blue artificial silk frock with white trimmings, flesh-coloured stockings, left one torn, brown shoes, and a small cream straw hat with a pink ribbon round it. What she had on beneath her frock, said Mrs. Maydew primly to the sergeant, was no concern of his. Best ask Tom Jenkins, or whatever his name was, if the police really wanted to know. "A hussy!" added the housekeeper vindictively. "Nothing but a common hussy."

Three days passed, and the search for Prudence Hill became as intensified as the search for Simon Selby; and in many minds the two activities were connected. As yet, however, there was no reference to this possibility in the press: the police did not wish to alarm the neighbourhood unduly.

"No sir, if you please," said Sergeant Crashaw to Mervyn Wilson, the representative of the Universal News Agency. "Not a word of it—can't go scaring folk like that. Not but what there may be something in it, of course, but we can't tell till we find one or other of 'em, or both."

"Which sounds like perpetual silence to me," rejoined Wilson rudely, and departed. Outside Burwood police-station he paused, deliberating what to do. Should he join one of the official search-parties? Or go back to the pub where he was staying and play darts till something fresh turned up? Or rout round by himself? The last idea appealed to him most, not so much because he hoped to find out anything about either Prudence Hill or Simon Selby on his own as because he disliked the idea of being ordered about by rural policemen, and he felt that he ought to be doing something. Besides, there were queer stories about the New Forest. People said there were nudist colonies hidden in its depths, though nobody seemed to know quite where to look for them. Perhaps he would be lucky enough to find one, thought Mervyn Wilson, and smiled to himself appreciatively: as Dickie Donovan had hinted to Beale, he was susceptible to feminine charms.

But he was definitely not susceptible to the patently displayed charms of Betty Trotter. As he walked up the street he saw her standing outside the *Horse's Head* drinking ginger beer, gave her one optimistic glance, and hurried on, for she was in his opinion everything that a girl ought not to be. Her bare sun-starved legs reminded him of two enormous wax candles, her shorts were inartistically designed and badly cut, the colour of her topheavily bulging woollen jumper was orange flecked generously with blue, and her hair was red. From a plain unattractive face her eyes protruded towards him in a stare which he fancied was meant to be provocative, and he hastily looked away.

'Has she escaped too?' he wondered, and glanced round to make sure that she was real. At this she smiled toothfully, and to his amazed horror raised her glass in his direction.

'Well!' he thought, further quickening his stride. 'Now say I'm not good-looking, somebody. And then say she is! Where do such freaks come from—and in May, too? Hike tristissima—these things are very sad-making.'

But he soon forgot about Betty Trotter. The day was fine, the sky blue and cloudless and the sun strong overhead, and presently he turned off the road to follow a narrow path among the trees.

'As well go this way as any other' he thought. 'If I hadn't left my map behind I'd know where it leads to. Not that it matters—I'll either be lucky or nothing, and May's a bit early, I dare say.'

The path had on one side of it a plantation of young scotch firs, and on the other open moorland in which flamed patches of yellow gorse; but this soon gave way to a belt of oak trees, thin at first but gradually widening until he could see no daylight through them.

When he had gone about a mile he sat down on a fallen trunk, pulled out his pipe, and slowly filled it. This was a change from London all right, he mused, as he stuffed down the tobacco carefully. In general the country bored him, and the first visit here after the story of Selby's escape had been deadly; but now he felt glad that he had been given the second assignment in connection with Prudence Hill. He had certainly been getting tired of inquests and police-court news day after day. 'The prisoner was discharged as stated—or remanded, or convicted. The magistrate looked like a slightly dishonest station-master in need of a dryclean.'

Not that his employers ever let him record such brutal truths, but he was still young, and had not yet lost all his early insistent desire to be allowed to describe things as he saw them. He was beginning to realize, though, that veracity, as such, was not necessarily a marketable commodity; and his own personal vision usually a matter of the supremest unimportance. What he was paid to hunt out were facts—dry bones for other hands than his to build upon, adding a feature here, ignoring one there, emphasizing this diminishing that, until the same material was fashioned into half a dozen different likenesses.

He found it pleasant, in retrospect, to get away from that sort of life temporarily: to sit instead on a hunk of wood in the New Forest. Although it might be no softer than a press bench, there was at least no need to go near a telephone till six o'clock. At that time, or thereabouts, he would drop in at the police-station again, be told that nothing had happened, and pass the news on to headquarters in appropriate language. Of course, he would be rather out of the running if anything *did* happen, but he felt ready to take the risk. He could always invent some plausible story about how he had preferred to follow up a likely clue rather than kick his heels in the town all day, drinking beer or staring aimlessly at the tawdry flags and bunting put up for Wednesday's Coronation.

It was after he had finished filling his- pipe that he remembered having used his last match an hour before. 'Confound that fat goggling hag in orange' he thought. 'I was going to buy some, only she made me forget. Better walk on till I meet somebody, I suppose—or shall I go back? But that wouldn't be very interesting.'

He pondered the question idly, and decided that it would be nicer to do neither. He could get on without a smoke: he would lie down in the sun and listen to the grasshoppers, or whatever they were.

He never woke up.

VII

CAPTAIN FELIX WYNDHAM shook his head solemnly, gave Superintendent Dane a consciously patient smile, and adjusted his horn-rimmed spectacles. They made him look anything but what he was: fifty-five, perhaps, instead of forty-six; studious and dreamy when in fact he rarely read a book, and preferred action to thought; a mild-mannered tutor, not a chief-constable whose sharp tongue was a by-word among his subordinates. It was when he smiled, as now, that he was likely to be rudest, and Dane knew this.

They sat in his private office at the county police sub-headquarters in Burwood: a room remarkable only for the hideous pattern of the flowered wall paper and the untidiness of the Chief-constable's desk. In Dane's opinion it reflected accurately the prevailing state of its owner's mind.

"You're being a fool," said Wyndham. "Not your fault, maybe, but annoying—I loathe and detest fools."

"Yes sir," murmured Dane, aware that he was not one, and also that Wyndham knew this too.

"You say there's no connection between any of these things," went on the Chief-constable. "I say it'd be incredible if there weren't. They sent you to school? Then you know what incredible means."

"Sometimes a synonym for the obvious and therefore unwelcome," returned Dane evenly.

"Eh?"

"Nothing, sir—it doesn't matter."

"I hope not. Just look at the sequence of events, man, instead of sitting there yammering. On April 29th our estimable friend Peake lets one of his lunatics escape—in the middle of the night, that happened. Eight days later, on May 7th, the second housemaid at Yewhurst Hall also disappears: time, evening. Three days after that, on May 10th, a reporter down here from London for the story also vanishes: time, unknown, but not before midday, as he was here with Sergeant Crashaw till then. On May 10th, too, a girl hiker called Betty Trotter is reported missing: at least, she was due to meet a friend at Lymington that night, and she never turned up. It's now the 12th, and we don't know where any of them are, though we've made the most thorough search possible in the time. Those are the facts—agree?"

"The girl Trotter was last seen at one o'clock," said Dane. "Walking towards Dunholm Enclosure, roughly the way that Wilson's believed to have taken. Yes, those are the facts."

"And you see nothing significant in the order? *First* the lunatic, next the lunatic's natural prey, a defenceless good-looking girl, then a nosy reporter, probably on his track and a sight too dangerous to be left alive, and lastly a girl hiker."

"More prey, sir?" suggested the Superintendent, with quiet sarcasm.

"Exactly—you're not so dull when you use your wits."

"Thank you. But I should like to make my position clear—if I can. I'm not saying there can't be any connection between those four disappearances—only that there *may* not be. There's a difference, you know. Very probably you're right, sir—but I still think it's worth while to consider other possibilities, and I must say there are one or two points that don't quite seem to fit."

"Fit?" echoed Wyndham. "What doesn't fit?"

"Well sir, did you ever see Betty Trotter?"

"Certainly not—sure of it. I saw her photograph, and that was quite enough."

"Quite, sir—that's what I mean. Would you expect her to be anybody's prey? She looked terrible to me."

"Repulsive—but what of it? Beggars can't be choosers, and a girl's a girl for all that."

"And yet," mused Dane aloud, "part of your reason for thinking that Prudence Hill was his victim is that she was good looking. If he chose carefully the first time, when you'd expect him not to be too particular, why should he be so entirely lacking in discrimination the second time, when you'd expect him to have the edge off his appetite, if I can put it that way, and a bit more pernickety?"

Captain Wyndham nodded.

"Fellow's mad, that's why," he said. "Does things back to front."

"In which case, why kill the reporter? Surely that's a sane fugitive's action: on the back-to-front principle you'd expect a lunatic to let him go with a good-luck kiss."

The Chief-constable stared at the Superintendent.

"Trying to make me wear your cap, are you?" he asked.

"Cap, sir?"

"Cap—fool's cap. I will if you can prove it fits."

He paused for some moments, frowning sternly at his chaotic desk.

"The fact is," he said at last, "we don't know enough to go forming theories like this. Don't even know that anybody's dead at all, if it comes to that."

"No sir, not till we find them. There's half a dozen search-parties going through the Forest systematically, though, so we may know one way or the other pretty soon."

Wyndham snorted.

"Not as easy as it sounds," he declared: which, Dane realized, was the truth. "Ever lost a golf ball when you knew darned well it was only a couple of yards from where you were standing, and yet you couldn't find the blamed thing?"

'* No sir."

"Well, I have. It's easy enough to talk about searching the New Forest, but you don't seem to understand what that means. Think of the size of it—think of all the thousands and thousands of hiding-places: up trees, down holes, in ditches, under bracken."

"Yes sir," agreed Dane. "Yet it's the obvious thing to do, and they're being thorough: two dead dogs, one petrol can, a picnic basket, and a sackful of old bottles to date. Were you thinking of hiding-places for bodies or people, sir?"

"Bodies, chiefly. Look here, Dane, let's be frank. Do you or don't you think any of those four are dead?"

The Superintendent shrugged his broad shoulders: he was a bulky loosely-constructed man who weighed half as much again as Wyndham.

"I wouldn't be surprised if they weren't," he said.

"Meaning you would be surprised if they were?"

"No, not exactly. I wouldn't be surprised either way, but I'm not *certain* they're dead."

"Then what else do you think can have happened to them? The last three in particular."

"Well sir, it's hard to guess like that, and to be quite honest, I can't make my mind up about the Hill girl. She may be dead, as you say, or she may have eloped, or gone off into the woods to meet somebody, and been done in by him."

Wyndham smiled amiably.

"That wouldn't amount to being dead, would it?" he queried.

"Not in your sense of the word, sir. You mean killed by Simon Selby, but I mean killed—if at all—by any other person. Barring us, of course."

"Barring me, certainly. And why exclude the most likely person?"

"In a minute sir, please. Then there's the Wilson fellow: what would you say to a practical joke there?"

The idea displeased the Chief-constable.

"Wouldn't it be worth his job?" he asked hopefully.

"Not necessarily: he might think he'd get a good story by showing up the inefficiency of the local police, and all that. 'How I hid in the New Forest for five days', by our special representative."

Wyndham shifted uncomfortably.

"Nasty thought," he said. "Hope to goodness you're wrong. What about Betty Trotter?"

"There again I'm not at all sure, but I wouldn't rule out either accident or suicide. I've been making one or two enquiries about her, and by all accounts she was a pretty hopeless sort of creature."

"In what way?"

"Oh, the usual, or too usual. She realized she was about as attractive to men as a pound of stale haddock, and she didn't take it calmly. From what I've been able to gather, she spent her life dithering between fits of despair and periods of flinging herself headlong at the nearest pair of male feet. Not her fault, really—a case for the psychologists. Even Peake might have been able to do her a bit of good, if she'd ever come his way. She put up at the *Roebuck* on the night of the 9th, you know, sir, and they don't speak very well of her. Apparently she ogled one of the waiters all the evening, and tried to make a date with him on his afternoon off. When that fell flat, she paraded round the lounge in the most appalling jumper and shorts. She was clumsy, too: broke her wash-basin and tripped over the mat in the hall, and didn't generally seem to have much control over her hands and feet. That's why I suggested an accident—plenty of roots about in the woods."

"Twaddle!" said the Chief-constable shortly. "Don't believe a word of it, and I don't believe you do either. For goodness' sake tell me why you won't have the sensible explanation—Selby escapes, and polishes off anybody he can lay hands on?"

"Partly because of what Professor Peake said, sir he wouldn't hear of Selby being violent that way. Admittedly he had periodic fits, but they definitely weren't homicidal, he said."

"Oh, Peake!"—and Wyndham laughed a little scornfully. "Queer sort of cove altogether, if you ask me. What else?"

Superintendent Dane hesitated.

"Can I speak unofficially, sir?"

"Well, I suppose you can if you must. What is it?"

"Thank you. Then in my opinion Simon Selby's escape wasn't the unassisted break-away somebody's been trying to make us believe. I think he was got out of Balmer's Court by his sister."

"Good God!" exclaimed the Chief-constable, really shocked: for, as Dane well knew, he was on terms of friendship with the girl.

"Are you sitting there and telling me that Lavinia—I mean, Miss Selby—helped her brother get away? It's unheard of—not even you could think of anything more cretinous. How *could* she have done? What grounds have you got for making such a bat-witted accusation?"

"No material evidence, sir—that's the trouble. All the same, it strikes me as being about the only explanation that covers the facts decently, however unpleasant the idea may be. I wasn't meaning to imply that she got him out entirely by herself, of course: only that she had the guiding hand in it."

"Then who helped her?"

"Peake's assistant, Dr. Wrench. You know they're very friendly?"

"Well—yes."

"And you know what Wrench did after the discovery that Selby was missing?"

"What?"

"Went out looking for him in his car. But just suppose for a moment that he wasn't looking: suppose Selby was snugly tucked away in the dickey seat all the time. It strikes me as an idea, sir."

"It strikes me as the sheerest tomfoolery," said the Chief-constable gruffly. "You won't go forgetting that Peake's short of a patient, will you? But just as a matter of interest, what do you base this precious idea on? Anything remotely sensible?"

"*I* think so, sir—and it wasn't an accusation," returned Dane equably. "I did ask if I could speak unofficially, you know. The thing that's been worrying me most is those missing iron bars. If Selby removed them from the window himself, which would take a deal of doing, incidentally, why in heaven's name take them away with him?"

"Good lord, fancy asking why!" said Wyndham irritably. "Can't you grasp the simple truth about the man? Don't you understand he's mad? That he doesn't do things the normal way round?"

Superintendent Dane sighed. At times he found his Chief-constable very very trying.

"Yes, I've fully grasped that fact," he answered. "All I'm grumbling at is that you want to have it both ways, sir. I don't pretend to be an expert like Professor Peake, but it seems to me that if Selby was daft enough to take away his prison bars with him as a memento, then he was too daft to do that little burglary at Farmer's place. It was a neat job, you know, sir."

Wyndham frowned.

"I'd forgotten about that for the moment," he confessed. "You think he wouldn't have had the sense to think of shaving himself?"

"Well sir, what do you think? And not only sense, but inclination. He hadn't had a hair off him for three years, because the Professor found he got on better like that—in fact, Peake definitely says that Selby would go to almost any lengths of violence to avoid being barbered, he hated it so much. I'm prepared to take that statement as true because I don't think Peake would have dared make it if it weren't—there'd be too many people to contradict him. All right: Selby escapes, Selby being a lunatic who has a strange horror of being barbered, and who's mad enough to take two useless iron bars with him. Does it make sense that his first action once he's free is to raid a lonely cottage lived in by a deaf author, carefully select just those things which'll be useful to him—clothes, shoes, food, money—and nothing else at all except a set of shaving tackle?"

"Well—it sounds odd, certainly, put that way; but as I keep saying, what in the world do you expect a lunatic to do? Still, I see your point—but why pick on Miss Selby?"

"Who else would have the slightest interest in getting him out? She's his only near relative. But I don't see how she could have done much by herself—after all, it's not a great deal easier to climb into Balmer's Court over a twelve-foot wall than it is to climb out of it."

"Not with a ladder?"

"Not for a girl by herself. Therefore I assumed an accomplice, and the obvious one is Wrench."

'Then what about the burglary—fake?"

"I wouldn't be surprised: done by the doctor, perhaps, because he reckoned it would be what we'd expect Selby to have done."

Wyndham stared thoughtfully for a moment, and then his face cleared.

"And the iron bars?" he asked. "Did he expect us to expect them to be missing too, and that's why he took them? Because we don't seem to have done, do we?"

Dane smiled.

"I've a different explanation for them, sir. The only way Wrench could get them out was by cutting or sawing them through, and then knocking the ends out of the stonework with a hammer, so of course he daren't leave them, or we'd know Selby wasn't responsible."

"Huh! Answer for everything, haven't you? Where do you think he is, then?"

"Miles away by now, I dare say."

"And why didn't anybody hear the hammering?"

"He used a pad to deaden the sound."

"Does Miss Selby know what you're thinking?"

"Oh no sir, of course not."

Superintendent Dane expressed as much astonishment as if he had been asked how often he had forcibly kissed her.

"I've questioned her pretty thoroughly, of course," he said, "and I've got a couple of men watching both of them, but that's as far as I cared to go without consulting you."

"So I should think! You'll be making a bigger fool of yourself than you really are if you don't look out. I still think it's all twaddle. For instance, why hasn't all this happened long ago? Why leave her brother bottled up in Balmer's Court for all those years?"

"I couldn't say, sir—maybe because she thought Peake could cure him."

"And again, *why* help him escape? What does she want a lunatic brother on her hands for? What's she going to do with him? Not so easy to hide or look after, surely—you'd expect her to prefer him to be in proper care."

"Oh, there might be reasons, sir. Peake isn't the only mental specialist in the world, even if he is one of the best. She may have found somebody she thinks could do more—abroad, say. She'd have had a devil of a job to get Selby out of the country by legal methods—he was properly certified, you know, sir."

"Don't keep saying 'You know'," remarked Wyndham sharply. "If I do, it's redundant: if I don't, it's a lie. Answer another question—if you can. How did Wrench smuggle Selby away without that male nurse knowing? They went out in the car together, didn't they?"

"Yes. The obvious answer is that Bellamy did know all about it."

"All right: if you're determined to make up a fairy story, I suppose you may as well be thorough. What about the other one—Nurse Spence? Is she in it too?"

At this Dane once more hesitated.

"By the look of her, no: but it would have spoiled everything if she'd decided to spend the night in the next room, and how could they know she wouldn't decide to? I tried to find out if she'd asked anybody's advice, but she swears she didn't."

"Well, don't let a little thing like that bother you," said Wrench sarcastically. "I think—"

But what he thought was lost in the sudden shrill tinkle of the telephone bell. The time was a few minutes after four o'clock on the afternoon of Thursday May 13th.

VIII

THE CHIEF-CONSTABLE picked up the receiver, grunted into the mouthpiece, as always, said 'Yes' twice, the second time with a rising note of interest, and thereafter listened so intently that Dane almost imagined he could hear him doing it. He knew from Wyndham's expression, and the way the fingers of his unused hand were gripping the arm of his chair, that something was up, and he suspected it might be serious. When the person the other end had finished speaking, Wyndham sat thinking for a moment. "Take charge till I get there," he said at last. "Be with you in half an hour."

Then he turned to Dane, and his face was very pale.

"That was Inspector Dalton, in charge of 'B' search-party—they've been going through Webbley's Enclosure. An hour ago he called for Sergeant Lee, also in the party, and discovered after a bit that he was missing. About three o'clock, that was. They started shouting for him, with no result, and eventually went back to look. It took them twenty minutes, but they found him in the end—lying dead near a pine tree with his helmet off and a hole in his head behind his right ear as big as a two-shilling piece. He'd been stabbed with something, so Dalton says—pretty ghastly, isn't it?"

The Chief-constable was obviously distressed: he even forgot, Dane noticed, to point out the fact that his theory was presumably proved wrong. He rose immediately, his face grave, for the news had shocked him too.

"I liked Lee," he said quietly. "It seems you were right after all, sir."

"Eh? Maybe. They're spreading out in a ring, but I don't doubt he got away. Yes, it's a pretty foul business. He had a wife and two children, didn't he?"

"Yes sir—will you be sending someone round?"

Wyndham adjusted his spectacles, and frowned heavily.

"Better go myself," he said, with evident distaste. "On our way. Tell Sergeant Crashaw to make arrangements for the other parties to join up with 'B'—I'll ring the doctor. Oh, there's one other thing I forgot—queer, too. His left boot was missing."

Dane showed his amazement at this information, and it was not lessened when, three-quarters of an hour later, he stood sombrely regarding all that remained of Sergeant Lee: the man with whom, only the previous week, he had discussed the problem of pruning pear trees to the best advantage. It was difficult to realize that Lee would have no further interest in pear trees, or in any of the multifarious activities, official and domestic, that made up his life as a country policeman.

The body lay on its face, both arms outstretched as if the Sergeant had tripped heavily over something, and had tried to break his fall. Behind the right ear was a blackened sticky mess, and below were marks on the neck where blood had run down and dripped on to the ground. A closer examination showed Dane the hole the Chief-constable had mentioned, though it would not now be possible to tell its exact size until the wound had been washed.

The Superintendent's careful eye went from the head to the hands again.

"Been photographed?" he asked Inspector Dalton.

"Yes sir—one of the party had a camera with him."

At this Dane nodded, knelt down, and gently raised first the right hand and then the left without difficulty: *rigor mortis* had not yet set in to any appreciable extent. The surface of the ground beneath was composed mostly of mouldering pine needles from nearby trees, and its condition, with that of the dead man's palms, convinced the Superintendent that his first impression from the position of the body had been correct. Lee had fallen forward violently, and had died where he fell.

Satisfied that he had not made a mistake, he turned his attention once more to the feet. To his mind there was an almost indecent incongruity in the way the right leg ended in a heavy regulation boot, and the left in a purple woollen sock. It provided the corpse with a touch of absurdity: as if, he thought, it were not really a corpse at all, but a dummy demonstrating a Father Brown detective story.

'Now why in the world would anyone take off a dead sergeant's boot?' he wondered. 'And if the left one, why not both?'

He could find no answer except the obvious one: that nobody would do such a thing unless he were mad.

"No sign of it anywhere?" he asked.

"No sir—and we've had a thorough look."

"Footprints?"

"Nothing worth anything, I'm afraid."

"And nothing else missing?"

"No sir. His helmet's over there"—pointing to a spot some ten feet off.

Dane rose, walked over, and picked it up. There was no sign on the outside that it had been in contact with anything but the ground, and he nodded: it had come off when Lee had fallen down.

As the Chief-constable was nowhere to be seen, he presumed that he was in charge.

"Your case, Doctor," he said, addressing a short middle-aged man who had been standing nearby with a determined air of indifference. Dr. Erwin looked as if he saw murdered police-sergeants with one boot missing every day of his life, and was no longer interested.

"Thanks," he answered. "I'll wait for the stretcher, I think—can't do much here."

"As you like. Been dead long?"

Dr. Erwin stared at the Superintendent coldly: he disliked being asked questions until he was sure of his facts, and he took no trouble to hide his dislike.

"Me? I'm not dead," he replied.

"Oh—I'm sorry."

At this riposte the doctor smiled glassily.

"About two hours, at a guess."

"Thank you."

"Not at all. I'd give you the exact time if I could, only I wasn't here."

Dane nodded: it would be waste of breath to ask for information about the probable nature of the weapon used.

"A pity," he said. "Otherwise somebody'd hang you."

Not sure what to do, he strolled away, and leant against a pine. The spot where they were was a mile and a half from the nearest road, he judged, and about two and a half from Burwood. It was also off the main path leading through Webbley's Enclosure, and as far as he could tell one of the most open places in the wood. The trees stood a dozen yards or so apart within a space of perhaps half an acre, yet it was impossible to walk on any ground that was not carpeted with pine needles, however thinly. As he gazed round him there came from far away in the depths of the enclosure the spasmodic call of a cuckoo: a slightly vulgar but mellowly pleasant sound which always reminded him of Tchaikovsky's piano concerto. When he turned his back on the small group twenty yards away—two living men and one dead one—he could almost imagine that he was alone here unless he listened very attentively. Then, faintly, he could hear sounds of other human beings: a muffled shout, an indistinguishable answer. That would be the search-party, he reflected: but he had no hope of their finding what they sought, even under Wyndham's energetic leadership. Something—perhaps the deliberateness with which the boot must have been removed—gave him the impression that the murderer had not been short of time.

'And yet he *must* have been' he mused. 'How could he know Lee wouldn't be missed at once? Or was he too daft to think of that?' And then a fresh thought struck him, and at once he was hurrying back to Inspector Dalton, tall and thin and consumptive-looking, although in fact he had a clean bill of health in seventeen years' service.

"I want a complete list of your search-party," said Dane. "Names and addresses of everybody in it, when and where they joined you, and who asked them. Let me have it as soon as you can, please.

Dalton looked uncomfortably surprised.

"Well now, sir," he began, "that won't be so easy. You see, we were a couple of dozen strong when we started, but there was more to come. Poor Lee himself had a couple of friends tacking on as soon as they could manage it—"

His voice tailed off into an embarrassed silence: it was plain that he had little clear idea of how many persons there had been in his charge, nor precisely who all of them were. Dane regarded him with displeasure, hating inefficiency in others scarcely less than in himself.

"Just what were you out here to look for?" he asked.

"Why, this Selby, sir, or any of the others that's missing."

"Splendid. And how would you recognize this Selby if you saw him—or Wilson either, for that matter?"

"Well sir, I've got their descriptions."

"And the rest of the party?"

"Oh, I told everyone what they looked like before we started."

"Then tell me."

"Beg pardon, sir? You mean you want Selby's description?" Inspector Dalton was plainly puzzled.

"And Wilson's. From memory, please."

"Yes sir. Simon Selby, thirty-one, fair hair, light-blue eyes, six foot two inches in height, heavily built may be dressed in dark-brown tweed suit, tennis shirt, and brown brogue shoes, may or may not be clean shaven, prominent mole on right forearm. Mervyn Eric Wilson, twenty-seven, dark-brown hair, hazel eyes, five foot eight inches in height, slight build, clean shaven, high forehead. When last seen was wearing biscuit-coloured sports coat, green pullover, grey flannel trousers, and brown shoes. No hat, wearing signet ring on little finger of left hand."

Dane nodded.

"Can you visualize either of those two men from their descriptions?" he asked.

"Visualize them, sir? Well, I couldn't say. I reckon I'd know them if I saw them."

"I wonder. Suppose Selby isn't wearing a dark-brown suit? Suppose he's changed his shoes, and got a hat from somewhere, and Wilson too, and suppose the pullover's been taken off?"

He paused, stared at Dalton again, and then sighed.

"I hope you see what I'm driving at, Inspector?"

"Well, no sir, can't say I do. Those were the descriptions I was given."

"Oh, I don't doubt that: but wouldn't it be funny if Selby joined your search-party without your knowing it? If you can't tell me who was in it, you can hardly expect the others to know. Anybody who wasn't obviously running away, or looking disreputable, might easily have been accepted as another member of the party, especially if he took pains to act the part."

"Good Lord, sir!" Dalton appeared thunderstruck. "I say, d'you think that's what happened?"

"I don't know, any more than you do: but it'll hardly be thanks to you if it hasn't, will it?"

At this an even more startled expression was registered on the Inspector's pallid face, and a shocked disbelieving look crept into his eyes.

"You mean it may have been *my* fault Lee was killed?" he asked hoarsely. "God, sir, I—I hope not."

"No, not quite as bad as that," answered Dane hurriedly: he was certainly cross with Dalton, but that was no reason for making things out to be worse than they were. "I just don't think you ran your search-party on very scientific lines, that's all."

IX

AT HALF PAST SEVEN Dane left the Inspector in charge, and began his walk back to the police-station. During the last two hours he had joined in an intensive search covering an area of approximately a square mile, the centre being the place where Sergeant Lee's dead body had been found. Nothing had been discovered which would give a clue to the murderer or his whereabouts, however, and he felt suddenly that he needed to be alone, to think things out.

Although it was against regulations, since he was on duty, he lit a cigarette as soon as he was far enough away from the rest, and presently sat down on a tree-stump. He wanted as far as possible to review the whole situation, so that when in due course the Chief-constable asked his opinion he would have some coherent answer to give.

There were two main problems confronting him. First, what was the probability that Lee's murder had been the work of Simon Selby, the escaped lunatic? Second, ought he to advise Captain Wyndham to call in Scotland Yard?

'Well,' he asked himself, dealing with the former question, who else would want to kill Lee? 'I suppose it's theoretically possible that he had personal enemies, but I don't believe it myself. He always seemed to me a harmless enough chap—a bit slow, perhaps, but solid and kindly. No, I don't think anyone could have been planning to kill him. But that means it was an unpremeditated murder, and if so, what about the weapon? Goodness knows exactly what it was, of course, but clearly some kind of a dagger, or something that was able to be used as a dagger. By the look of things he was pushed or tripped over, and then stabbed behind the ear.

'All right, let's suppose that's what happened. Then it seems likely he was attacked from the rear, since he fell on his face. By the amount of stuff on his hands, though, and the distance his helmet rolled, he was standing up when he was pushed or tripped, not bending down. Still, that's not certain—he was a big chap, and he'd fall pretty heavily. At all events, it's obvious he was taken by surprise, and probably dead before he had time to raise much of an outcry.

'Now, in what circumstances would that sort of murder be possible? When he'd every reason to believe he was alone—that's one;

or when he was with somebody he thought he could trust—that's the other. Yes, that seems fairly sensible—curse that fool Dalton for not knowing who was in his search-party and who wasn't. But it mightn't help much: someone from another lot could have called or beckoned to Lee, got him looking at something, walked round, and sent him sprawling. But that seems to make the murder premeditated, hang it—I'm getting in a muddle.

'Suppose he thought he was alone, then—does that lead anywhere? Straight to Selby, apparently. It's certainly not likely to have been Prudence Hill or the Trotter girl—the idea's ridiculous; nor Wilson unless he was mad too. And I don't fancy an unknown murderer—somebody quite unconnected with the whole business of Selby's escape. Anyway, I shan't consider that till I've got to. No, Selby's the safest bet. Very well, then is there anything else to suggest that Lee was killed by a lunatic?'

That Superintendent Dane considered the question for even so long as a minute was merely in the hope that he would find some sensible excuse for not accepting the obvious; but he found none. Nothing could get over the fact of the missing boot, and he could think of no sane reason for removing a dead policeman's footwear. A dangerous fingerprint, even if its presence could be satisfactorily accounted for, could easily have been wiped off, and although French peasants were vaguely supposed to conceal their wealth in old stockings, he had never heard that English police-sergeants kept theirs—if any—in their boots. 'It's a mad thing to do' he told himself: 'therefore it was done by a madman. Is that logical? I doubt it, but I can't see any other solution.

'Professor Peake must be wrong, then, and Selby *is* a homicidal maniac after all. Incidentally, I was wrong myself in suspecting Lavinia Selby. But I still don't understand that business of climbing over the wall, nor about the missing bars outside his bedroom window.'

And then, a moment later, he suddenly snapped his fingers with unaccustomed excitement.

'Iron bars, by hokey! They were about a foot long, weren't they, and as thick as a walking-stick? And the hole in poor Lee's head was the size of a two-shilling piece, so Wyndham said—presumably Dalton saw it when it was freshly made. I wonder—it looks convincing all right. One of the bars would make just the sort of weapon to leave that sort of wound. I must see if I can prove that definitely. Not so easy, I suppose—can't very well go 'round doing a murder or two of my own just to fee what the results look like, but maybe I can think of some way. I could even get a butcher to lend me a dead pig—why not?

'Yes, Dalton's not the only one who's slow—I ought to have thought of those bars the minute I saw Lee's head. So I was wrong, and Wyndham right—for once. How he'll crow! Still, we were only guessing, both of us, and nobody can guess right—or wrong—all the time. Picture of a sportsman being glad the best man won.

'Well, this opens up a lot of fresh problems—or old ones that I hoped needn't bother me. How in the world has Selby managed to exist all this time? Where does he get his food from? Where does he sleep at nights? How does he contrive to hide himself so well? Up a tree, I wouldn't be surprised. I ought to have looked more closely at the one Lee was lying under—maybe Selby jumped down on top of him. But that would be making it all terribly fluky, and anyway he wasn't exactly under it, and I'm certain he was killed where they found him.

'Ah well, I'd better be getting back to Burwood, I suppose, or they'll be sending a party out to look for me.'

And at that point Superintendent Dane forgot all about his second problem. It was swallowed up in the sudden terrifying realization that for all he knew he might even now be in imminent danger of never reaching the police-station alive. In an instant he was on his feet, a cold tingle of fear irritating the small of his back, and the tips of his ears burning. Why hadn't it occurred to him before? he was wondering as he stared round apprehensively, scenting danger in the still silence of the evening. Prudence Hill had been alone, and Wilson, and Betty Trotter, and Sergeant Lee almost certainly: and here was he doing his damndest to provide a fifth victim.

'Silly daft fool!' he told himself, still gazing round: but he could see nothing that suggested the presence of any other person near him. He was seemingly alone with the motionless trees under a sky which he fancied would be a darkish lavender colour if he could see enough of it to judge. Dusk was approaching, and the air becoming chilly: it was time to go, while going remained possible.

'I'm lucky' he thought, as he moved towards the path. 'Lucky—and confoundedly careless.'

He was also nervous, he realized. The unexpected sharp twitter of a bird on a branch above his head made him start violently, and he felt uncomfortably ashamed. This was no way for a man to behave who had sat for two hours in a shell-hole in no man's land dodging machine-gun bullets, and not doubted he would survive.

'But that was because I was so perishing hungry' he remembered. 'All I could think of was stew for supper—and what a stew!'

He was walking fast now, keeping his eyes watchful and his ears vigilantly alert. Every few moments he stopped short and swung round, and each time he was consciously relieved to find no one behind him.

'Good job Wyndham can't see me now!' he thought. 'He'd want to know what I was afraid of if I believe Selby's miles away, and I'd have to climb down. Not that I'd mind that, only he's apt to chortle so. Still, he's a decent enough chap at heart, and he *is* keen on his job. And anyway, Lee was killed all right just now, so there's plenty to be scared of. I wonder if he'll suggest Scotland Yard, or if I ought to? I'd like to tackle the thing myself, but then I have, more or less, for a fortnight, and where am I? Out alone in the twilight hurrying away from bogies. Better have somebody down if Wyndham'll stand for it. He's never had a murder on his hands before, though, so there's no telling which way he'll look at it.

'I must be pretty near the road now, I should think not more than a couple of hundred yards off. I'll feel better when I've got something solid under my feet though I'm sure I don't know why, come to think of it. Prudence Hill probably felt safe on her bicycle, and the lord knows where she is now. I wish I did. But young Jenkins is out of it, I'm certain. He looked—'

And then, again Dane's thoughts were cut off as abruptly as if his nerve centres had fused. Once more he was assailed by that prickle of fear in his back, and sight and hearing strained themselves to detect what it was that had startled him. Behind, some distance away, had come a sudden unnatural sound: between a shout and a shriek, so his fading memory of it told him.

A less scrupulous man would have disbelievingly put it down as the call of an unfamiliar bird, and hastened on his way before it came again; but Dane stood waiting, so rigidly still that his feet felt rooted, as if it would take more strength than he possessed to lift them.

Then the sound was repeated, distinctly a human cry, though not to his mind so urgent. It seemed like a girl's voice, and he debated for the fraction of a second about how best to answer it. As he did so he felt in his breast pocket; yes, he had his whistle with him, and it would carry farther than his voice, besides indicating who and what he was. Would that be a good thing or a bad one? He had hardly time to decide before he had blown, two short blasts that echoed piercingly among the trees.

It was becoming increasingly difficult to see: in quarter of an hour it would be dark, and he must hurry. First, though, it was necessary to stand still again, in case the voice answered. His feet had regained their power of motion quite without his noticing.

Within ten seconds there was a third call, from a distance of perhaps a hundred and fifty yards, he guessed. He began hurrying towards it, leaving the path to make his way through an assembly of ancient beeches, and arriving on open ground spread out with heather. Almost at once he spotted the figure of a woman in a light dress waving, and broke into his clumsy run. As he came up he saw that it was Lavinia Selby, hatless as always, her fair hair the colour of ripe oats.

"Oh Mr. Dane!" she exclaimed. "I'm so glad it's you. I had such a fright, such a terrible fright just now. Mr. Dane, there's a dead body over there"—pointing roughly west, where the last streaks of sunset lingered on the rim of the sky.

"A dead body, Miss Selby?" he queried, regarding her very steadily. "Was that what made you scream?"

"Yes—I'm afraid I lost my head for a minute. You'd better let me show you where it is—only I don't want to go near it again, if you don't mind. I only saw its foot, and that was quite enough."

"Then you can't be certain it's dead?"

"Oh, of course it is—else it would have got up when I screamed, wouldn't it. I needn't come with you?"

"Of course not."

Dane spoke calmly: he could see that the girl had had a considerable shock, or looked as if she had done. Her face was pale, reminding him even more than usual of a Greek statue's, the nose very straight, the brow broad, and the lips firmly modelled. It had also, in repose, the peculiarly aloof vacancy of a statue, as if her thoughts were always of yesterday or tomorrow.

'She's very beautiful' he thought, not for the first time. 'A bit too tall, perhaps, and a bit too slim but beautiful, all the same. I wonder if I still suspect her of anything?'

"Of course not," he repeated. "Did you come across it by accident?"

(His mind was concentrating on the business in hand again. 'Another body' it was saying. 'That means Scotland Yard without question—I'm glad.')

The girl put her own interpretation on his query, and smiled suddenly, wanly.

"You're wondering what I'm doing out here all alone," she told him.

"In a way," he admitted: "but it'll be dark soon, and I haven't a torch with me, so you'd better explain about that later. Just come far enough to show me where this body is, please, and then wait. And is it a man or a woman, do you know?"

"A woman, I think—anyway, it's not Simon."

'Which one?' he asked himself immediately. 'I was wrong—it's Selby's work all right. But I mustn't say so. She knows her brother's a lunatic, but she needn't know I think he's probably a murderer. Though she must be thinking the same anyway—it's the only rational explanation. There couldn't be any possibility that she's mad too, could there? I'm glad I'm not her.'

"Thank you," he said aloud, and listened to her directions. Then he walked on alone, his nerves taut, his whole being expectant. He was about to look at a corpse: but how easily, it seemed to him, it might have been the other way round—someone else stepping reluctantly to view his own still hulk.

He pulled aside the branches with which the body had been roughly covered, and recognized at once that it was Betty Trotter's. All that Lavinia Selby could have seen, he noted, was a foot, as she had said: one bare shoeless foot, the left one. The girl hiker was lying on her side, her right arm doubled under her and both legs bent at the knee, though not to the same extent. She had obviously been dead some time, and was not pleasant to regard, but he forced himself to take in all the details, straining his eyes to do so.

Her canvas knapsack was still attached to her shoulders, and apparently no attempt had been made to unfasten it: both straps were still done up. Nor, as far as he could tell by looking, had she been interfered with in any way. The orange and blue jumper was still in place, or at any rate tucked into her shorts all the way round, and these in turn appeared intact. The only thing wrong with her clothing, as far as condition and outer completeness went, was the absence of her left shoe, assuming her to have worn neither stockings nor socks. He looked round carefully, but could find no trace of the missing article.

Returning his attention to the body, he remained a moment staring at the stiff dead toes of her left foot. Then his glance travelled upwards to the head, after he had decided that her legs were the ugliest he ever remembered seeing. 'Yes, there was certainly something wrong with her, poor wretch' he thought. 'Any normal girl would have covered them with the longest skirt she could get, not pranced round half naked in corduroy pants. She was definitely abnormal, I reckon: but that doesn't explain how she comes to be lying here so quiet and horrible.'

The cause of death was clear: she had been killed in the same way as Sergeant Lee, by a stab behind the right ear into the brain. Her head was at such an angle—thrust forward, nose touching the ground—that he was able to determine this without difficulty. There were no other marks of injury visible.

When he had finished his examination he returned to Lavinia Selby, standing with her back to him smoking furiously. He was relieved to find that she had apparently recovered most of her composure, though by now it was too dark to tell if her colour also had returned.

"Is she dead?" she asked, offering him a cigarette, which he accepted.

"Yes," he told her, but volunteered nothing further.

"What are you going to do?"

"We'd better get back to Burwood, I think."

"Both of us? But is it all right to leave—?"

She seemed not to be able to find suitable words for the end of her question, and it remained unfinished. Half a dozen answers crowded his mind, from the vulgarity of "It won't run away," to the sober truth of "We'd much better stick together—nobody's likely to attack two of us." He chose a compromise.

"You probably aren't too sure of the way back in the dark," he said, "and I wouldn't dream of asking you to stay here alone."

"No," she agreed: "and I wouldn't if you did ask. But will you be able to find the place again?"

"Oh yes—I was born not five miles from here, you know."

(' Which isn't an answer at all' he thought: 'but I'm pretty sure I can find it.')

"And now perhaps you won't mind if I ask what you were doing alone in the woods?" he asked presently, when they were safely on the road.

"Well, I was out searching for my brother this afternoon with a lot of other people—"

"Which party?" he interrupted.

" 'C', I think it was: a fat man who didn't know his way about was in charge."

"Yes, that would be Inspector Sibble from the other side. How did you get mixed up with his lot?"

"Well, originally I was going with Dr. Wrench, but at the last moment he couldn't get away because Nurse Spence sprained her ankle, so I went with Professor Peake instead—and Bellamy, the male nurse. I've been out every day since my brother disappeared, you know, and we just joined up with the first lot we came across.

"Anyway, about six o'clock I suddenly noticed I'd lost my bracelet—a gold one I was very fond of. I didn't want to leave it, and I thought I knew where I might have dropped it, when I had to take my shoe off because I got something in it, so I went back."

"Without telling anyone?"

"Yes. You see, we were all spread out, and it didn't seem worth making a fuss over. Besides, people might have thought I oughtn't to be bothering about a little thing like a bracelet when my brother was still lost, and it would have taken too long to explain that it was the last thing he gave me before—before he went mad, and that was why I wanted to find it. And I couldn't see the Professor or Bellamy, so I just went back by myself. It wasn't where I thought it might be, though, and so I tried returning the way I'd come. Quite hopeless, of course, but one does stupid things like that sometimes. I must have been looking far longer than I realized, though, because I suddenly noticed that it was getting dark. Then I almost walked on top of that body, and just screamed. It was an awful shock."

"I'm sure it was. Did you find your bracelet?"

"No. I oughtn't to have worried about it, I suppose—though it's probably a good job I did. Tell me, Mr. Dane, was the—I mean, has anyone been killed? Murdered?"

The Superintendent remained silent for a moment. In half a minute they would reach the first of Burwood's street lamps, and he wanted to see the effect of his answer.

"Yes," he said, timing things carefully, and slowing his walk. "It was the girl hiker."

At this she gave a little gasp: not so much of astonishment, he fancied, as of relief that what she had been dreading had happened at last.

"And you probably don't know about Sergeant Lee," he went on, as they approached the next lamp.

"Sergeant Lee? The big one with the moustache?"

"Yes, that's him."

"Then what?"

She had paused now, and was facing him, her mouth slightly open and her eyes regarding him intently.

"He was murdered this afternoon about a mile away from where you found Miss Trotter. In exactly the same way."

"This afternoon—in broad daylight? My God! Then he's still near—he must have been right close by all the time. Why the hell don't we see anything of him? This is simply terrible—killing two people the same day. But it isn't his fault, really it isn't. He's mad, you know—he can't help it."

By now she was almost in tears, and very distressed, and he did his best to soothe her.

"I know," he said, as kindly as he could. "And you're not quite right: Miss Trotter had been dead some time."

They remained silent for the rest of their walk, and as they entered the police-station the Superintendent, curiously enough, was thinking not about Lavinia or her brother Simon, nor about Lee and Betty Trotter. He was wondering what sort of a man they would send down from Scotland Yard.

X

THE MURDER OF Sergeant Lee, and the tragic discovery of Betty Trotter's dead body on the same day, turned the affair of Simon Selby's escape from a local concern into almost a national one. It was a long time since a policeman had been so brutally killed on duty, and the fact that his left boot was missing intrigued the public's imagination. In drawing-room and restaurant and saloon bar the fancifully minded strove to provide some plausible explanation for this curious feature of the business, but without much success. The truth seemed so very obvious: the murders had been done, and the footwear taken, by a madman, and what was the good of trying to find reason in a madman's actions? So, anyway, said the supporters of common sense without frills. What must be done was to catch him, and not only quickly, but if possible without further loss of life. Nobody quite believed that that would happen, however. The papers were eagerly scanned, and the wireless news bulletins as eagerly listened to, for reports of the finding of Prudence Hill and Mervyn Wilson. Both would be dead, the public anticipated, both would have at least one shoe missing, and many expected the girl to lack far more than that.

Chief-Inspector Beale's immediate superior, Superintendent Vinney, had serious thoughts of going down to the New Forest himself, but decided against it on the strength of his subordinate's knowledge of Hilary Peake and his history.

"All right, take Matthews and see what you can do," he said. "And don't mind how the Chief-constable down there treats you—he's apt to snarl a bit."

"So you've got something to thank me for after all," remarked Dickie Donovan smugly, when he heard the news. "Is Tony coming?"

He referred to Anthony Purdon, assistant editor of *The Stockbroker,* and Beale's closest friend. When sudden death was in the air, or its results stretched out in some cold rural mortuary, he could always find an excuse for leaving his desk and placing himself and his Bentley at Beale's service. He liked watching his friend tackle a case from the beginning, on equal terms with himself in the matter of information, as often as not; and he liked to maintain the pretence of keeping up with powers of reasoning and perception acuter than his own. He was the amateur, Beale the professional, and he was never reluctant to admit that for once the professional was in a different and far higher class.

"Yes, I know you can give me five clues and a beating," he had said once, "but I don't despair. One of these days my simple mind will interpret a simple fact simply, and correctly, while you're still weaving subtle and complicated theories for it to fit into."

He was tall, ugly where Beale was merely plain, powerfully built, and a confirmed bachelor at thirty-seven—five years younger than his friend. He was also an expert if hair-raising driver.

There were four of them in the Bentley on Friday May 14th as it swept towards Winchester at a steady fifty-five: Tony for once was not feeling much like hurrying. The third member of the party was the reporter, and the fourth Detective-sergeant 'Horsey' Matthews, as perkily cheerful as ever, and far too small, someone had remarked uncharitably, to be even a boy scout, far less a policeman. In appearance he resembled a jockey who had grown to resemble a favourite mount, and he was quite untroubled by the fact.

The journey proceeded mostly in silence, because Beale was busy reading and re-reading Superintendent Dane's confidential report, a hastily-composed and lengthy document containing full details of what had happened since Simon Selby's escape on April 29th. It made little or no mention of the author's own opinions, however. When he had finished with this he passed it on to Matthews and Dickie in the back, and sat brooding, while the car maintained its steady progress. Then, about two o'clock, with another twenty miles to go, he took out his note-book and made a few entries. He had long ago learnt to write without difficulty in almost any sort of vehicle.

'Interview Alfred Farmer' he scribbled. 'Had Selby ever been to the house before? How did he enter? Where were clothes, shaving things, etc?

'Get Supt. Dane's ideas—must have some unless nitwit.

'Find out if Peake still thinks Selby's sister helped him escape.

'Weapon one of missing bars?'

Burwood proved to be a small compact town which might conceivably have been attractive without its tawdry decorations. These consisted mostly of bunting and limp union jacks, some made of paper and some of cotton, with an occasional aristocrat of silk, but all hung without regard either for correctness or harmony of effect. They sprouted from casements, jutted over porches, flapped dismally in suspension from wires stretched across the main street, and draped almost every shop.

" 'Whose flag has braved a thousand years, The battle and the breeze'," murmured Tony. "Notwithstanding that it dates only from 1801. My country, right way up or wrong. 'The English of the twentieth century' some future historian will solemnly write 'were in many respects a primitive people. They loved bright colours, and although on occasion they could evince intense patriotism, they did so both crudely and garishly: all heart and no art, as it were. The boldness and extent of the display alone counted: quality found little esteem. Doubtless much may be pardoned to such childlike enthusiasm, but at times it was bound to degenerate into absurdity. It is actually on record that one Anthony Purdon, in the year 1937 and upon the occasion of the king's coronation, having chanced to visit the old-world town of Burwood, saw hanging from the upper front window of a gentlewomen's upholstery emporium seven flags of different and chiefly irrelevant nationalities, including those of Albania and San Domingo.' "

This monologue, whose composition rendered his driving erratic, was terminated by their arrival at the police-station at half past two. Beale and Matthews at once went in leaving the others to fix up rooms. They found Dane and Captain Wyndham waiting for them, though the latter almost immediately excused himself.

"Simply must get along to take charge," he said. "We're doing Broad Walk Enclosure, and there's two more bodies to find, you know. At least two, and I hope it'll be three—save a lot of trouble."

"Undoubtedly," agreed Beale. "I hope you'll be lucky, sir."

Wyndham nodded. He was clearly worried, and stood at the door a moment frowning at Beale through his spectacles: and his ultimate expression seemed chiefly one of disappointment.

"Glad to do anything you suggest," he grunted at last, and strode out.

"And I echo Captain Wyndham," said Dane with a smile. "You got my report all right, Inspector?"

"Yes, thank you sir—and very clear it was, as far as facts go."

"Yes? What wasn't clear, then?"

Beale hesitated, regarded the Superintendent again, decided he liked the look of him, and spoke without reserve.

"You were rather sparing with your opinions, sir."

"Oh, I hardly thought you'd want to be bothered with *them.* You'll be forming your own, surely?"

"I hope I shall: but I'd still like to know something of yours, if only for purposes of comparison. Perhaps you won't mind if I ask you one or two questions?"

"Of course not—carry on."

"Thank you. Then what do you really think about Selby's escape? Was it all that it seems to be on the surface?"

"Well, that's a bit difficult to say. I used to be a little doubtful, I don't mind admitting, but I don't think I am now. There doesn't seem to be much room left for doubt."

"Why not?" asked Beale quietly. "I take it you were suspicious partly because of the difficulty of climbing the wall, partly because of the window bars, and partly because of the burglary at Mr. Farmer's place?"

Dane stared at him with some little surprise.

"Those were certainly the chief points," he agreed.

"Then what's happened since to lull your suspicions? The two murders?"

"Why, yes. Since Selby's so obviously alive, there can't be any question about his escape, can there?"

"Not about the fact of its having happened, no. He's definitely vanished, and two persons have been murdered, or have been found murdered, in the New Forest. Both were apparently killed in the same unusual way, and therefore presumably by the same person, and there's every reason to suppose that that person was mad. Yes, I agree with all that,"—as Dane nodded: "but it still doesn't seem to tell us anything about the manner of Selby's escape from Balmer's Court. He's there one day, and gone the next, and the point that interests me at the moment almost more than any other is, how did he go? I mean, off his own bat, or with someone else's help or persuasion? As far as I can see, if he was helped there's nothing to make us say that he couldn't afterwards have escaped genuinely from whoever got him out."

"Good lord!" exclaimed Dane. "I never thought of that, Inspector—it would explain a lot of things, wouldn't it?"

"If they can't be explained in any other way, sir. Which point seemed most suspicious to you, the climb, the bars, or the apparent saneness of the burglary? I except the dummy in the bed, because we know we're dealing with a lunatic. I suppose I ought to except the bars for the same reason," he added with a smile, "but I'm not quite happy about it. The wall would be hard enough to climb anyway, by all accounts, but surely impossible in pyjamas if he was holding the bars? Then that would mean that he threw them over first, and picked them up afterwards on the other side, which seems just a trifle too deliberate to be plausible. Quite probably I'm wrong, though, so I won't press the point."

"Just a minute," said Dane. "I'm sorry to be dense, but do you mind explaining about the dummy? Do you mean it was too sane of him to leave one?"

"More or less—the whole thing seems a little contradictory. Can he be sensible enough to make a dummy at all, and yet at the same time stupid enough to make one out of his day clothes and escape in his night things? Has the point been queried?"

"Not by me," answered Dane frankly. "I'm afraid you're showing us up, Inspector. By the way, it's very probable that one of the missing bars was the weapon."

"Good—I was ready for that from the description of the wounds. But did he take them in order to do the murders, or did he do the murders because he had the bars with him? The first seems to show definite forethought, but I suppose he may have been capable of that even though he was mad.

"Now, about the wall: as a question of fact, *could* he have climbed over it without assistance?"

Dane leant back in his chair, smiling again.

"The only fact I can tell you is that I don't know," he answered. "The wall's just short of twelve feet high, and at one point there's a chipped brick which might have given him a hand-hold, and another lower down for his feet. All the same, it's not an easy matter to say plain yes or no, Inspector. I put a couple of men on to seeing what they could do, and they couldn't do anything except break their nails and lost their tempers. Then I put a third man on the job, and he got over without much trouble. After that the first two men tried again, and one of 'em managed it this time, but the other still couldn't get started.

"Well, that's all right as far as it goes, but I simply can't say if it would hold good for Selby. For one thing, he's supposed to have escaped in canvas shoes, plimsolls, which wouldn't be the best things to climb in. For another, he was in the dark, when he probably wouldn't have been able to see the holds at all."

Beale nodded.

"It's certainly harder to settle than I realized, sir," he said. "About the most we can say is that it may have been possible: very grudging in view of subsequent facts, I suppose, but there you are. We can't afford to assume he was capable of doing the impossible just because he's a lunatic."

"Exactly," agreed Dane. "I tried to make somewhat the same point to Captain Wyndham."

"With success?" queried Beale; but the Superintendent merely shrugged his vast shoulders.

"And lastly the burglary, sir. Can you tell me if Selby had ever been in Mr. Farmer's house before?"

"When he was sane, do you mean?"

"At any time. Can he possibly have known his way about, or even that such a person as Farmer existed?"

"He may have known that, but nothing about the house, as far as I can find out. His sister says not."

"I see. He didn't leave any fingerprints?"

"No, nor footprints either. But Farmer's garden path is gravel, and goes right up to the door."

"They're about the same height and build, I take it?"

"Almost exactly—somewhere round my size. It was the first point that struck me—so very convenient, you know. The first place he goes into has just what he wants."

"And the owner obligingly as deaf as Baal. You're sure it *was* the first place?"

"Pretty sure. We've made extensive enquiries but nobody else seems to think they've been burgled. One trouble is that it's difficult to say exactly when the things were taken. Farmer's a careless sort, besides being deaf, and he can't be certain if it happened on the Thursday night or not. He isn't even too sure where the various articles were—shoes and gloves and shirt, I mean. The suit was done up in a parcel in his bedroom, he thinks—it came back from the cleaners a few days before. All he knows definitely is that his stuff was gone by Saturday morning."

Beale seemed a little surprised at this.

"But wouldn't he miss his shaving tackle?" he asked. Dane shook his head.

"Wait till you meet Mr. Farmer," he advised. "I shouldn't think he shaves more than once a week, if that."

"Yet he has his suits cleaned."

"His suit. He was going to a party or something on the Saturday, and wanted to make a good impression, I think. That's why he was in such a fury when he found he'd nothing decent left to go in—came tearing over here to demand that we get the stuff back by midday."

Beale smiled.

"He sounds a little eccentric," he said.

"He is."

"Been in the neighbourhood long?"

"About ten years. He writes, you know—very intense psychological novels. I haven't read any, so I can't tell you what they're like."

Beale nodded, and returned to the business in hand.

"What else bothered you about the burglary, sir?" he asked: and was prepared to judge Dane's intelligence as a detective by his answer.

"Well, there was the matter of the mirror," said the Superintendent.

"Oh, then he did take a mirror?"

"No—I meant the one he didn't take: a Sherlockismus, I'm afraid. It was on the shelf in his kitchen with the rest of the things—he hasn't a proper bathroom—but hadn't been touched. We tested all the prints, and they were all Farmer's. I gather you'd spotted the point."

"Yes, it certainly occurred to me—as also the kind of razor involved. I understand it was a safety."

"Yes, though I'm not sure how you know—nor about the mirror. I don't think I mentioned it in my report. Oh, I see—because I didn't, I suppose? But that still doesn't explain the razor. You see, the significance of that only struck me this morning."

He paused, obviously waiting for an answer; and the one he got surprised him.

"In a way you could put it that Mervyn Wilson told me," said Beale.

"Wilson?"

"Yes, though not directly,"—and he summarized the circumstances. "It made me wonder," he went on. "I was curious about how anyone with three years' growth of hair on his face was to do much with a safety razor. He didn't take any scissors?"

Dane shook his head decisively.

"Not from Farmer's, nor from Peake's place," he answered. "I asked this morning—late, admittedly: you're sharper than I am. Incidentally, thinking about it now I'm almost inclined to renew my old suspicions."

"Just of Selby's escape in general, or of any particular person as accomplice?"

"Well, I'd prefer you not to let it go any further, but I've thought quite a bit about the idea that his sister and Dr. Wrench may have got him out."

"Now that's interesting," said Beale, sitting forward. "Don't be offended, sir, but is it an original idea?"

"As far as I know. The only person I've discussed it with is Captain Wyndham, and he says it's nonsense: but then, he's a friend of Miss Selby's. Why did you ask that?"

"Because—on similar terms, that it doesn't go any further—I also understand from the same source that Professor Peake suspects precisely the same thing, or did at one time. He may have changed his mind, of course."

"Peake, eh? That's queer—maybe there's something in it. What do you think?"

Beale shook his head.

"I haven't seen Miss Selby or Dr. Wrench," he answered. "Are they at all likely suspects?"

"Not as people, no," said Dane with a frown. "They both seem perfectly honest about everything, and very worried indeed about Selby's disappearance, especially since the murders. Her bracelet's been found, too, in a suitable place—the one she was looking for yesterday when she came on Betty Trotter's body: which bears out her story. All the same, if there's to be any doubt about how Selby escaped, then I don't see anyone else to go for. His sister's his only living relative, and seems to be the only person who's got any interest in him. Wrench, of course, if he had a hand in it, would be helping her. They're more or less in love, I believe, though no question of any official engagement. But you were probably told that too—they don't attempt to hide it."

"Yes," agreed Beale quietly. "Wilson seems to have spotted the attachment. Have you been keeping any sort of watch on them, sir?"

"Yes, but they've both been behaving quite normally, considering the circumstances: and previous to Selby's escape too, as far as we can find out. She goes out every day with one or other of the search-parties, and the doctor with her, except yesterday."

"Which reminds me: how was it that nobody else found the body first? You spoke in your report about her going back the way she'd come: then hadn't that part been already searched?"

Dane shook his head.

"She'd wandered off into another enclosure," he explained. "Yes, I see what you're thinking,"—as Beale frowned. "Why couldn't her brother do the same—dodge us here, there and all over the shop? It looks to me as if that must be what he's up to, but I honestly don't see how we're to stop it short of getting half the army out and doing the whole Forest at once."

"It's an idea," agreed Beale with a smile. "Have you used the air at all?"

"Yes, we had a couple of private planes flying low on and off during the first week, but with no result."

At this point 'Horsey' Matthews decided he had been silent long enough.

"What about the Professor, sir?" he asked, addressing the Superintendent. "Does he go along with the doctor and Miss Selby?"

"Most days, Sergeant—why?"

"Well sir, I was wondering if he'd keep an eye on them too, same as you've done, seeing he thought the same."

"Yes, quite probably that's why he did go—a good point."

"And what about whoever you put on to tag them, sir? What was he doing to let Miss Selby go back for her bangle alone like that? If it'd been me, I'd have been thinking maybe she was sneaking off to meet her brother."

Dane acknowledged the shrewdness of the question with a smile.

"Another good point, with an unsatisfactory answer, I'm afraid. The man I put on to Dr. Wrench hung about Balmer's Court all the afternoon and evening, and of course saw nothing, but the one who was looking after Miss Selby had to join her search-party. At that time I hadn't told the Chief what was happening: he's a friend of hers, as I said, and I thought he mightn't like the idea too much. In consequence Weller was acting more or less unofficially, though under my orders. When he found himself detailed by Inspector Sibble to do something else he wasn't quick-witted enough to make an excuse, unfortunately. Sibble comes from the other side of the Forest, and was in charge of the party. He doesn't know his way about here much, though, and got Weller to lead. I ought to have foreseen a muddle like that, but I'm afraid I didn't."

"Captain Wyndham knows about the watching now, doesn't he?" asked Beale.

"Yes—I told him that same afternoon. The only question is whether to go on with it or not. What do you think, Inspector? After all, it's not much good your coming down here unless you have a say in things."

"Thank you. Then I suggest that you get a couple of plain-clothes men from another part of the county, and put them under Sergeant Matthews here."

"Certainly, if you think that's best."

"Thanks. By the way, have you found out what Peake thinks of the latest developments? Does he still maintain that Selby had no homicidal tendencies?"

"No, I wouldn't say that, but it's clear enough he doesn't like the idea. I think you'd better see him yourself, and then you'll be able to form an opinion."

"Yes: I might do that right away, really. After all, I shan't be much good in a search-party, because I don't know the country either. I had a fortnight down this way ten years ago, but that won't help."

He paused for a few moments, thinking, and then asked a blunt question.

"I've been wondering why you called in Scotland Yard at all," he said: "why?"

The Superintendent looked uncomfortable.

"If you want the truth," he said, "I didn't feel I could cope with it myself. Or perhaps not that so much as that I oughtn't to try to when there was expert help for the asking. With all due respect, Captain Wyndham isn't much of a detective, and when he mentioned the possibility of calling your people in I agreed at once.

"On the face of it the thing's simple enough, I know: all we've got to do is to find Simon Selby, and anybody else he may have murdered before we do catch him. On the other hand, we've been after him for a fortnight, and got nowhere. Exactly what you're going to be able to do about it that we can't remains to be seen: all the clues are probably stone-cold by now, if there ever were any. I only know I feel a lot happier about it now you're here.

"I'm not suggesting that all murder cases are alike, of course, and that you've only got to do what you've done before to solve the whole business. They're probably as different as one day's cross-word puzzle from the next day's. All the same, somebody who's used to doing cross-words will usually get on better with one than somebody who's stuck to anagrams, say."

"Well, I only hope we shan't let you down, sir," said Beale. He thought he understood Dane's problem, and sympathized.

"I'm sure you won't: and—if the sergeant isn't listening—there's really no need for the 'sir'. I'm dead certain I shouldn't be a superintendent if I were at Scotland Yard."

XI

IT WAS AFTER half past four when Beale and Tony set out for Balmer's Court. Matthews remained at the police-station, and Dickie Donovan elected to go off on his own.

"Then for heaven's sake be careful," Beale warned him. "By all accounts that's exactly what Wilson did—cleared off by himself and hasn't been seen since." Dickie merely nodded, his face quite serious for once. In general he took life cheerfully, but the disappearance and probable death of Mervyn Wilson had temporarily shocked him. Although he could contemplate the murder of anyone unknown to him with no more than professional interest, when it came to one of his own friends he found, a little to his surprise, that he was not so dispassionate in his view. He was surprised at this discovery because for some time past he had imagined himself to be singularly devoid of sentiment in any form. People were mostly not worth getting fond of, he had said cynically in his extreme youth after being turned down by a girl he had really cared about; and he had repeated the statement so often since that he had almost come to believe it. People were feather-less five-toed bipeds who differed among themselves only in the degree to which they lacked the more desirable qualities of mind or character. If by chance you found something good in Smith, you could almost certainly duplicate it in Brown or Jones or Robinson, or another; and if you could not, it was likely to be no great loss. Why then grow over-fond of Smith?

From this seeping condemnation of the human species he excepted perhaps half a dozen persons, among them Beale. He also excepted himself, which reassured those observant enough to notice it that his trouble was curable: the cynic to despair of is the one who despises himself more than others.

It began to dawn on him now, however, that possibly he had been making a mistake for years: that perhaps after all he was not incapable of affection. Although he could imagine no one more ordinary, in general, than Mervyn Wilson, and although he had not been particularly intimate with the man, nevertheless the fact that he was probably lying dead in a nearby wood with a hole in his head behind his ear, and beyond reach of all human aid, moved Dick considerably. He had known Wilson, though sketchily: therefore he had a special interest in him. If the missing reporter should in fact be dead, it would mean that he—Donovan—had suffered an irreparable loss, if not a deeply wounding one.

It seemed obvious to him that he could do little by himself towards proving or disproving Wilson's fate directly: that business was in better hands than his, being done by people who were familiar with the country, and must eventually come across the body if there were one. The person to concentrate on seemed to be Simon Selby, who was almost certainly not dead. The three likeliest sources from which to gather information about him were Balmer's Court, Lavinia Selby, and Alfred Farmer's cottage, the last dwelling-place which the lunatic was thought to have visited. Beale was undertaking the first, the second would be better done after an introduction, but the third he could tackle himself straight away. He therefore resolved to see Alfred Farmer, and get first-hand details of the burglary.

Balmer's Court turned out to be a rambling old-fashioned house set in two acres or so of gardens, and bounded on the north and east by the Forest. The approach led by way of an ornamental iron gate through pleasant lawns to the building itself, which struck Tony as a most improbable place for a private lunatic asylum. It conveyed to him more the atmosphere of a country rectory where tennis is played discreetly on sunny summer afternoons, except Sundays, when sermons would be laboriously pieced together within smelling-distance of the roses. He said as much to Beale, as they waited for someone to answer the bell, but was contradicted with a shake of the head.

"No sermon worth hearing was ever composed later than a Friday," said his friend, with an air of superior knowledge.

"Which only proves my point."

"Nonsense—I wasn't talking about school sermons. You could count all the ones you've heard since on your tail. I suppose there *is* someone in?"

He rang again, and presently a maid appeared. No, she was very sorry, but neither Professor Peake nor Dr. Wrench was at home. Yes, they could certainly wait for a while if they liked, but she wasn't able to say for sure what time anybody would be back.

They were shown into what seemed to be a lounge, whose windows overlooked flower-beds massed with stately tulips.

"Florid," remarked Tony, when they were alone, gazing at the display of colour. "Don't they look exactly as if they were made of wax, and proud of it? I prefer something a bit more friendly—

common things like snapdragons and stocks and candytuft, not rows and rows of expensive snobs."

"The black ones show up well, though," said Beale. "They must be nearly good enough to have satisfied Dumas."

"Which one? All right, I'll answer myself.

> "Dumas *pere*
> Wrote *Les Trois Mousquetaires:*
> But it was probably Dumas *fils*
> Who responded to the cries of *Bis!*"

The last line was rather gabbled, however, as there came a sharp knock at the door, and a middle-aged man entered. He was as tall as Tony, dressed in a worn tweed suit, and his lined face was almost without expression.

'The male nurse' Beale told himself instantly and correctly, and listened while Abel Bellamy explained who he was, why Peake and Dr. Wrench were out, and asked if he could be of any help.

"Quite probably: if I give you my card I expect you'll be able to guess what I've come about."

Bellamy bestowed on it a brief glance, narrowed his eyes a little, and nodded.

"It's a bad business, Inspector," he said. "Mr. Selby's been gone a fortnight now, just over. I hope you'll be able to do something—it's worrying the Professor. He hasn't hardly eaten anything for days."

Beale made a commiserative noise.

"While we're waiting, could you show us the courtyard?" he suggested.

"Why, yes—come with me, sir."

He led the way out of the lounge, down a carpeted passage which smelt faintly of disinfectant, and paused beside a door at the end on the right. It had a small sliding panel in it, and nearby were two electric-light switches.

"This was Mr. Selby's bedroom," he remarked: "the one he escaped from. Would you care to have a look round it first?"

"Yes, thank you."

They gave its felt-lined interior only a cursory examination, however: apart from the low bed clamped to the floor, and a built-in cupboard full of clothes, it was quite empty. Beale soon went over to the window, projected his head as far as possible, and spent some moments studying the cement work outside it. There were still five bars in place of the original seven, three on one side of the gap and two on the other. They were set about five inches apart, he reckoned, which would allow Selby ample room to have squeezed through, even if he had worn his outdoor clothes. That, then, was the end of one tentative theory: that the lunatic had escaped in pyjamas because only so would his body pass through the opening he had made. He tried one after another of the five bars, but could make no impression however hard he pulled or pushed, and when Tony assisted there was still no noticeable result.

"Maybe it's easier from outside," suggested Beale. "We can't get much of a grip in here because of the window-sill."

He turned to Bellamy, silently watching them.

"How long have you been with Professor Peake?" he asked.

"Close on two years, sir."

"Were these bars here before your time?"

"Oh yes, sir—one of the first things he had done when he come here, I think."

"And do you happen to know if any repairs have been necessary recently?"

"No, nothing—never had a workman in the place that I can remember."

"All right, let's go outside. By the way, I'm not keeping you from anything else?"

Bellamy seemed slightly surprised at the question, the first time Tony had noticed his features register a recognizable expression. He was a dreary-looking man except for his eyes; even his voice was unusually slow. He spoke with an accent which Beale was unable to place: it was a rasp rather than a burr, yet it was not the accent of a townsman, he judged.

"No sir, I'm not busy," was the answer. "There's only Miss Vining to look after now, and she don't give much trouble."

"The other patient?"

"Yes sir—she suffers from religion."

"How did she and Mr. Selby get on?"

"They didn't, sir—always kept strictly separate they were. It'd have been as much as my job's worth to let them meet. Mr. Selby didn't like but a few people, and women upset him more than men."

"Except his sister, I suppose?"

"Yes, except Miss Lavinia. He was more like a sane person with her than with anyone else, but even she couldn't do anything with him when he had one of his bad times. He'd just stare through her like she wasn't there. But the Professor'll be able to tell you about all that better than I can."

By now they were in the courtyard, a confined space about forty-five yards by twenty. In spite of its unpleasant associations—a lunatic walked here daily—it seemed to Beale to be one of the most peaceful places he had ever seen: the impression struck him the moment the glass door was closed behind them. He felt that he had entered a tiny unknown world where voices would fall naturally to whispers, and one's heart-beat become the muffled sound of a hammer: the air was cool and fresh, and the grass a brilliant green. It was crossed and surrounded by stone-paved paths, bordered with dwarf anemones and London Pride, and their placing, he thought, might have made a coherent pattern if he had been able to view them from a sufficient height above.

On three sides of the courtyard was the twelve-foot brick wall, and on the fourth the house, completely blocking it, a mass of old grey stone studded with windows. Only odd ones here and there were barred on the upper floors, but all on the lower. Beale at once noticed the absence of drain-pipes or any means of climbing towards the roof. Moss prevented the house from looking naked, but there was no ivy and no creeper: Selby could not have got in upstairs without the help of a ladder. His bedroom was in the south-west corner of the courtyard, its missing bars as conspicuous as absent teeth. Fifteen feet or so to the left of this came three steps leading down to a battered wooden door, which he realized must be the outer entrance to the cellars. For a moment he was inclined to investigate, but decided not to: he could surely trust the Superintendent to have covered all the elementary work.

Instead he walked over to the wall, and began to look for the foot-hold Dane had mentioned. After some trouble he found it, and the corresponding hand-hold above.

"New, by the look of it," said Tony, pointing to the latter. "Newer than the other, anyway. Did he make it himself, d'you think?"

He included Bellamy in his query, but the male nurse shook his head.

"We hadn't noticed either of them before," he replied, "though they may have been there, for all that."

Beale raised his eyebrows a little, and then with a word of explanation removed his jacket. His first attempt to climb the wall failed, and his second, but the third time he succeeded in getting astride it at the cost of a bruised knee. Tony clapped gently, helped him down, and declined to see what he could do himself.

Back on the ground Beale turned to Bellamy, watching without marked interest, and asked what sort of a night it had been on April 29th.

"Well sir,"—after a moment's thought, "not too dark and not too light. There was a moon all right, just past the full, but it was under the clouds mostly."

"You must have a jolly good memory," remarked Tony.

"Oh, I don't think so, sir—I was out a good while looking for him with the doctor."

"Well, I don't think I'd like that climb in the dark," said Beale. "Nor in pyjamas. Nor in plimsolls. Let's look at the window again from the outside."

They came to the conclusion, after rigorous scrutiny, that if both exerted all their strength they would probably be able to pull two of the bars out, but not the other three.

"And maybe one of the missing ones was specially weak," suggested Tony hopefully. "Then he could have used it as a lever on the other one."

"From inside?"

"Oh, I don't know about that."

Beale turned again to Bellamy.

"What was the longest that Mr. Selby was ever alone here with nobody watching him?" he asked.

"An hour, sir—fine days he and Miss Vining took share and share about. You see, we never reckoned anyone could climb over."

"Ha!" exclaimed Tony. "I have a query to make. If—"

But he got no farther, because of Beale's discouraging expression.

XII

PROFESSOR PEAKE returned at six o'clock, but without Dr. Wrench, who had gone on to Lavinia Selby's cottage two miles away. Within a few minutes of arriving he was sitting at his desk facing Beale and Tony, and both thought he looked worried as well as tired. There were rings under his brown eyes, his cheeks appeared pouchy, and his manner had a listlessness which, Beale suspected, was not natural to him. The furniture in his study was made for use rather than for comfort, and the most striking thing in the room was a large lacquered screen standing to the left behind the Professor's chair. From it grinned the face of a red dragon, and this fascinated Tony, who had a secret fondness for such beasts.

"I dare say you want to ask me a lot of questions," remarked Peake, with his recognizably American intonation. "Be as short as you can, will you? I'm not feeling up to much lately. You see, I can't help continually telling myself that I'm responsible for this wretched business, and yet I'm durned if I know what I could have done to prevent it. I simply don't know at all."

He paused, staring glumly at his visitors as if they had been brokers' men, and then gave them a weary smile.

"Care for a drink?" he asked. "I would. I don't generally take anything till later, but for once—"

He rose, moved across to the bell beside the main bookcase, and a moment later Bellamy appeared. His bearing was quiet, almost stern, but he favoured Beale and Tony with a slight nod of recognition.

"Will you bring the decanter, please, and three glasses?" requested Peake.

But, to the surprise of both his visitors, what they were presently offered was not whisky but sharp red wine. Both asserted, mendaciously, that they liked it.

When the male nurse had finally departed, Beale ventured a question.

"What exactly is Bellamy's position here?" he asked.

The Professor seemed a little surprised.

"Bellamy? Oh, he's supposed to be a nurse, though he isn't qualified in any way. He does a lot of the heavy work, and helps generally wherever he'll be most good. A dry old stick, but pretty efficient with his hands. You're wondering why he brought the drink up, I suppose? He's rather taken it on himself to look after me—always has."

Again he paused, regarding Beale intently, as though he were wondering if so quiet and ordinary-looking a person could be worth confiding in.

"I reckon I oughtn't to tell you, maybe," he went on, "but it'll save you asking him questions. Two years back, about, I nearly ran him down in my car—he lurched right across me, and I had all I could do to miss him. The poor chap was starving—on the roads with no money and nowhere to sleep and so on. I brought him back here and gave him a square meal, and the end of it was that he begged me to give him a job too. I was a bit dubious, but he's turned out far and away better than I hoped, and I really believe he'd do anything for me. He doesn't say much—I guess you found it hard work to get anything out of him at all: but I think he feels I helped restore his self-respect."

"I see," said Beale. "What was he before he came to you?"

"Don't know, really—he never volunteered much, and I haven't bothered him. I take people more or less as I find them, I'm afraid—always have done. I think he said something once about being at sea for a time, but how long I don't know. Anyway, it doesn't seem to matter much."

He broke off to finish his wine, eyeing Beale shrewdly.

"Why not get down to business?" he suggested. "You're here about Selby—well, what is it you want to know? I've told a dozen people already, so one more won't make any odds. Only it's no manner of good asking me where he is, because I don't know."

Beale considered for a moment.

"Actually, there isn't a lot I want to ask at the moment," he said. "In fact, only four questions that really matter—but they're quite important."

"Good," remarked Peake quietly. "But your friend?" he added, turning his head.

"Oh, I never ask questions," Tony assured him. "I'm nobody—just a sort of chopping-block, and so I have to be about to know what's being chopped. But when Inspector Beale says four he probably means forty-four—it's only fair that somebody should warn you."

"Thanks—though I took it as a figure of speech anyway."

"Oh, but I meant it," said Beale, smiling: "four main ones, and any subsidiaries they give rise to. First, give me your frank opinion about these murders. Did Simon Selby do them?"

Hilary Peake gazed at him for quite five seconds, and then jerked his head in a puzzled way.

"Is there any possible doubt?" he countered.

"I don't know—I'm asking you. Briefly, had he any homicidal tendencies?"

"Am I to answer from my own experience, or in view of what's happened?"

"From experience, please."

"Then I can only repeat what I've already told other people: that I never noticed any. I can't conceive how I could have been taken in, but there you are—apparently I was."

"Is there anybody else in a position to bear out your views? Qualified to do so, or express any at all, I mean. Dr. Wrench, for instance?"

Peake shook his head.

"Not Wrench, no. He's a clever chap, and he'll go a long way if he perseveres, but at present he's a comparative beginner at the game. He's only been with me three years, you know. I took him on so that he could look after Selby's health during a temporary absence I had to make, and found him worth keeping."

"And you?"

The Professor smiled faintly.

"Forty years," he said. "I'm sixty-five now, and I was twenty-five when I started; and it seems I know very little, after all that time. But I'm not answering your question. Yes, there is someone else who's fit to give an opinion—Sir Digby Grant. Have you heard of him?"

"Vaguely."

Again Peake smiled.

"You English!" he said. "Most of you know the name of your Prime Minister, and you're pretty hot at boxers and cricketers and film stars, but I'm darned if any of you know who does the real work. At least, maybe I'm prejudiced, but I reckon it does more ultimate good to turn mad minds into sane ones than to play the fool at Westminster or on the movies. Digby Grant's about the best of your psychiatrists, and he was down here for some months a while back studying Selby's case. Admitted he didn't get anywhere much, but I think he'd bear me out that there was no earthly reason to suspect the man of having homicidal tendencies."

"Thank you. He was violent at times, though, wasn't he?"

"Sure he was: but all lunatic violence isn't homicidal, any more than everybody who runs is running to catch a train."

"No, quite. Then how do you reconcile what's happened with his and your opinion?"

Peake made a gesture of impatience.

"My dear man, there's only one way: by admitting I was dead wrong. I was out by a mile—I'm a sucker at my job. I don't know a potential killer from a sister of mercy."

Again Beale nodded.

"And do you believe that in your heart?" he asked seriously.

"Believe it? I haven't any choice."

"Oh, but you have: the choice of all intelligent men to back themselves up when they know they know best. To believe the evidence of their own eyes and ears and experience instead of other people's common sense. Especially when the experience is specialized knowledge, like yours."

But Peake at once exposed the weak point in Beale's argument.

"Specialized, certainly: but knowledge? I doubt it. Not in any absolute meaning of the word, at all events: not the sort of knowledge that knows why watering's good for flowers or pills for the belly-ache. A kind of experimental guess-work, I'd call it."

"In other words," suggested Tony, "the science of detection as practised in all the best circles. The snobs call it deduction, and the superstitious intuition, and they're both right, only one stresses the conscious side, and the other the unconscious. Pardon my interrupting like this: but now I have got my mouth open I may as well ask the question I said I wouldn't. What about the missing boots and shoes, Professor? Can previous knowledge account for them?"

Peake smiled more cheerfully.

"It can and it can't," he said. "As shoes, no: as missing things, yes. Selby was a born collector—always has been, so his sister says, even when he was normal. Then it used to be ordinary things like stamps and butterflies and snuff-boxes, but while he's been with me it's varied from the dust-jackets of novels to drawing-pins and crackers."

"Crackers?" interposed Beale.

"Well, sorry—biscuits to you. The last thing before he escaped he was collecting matches, but he used to change about very abruptly, and to my mind there's nothing intrinsically impossible in the idea that he suddenly directed his collecting energies towards shoes. And what you call boots as well, of course," he added. "We don't use the word except for high boots—Wellingtons."

"Really?" said Beale. "We're learning something, anyway. Do you think he might have escaped solely in order to collect—shoes?"

"I don't know," answered Peake, with a grin of acknowledgment at the careful wording. "I'd have expected him to try getting hold of ours first, I think—mine or Bellamy's or Wrench's."

"And he didn't?"

"No—I enquired this morning as soon as I heard the details."

"And another point, with just a shade of difference: is it likely that he's done the murders solely to acquire shoes?"

"Well, that seems the obvious conclusion to draw."

Beale nodded.

"Then why only left ones?" he asked.

"Oh, don't let that vex you. Why brown eggshells instead of white ones? Why back-collar buttons and not front ones? He collected both those for a spell last year, but never gave a rational explanation of why he imposed such arbitrary limits on himself. 'I like them better'—that was his line."

"I see—thanks. And now for the second real question—"

"But the thirteenth actual one," murmured Tony.

"Hush—don't count aloud. Is the method of murdering consistent with the idea of Selby's guilt?"

"Guilt?" queried Peake sharply.

"Well, with the idea of his having done them, then—I wasn't meaning to imply any moral condemnation."

"Good—I fancied just for a moment that you were, like that bone-head Wyndham. Yes, it is, as far as I can judge. At all events, he'd find it natural to use the same method in every case, but why he didn't stab them through the eye or the throat instead I can't say, of course. Nobody in the world could—it's just one of those things."

"It makes sense that he wasn't particular about the sex of his victims?"

"If you look at it in another way, that he wasn't particular about the sex of the shoes he was collecting."

"Thank you—that's nicely put. And here's another one, while I think of it: was there any special reason for his taking his watch with him?"

"A good enough one: it was a present from his sister, and he attached a good deal of sentimental value to it. Maybe what he used to say himself will explain: 'It reminds me of when I didn't make her cry'."

"Poor devil—then he knew he wasn't normal?"

"Yes—it was one of the most curious features of his case."

"And now number three: do you believe he escaped without help, or not?"

Again the Professor stared.

"You do ask the durndest things, don't you?" he commented. "Does it matter what I believe?"

"Yes, I think so. After all, you were the person who took precautions against his escape—and yet it happened. If I tied you up in an attic, and locked and bolted you in, and went out for a stroll in the garden, and when I came back you opened the door to me—well, I'd be pretty certain somebody had helped you."

Hilary Peake smiled.

"I used to think the whole thing was a bit fishy," he said.

"But you don't any longer?"

"No, not now."

"Why not?"

"Because I've had an opportunity of studying the people I suspected in the light of my suspicions,"—Peake was choosing his words carefully. "I've come to the conclusion that I was wrong."

"In other words, you don't believe now that either Dr. Wrench or Miss Selby had anything to do with whatever happened on the night of April 29th?"

"Exactly—good guessing. But how—?"

Briefly Beale explained what he had learnt from Dickie Donovan about the Professor's opinions: but made no reference to his knowledge also of Peake's previous history.

"And what made you suspect those two in particular?" he asked.

"Because they were the only ones I could think of with a possible motive, and I wasn't easy about the idea of Selby pulling those bars out on his own."

"I see: and how do you account for that now? Mr. Purdon and I tried the remaining ones before you came, and we didn't get on so well."

"No? But if Selby was a homicidal maniac, and I never noticed, what's to stop him having been Sandow and Samson combined? I guess I still wouldn't have noticed. And anyway, you never know how strong a man is till he really tries."

"And the climb over the wall?"

"Oh, the local Superintendent showed me where he probably got over. I don't doubt it was the place all right."

"You're quite certain now that neither Dr. Wrench nor Miss Selby know anything about the escape?"

"Yes—at least, as certain as I've any right to be. Allowing for the fact that I don't seem to be much of a judge of things, I mean."

"Now now, Professor!" reproved Tony. "Do please stop frog-marching yourself—it makes me uncomfortable."

"Sorry, sir—but I feel I deserve it."

"And the two nurses?" continued Beale.

"Oh no, quite out of the question."

"I see. Now, what about the burglary at Mr. Farmer's place?"

"I know very little about it, I'm afraid. It doesn't seem to have been beyond his capabilities—I understand the door only has to be shoved hard, and it opens."

"Do you know the place?"

"Only by sight—I've never met the man."

"And it's no good asking what you think Selby would do the moment he got over the wall, I suppose?"

"Not much. He probably did the same as you or I would have done: ran like—like—"

"Like a madman," suggested Tony gravely.

"Just so. What was the point of your question, though, Inspector?"

"I was trying to find out if you thought Farmer's place too near, or too far away, or in the right direction."

The Professor made a clucking noise.

"I honestly hadn't thought about it," he confessed. "I should say it's all right, though—three miles off, and you can get to it through the woods, if you go the right way. That's a thing that nobody can say, though. The burglary seems to show he did, doesn't it?"

"Yes, it seems to," agreed Beale. "Now, here's my fourth question: what about the dummy?"

At once Peake nodded, and his manner became more alert.

"You're the first person who's had the gumption to ask about that," he said. "I tried telling that fool of a Chief-constable, only he wouldn't listen. You think it's queer that he cleared off in his night robes and left his day clothes behind? But it isn't, really—or that isn't the queer thing about it. The fact is that he very often slept in his ordinary things—more often than not. What puzzles me more is that he went off with so little on. He felt the cold worse than anybody I know—he'd shiver when most people thought it was warm."

"Would he have had enough sense to realize that a dummy made out of his suit would be more likely to deceive than one made out of his pyjamas?"

"Yes, I reckon so. At his brightest, anyway."

"And now my turn," put in Tony. "How did Nurse Who-is-it see the thing, or spot that anything was wrong at all? Did she have a torch?"

"No need," answered the Professor. "There was always a light on in his room at night."

"Yes," said Beale. "I saw the two switches outside the door, and also the two bulbs. Lastly, what about the beard? I understand you don't like the idea of his cutting it off himself?"

Peake shook his head decisively.

"I don't, and that's flat: but what am I to do? If I say he wouldn't have meddled with his hair under any circumstances, then I've got to disbelieve in the burglary. Not that it happened, of course, but that he did it. But if I go as far as that, I've no choice but to believe he was helped, and the razor and so on taken for a blind. Then I start looking for the people who helped him—as I have done: and I get no place. Not to make any bones about it, Inspector, I'd rather wait till he's caught before I make my mind up."

"Just a bit," interrupted Tony, as Beale was about to speak. "Has anybody considered the idea that what really happened was that Selby suddenly recovered his sanity? Wouldn't that explain a lot of things?"

It seemed to him a sparkling idea, and he smiled amiably at the lacquered dragon as he formulated it.

"All but one," said Peake in answer, half turning to see where his questioner was looking. "Oh, it's my screen you're staring at," he remarked. "Nice, isn't it? Yes, that would clear up all but one thing, sir: that people in Selby's condition don't suddenly recover their wits like that. Not in ten minutes, nor even in ten days, without a major miracle, and I'm getting a trifle old to believe in such things. Till they're proven, anyway," he added. "Then I might."

"Well," said Beale, "that's about all my questions—ones I've any right to ask. There is one other point, though, if you'd be so kind."

Peake looked at him steadily, and—it seemed to Tony—rather suspiciously.

"You could always ask," he remarked at last.

"Thank you—then I will. Why did you leave America, Professor? To put it crudely, were you driven out?"

"On account of what, pray?"

"On account of Thomas Jefferson Jay."

At this, to Beale's surprise, Peake's face at once cleared, and he looked almost cheerful.

"You know the whole story?" he queried, a note of eagerness in his voice."

"Yes, I think so."

"Good—good. I reckon I ought to have guessed you would, only I rather came over here expecting everybody to, and they didn't. But it's your job to know things, of course."

Beale managed not to blush.

"Put it that people tell me things, anyway," he said.

"And you want to know if I was driven out. Why?"

"Partly from curiosity, and partly because it occurred to me that you might have active personal enemies. Admittedly it's a bit preposterous to suppose they'd be active enough to kidnap Selby just in order to embarrass you, and it wouldn't explain the murders at all: but the improbable does sometimes happen. Is that a satisfactory answer?"

"Very—at least you're honest, and not devoid of imagination. I'll be equally honest: I left the States of my own accord so that I wouldn't be driven out. You see, I had Mrs. Cornelius Jay after me, and she's got a deal of power behind her still. Far more than she has now—I hope."

"You hope?"

"Yes. Tell me, Inspector, have you ever had a brickbat fall right by your ear off the top of a twenty-story building?"

"Well, no—they don't go so high over here."

"Or a black sedan do a peach of a skid your way, and only by God knows what stroke of luck did you fling yourself on the sidewalk in time? Mind you, I'm not making any accusations—I didn't then and I shan't start now. There may have been some connection and there may not: but those things happened to me, and others too, and I didn't wait to argue—I quit while I could."

"Well, it certainly sounds as if you were being prudent. But why do you still hope?"

"Why—or what?"

"Both."

"Well, I hope bricks don't begin flying around over here, or cars skidding, or any other little unpleasantness. As for why, you'd best read this."

As he spoke he took an envelope from his pocket, removed the single sheet of notepaper inside, and put it into Beale's hand.

The die-stamped heading was that of the Falcon Hotel, Burwood, the date that of the previous day, the 13th, and the letter short but pointed.

"Dear Professor Peake,

You will doubtless be surprised to hear from me. I docked in England on Monday, having come over chiefly to see you, and I shall be grateful if I may call at three o'clock on Saturday afternoon. Please make this time convenient if you possibly can, and oblige

Yours truly,
Caroline Jay (Mrs. Cornelius Jay)."

Beale sat frowning over it a moment. The writing was bold and clear, bearing the unmistakable stamp of self-assurance, and the signature not entirely devoid of flourish.

"No hint given about the nature of her call," he remarked, returning the letter. "What do you suppose she wants?"

Peake shook his head, looking suddenly tired again.

"I'll wait till I've seen her," he said. "Have another drink—yes, do. You can't often get the chance. If you really do know the story, and believe what I said just now at all, you can guess I'm not quite easy about it. Why should the woman come all the way to England just to visit me? What can she have to say that couldn't have been done equally well through the mails?"

"Well, it's always possible that she exaggerated a little, of course: she really came to see the Coronation, and thought she'd look you up. Otherwise the obvious answer is that she wants to make some sort of a personal plea. At least, provided my information's correct. Would you consider it true to say that if you'd reversed your previous verdict, her son would now be at liberty?"

"Grandson," corrected Peake. "Yes, I think you could go as far as that, without wanting to boost myself. Yes, I reckon you're about right, but I still don't like it—she can't help but know perfectly well that I won't fake an opinion to please her. The first time I saw Jay he was mad, and I said so. The second time I saw him he was still mad, and again I said so. The most she can possibly hope is that I'll agree to examine him a third time, and I doubt if she trusts my judgement enough to want that."

"*Would* you examine him again?"

"I don't know. Not till this business with Selby is all cleared up, anyway. Then I suppose I might, if she could satisfy me there'd been some appreciable change in his condition."

"If it isn't rude to ask, who paid the expenses of your last visit?"

"I paid them myself—you don't imagine I could afford to have her do it, do you? Or anybody else. Not one cent have I ever had from either side, thank the Lord."

He spoke with what seemed to both his listeners to be undoubted sincerity, emphasized his words with a decisive head-shake, and sat silent for some seconds.

"I don't reckon there's much in your idea about kidnapping," he said at last. "It's a bit too tall for this country, and it doesn't explain the murders at all, as you said."

"No, it's the wrong way round," agreed Tony. "If she was trying to blackmail you into saying her grandson was sane, she'd start by only threatening to do them. Anyway, I know I would."

Nevertheless, Peake's face still expressed some uncertainty.

"You haven't met the lady," he said. "She's a bit like that—above the ordinary rules. Look here, Inspector, I hope you don't take offence, but I'm going to ask you a favour. I know you're going to be busy, but can you possibly spare time to come along tomorrow afternoon?"

"To meet Mrs. Cornelius Jay?"

"To do just that—and ease my mind. I'm a grown man, a good few years older than either of you, I guess, and I never reckoned I was a bigger coward than most people—except over fire: but I don't mind telling you I'm just a bit scared. Not of anything in particular—way inside me. Don't misunderstand—I'm not expecting her to pull out a gun and do a bit of target practice on my shirt bosom, but I'm not looking forward to her visit. I don't see why she's coming at all, and I don't like her when she turns nasty."

He waved his hand vaguely, as if to express his state of mind.

"It's all a sight too queer for my taste," he said. "First this affair with Selby, then a couple of slayings and a couple more bodies to come, and then that letter. I don't get it clear, but I can't help feeling there's something up that oughtn't to be, and I'd be much obliged if you could come."

"But how *can* there be any connection between her visit and Selby's escape?" demanded Tony. "After all, it ought to be possible to check her story about landing in England on Monday. If her name's on some passenger-list or other, then that'll be the end of the idea, won't it?"

Peake shrugged his bent shoulders.

"I tell you, I just don't like it," he repeated. "Maybe I'm wrong—probably I'm wrong: but the fact that she wasn't in England before Monday wouldn't prove a darned thing. You see, sir, you don't get women like that over here, any more than you get a Capone or a Dillinger. Oh yes, she's just as much a racketeer in her own way as they ever were in theirs. She wants the same thing, power, only she wants it in terms of social position instead of money. She's already got ten men's share of that.

"Oh, I don't blame you for wanting to laugh. You probably think I'm a lily-livered fool shivering because an old woman crosses the Atlantic, and all I can say is that you don't know the woman. Now, I don't know her well, but well enough to assure you that if she was in Spitzbergen, say, or Cape Cod, and she got the idea she'd like nothing better than to have a knife stuck in the ribs of a Kansas City cop named Maloney—well, Mrs. Maloney would be out buying crape the same month.

"Folk tell you the States aren't half as bad as they're painted. All these gangster films and so on have got nothing to do with real life, they say—just Jack the Blue-beard up to date. But don't you believe them—not all the way. Ninety per cent of the population may be honest and law-abiding, same as yours, but the other ten per cent's a durned sight more dishonest. If somebody knocks off a policeman in England there's a terrible to-do, like there is over that poor fellow Lee; but if that had happened back home he'd have been lucky to get a fair-sized paragraph. Anyway, that'll serve as a comparison. Maybe eighteen Americans out of twenty wouldn't believe me any more than you do, but the other two would know I'm not laying it too thick. If you've got enough dollars and enough pull—and Mrs. Jay's got both—you can get hold of the right man for any dirty job you have in mind over there, short of committing suicide."

XIII

BEALE left the Professor's invitation open, promising to be present at Mrs. Jay's visit if he could manage it. He then asked if he might see Nurse Spence before he returned to Burwood.

"Certainly," agreed Peake. "She's in bed, though—fell over a bucket or something the other day and sprained her ankle rather badly. I'm afraid you may find her a bit long-winded, but she's a good sort."

"How long has she been with you?"

"Five years, and I couldn't wish for a better nurse. It wasn't in any way her fault that Selby escaped."

He led them from his study, which was on the first floor, along a corridor to the main landing, a bare draughty place. As far as Tony could see, all the walls inside the house were distempered in faded pastel colours, which gave a depressingly cheerless effect: the contrast between the interior and the gardens was most marked.

Presently they stopped before an obvious bedroom door, from beyond which came faintly the sound of women's voices.

"That'll be her friend Mrs. Montgomery in there," remarked Peake in an undertone. "She's another chatter-box."

"Oh dear!" said Beale. "I'd much rather see Nurse Spence alone."

"Then you'd best leave it till tomorrow afternoon."

"An added inducement to turn up, eh? All right—"

But before he could say more the door of the bedroom suddenly opened, and Mrs. Montgomery appeared. She was a tall large-boned woman, dressed in a tight-fitting black coat which drew attention to her size, and an imposing hat, and she had a round smiling face. One of her blue eyes, Beale noticed instantly, was a shade lighter than the other, and for a moment he had the ridiculous feeling that both were made of glass.

"Oh dear!" she exclaimed, which made Tony smile involuntarily: she might for all the world have been deliberately mimicking his friend, he thought. "Oh dear, so many men all at once! I'm sure I'm in the way, Professor—is there just room for me to squeeze by, do you think?"

She managed to do so, still wreathed in smiles, and left behind an impression of good-natured commonness momentarily encountered. From the last possible vantage point she looked upwards, but turned away quickly as she caught Beale's eye. It crossed his mind, unaccountably, that she had behaved precisely as if she knew him to be a policeman, and was off to tell someone about it; and as he entered the bedroom he was asking himself why he had bothered to stare after her.

He got very little out of Nurse Spence apart from an emphatic repetition of what he had already been told by Superintendent Dane. She lay propped up on pillows, a high-complexioned homely woman of about fifty, whose false teeth were noticeably some dentist's failure. They clicked and clattered whenever she spoke, which was almost incessantly once she was started, and the sound, punctuating that of her rather shrill voice, irritated him. When he had the chance he put again to her Dane's specific question: had she sought or been given advice of any kind by anyone about sleeping in the room next to Simon Selby's on the night of April 29th?

"No, Inspector, certainly not. I've never been one for hanging on to other people's apron-strings—nobody could say that, however sharp their tongue. I looked in last thing before I went to bed, like the Professor asked me to—that's right, isn't it, Professor? Half past ten that was—eleven o'clock's my time for bed, summer or winter, fine weather or foul. Make a good habit and stick to it, they taught me when I was young. Not that you always can, of course, being a nurse—duty comes first. Still, we mustn't expect everything our own way in this world, must we now?

"Well, Mr. Selby seemed all right—not looking as if he'd be likely to give any trouble in the night, I mean. He answered me quite civil, which he didn't always, not liking women much barring his sister, and everybody likes her. 'Yes Nurse, I'm quite all right, thank you' he says, and as far as I could tell he was, too. But I didn't stop at looks—not me. When you get to be my age you go a mite deeper. But he didn't mind a bit when I made to take his temperature, though often enough he'd grumble, and sometimes even refuse point-blank. I used to have to get Bellamy to do it then if I couldn't humour him myself, and some trouble that was, I can tell you, but that night he was as good as gold. You see, whenever he had an attack coming on his temperature used to go up a bit. Nothing to worry about, 99.6 or thereabouts but just enough to tip you the wink, as you might say. The Professor told me he was restless, so naturally I did what I thought was best, but normal he was, not a fraction over, so I said to myself 'You for your own bed tonight, Esther—nothing's going to happen to *him'*. Those'd have been my very words if I'd spoke my thoughts aloud, that they would.

"Well, as I was telling you, I woke up all of a fluster about a quarter to four—sitting bolt upright in this very bed I was, listening hard, though what it was had roused me I don't know any more than a new-born child, and I was never one to make up stories for what I couldn't rightly explain. Well, I went on listening, but nothing seemed to happen, but I thought I'd best be on the safe side, so I jumped out of bed and put on my dressing-gown nice and tidy and tiptoed down and along the passage to Miss Vining's room. I just peeped through the door, but she was sound asleep, poor lamb, and—"

"Why did you go to her first?" interrupted Beale heartlessly, and Nurse Spence gave him a reproachful look. She explained that it was first on her way, and she was never one to let a chance slip; went on to describe her further journey to Simon Selby's room, what she saw when she looked through the spy-hole, how she was never for a moment taken in by the dummy, though many a less observant person might have been; and ended with her subsequent actions on finding that Selby had entirely disappeared.

The phrase stuck in Tony's mind, and he repeated it to Beale on the way back to Burwood in a passable imitation of Nurse Spence's tinny voice.

"Not just half of him gone, mark you, or even three quarters, but absolutely and entirely not there."

"And he doesn't seem to be the only one," said Beale. "Did she really say 'entirely'?"

"She did—and I quite expected her to add that he was never one to do things by halves. By the way, what do you make of Peake? Seems a windy old boy, doesn't he?"

Beale nodded thoughtfully.

"And possibly not without reason," he said. "I'm rather looking forward to meeting Mrs. Cornelius Jay tomorrow."

"Then you'll go?"

"I think so. Her turning up at a time like this certainly stimulates the imagination."

"You mean you really swallow the idea of a possible connection between her visit and Selby's disappearance? You're absent too."

It was already dark by the time they left Balmer's Court, and in the five miles to Burwood they passed neither pedestrian nor cyclist. A brief call at the police-station elicited from Captain Wyndham that nothing further had happened. He readily agreed with Beale's suggestion that the local inhabitants were scared, and went on to explain how much so.

"You won't find anybody out alone at night round here," he said: "not even a constable. I've given instructions that all outdoor duty's to be done in pairs. That blasted lunatic'll have his work cut out to find anyone to murder from now on, I promise you."

"We'll hope so," murmured Beale, but without much warmth. The Chief-constable noticed this, and glared through his spectacles.

"Meaning what?" he enquired brusquely.

"Nothing special, sir: but somehow I don't fancy the idea of his hiding out there all alone for so long."

He waved his hand towards the window, and the Forest a mile beyond.

"Do you know the country well?" he asked.

"Me? Of course I do—born here."

"I was born in Croydon, so they tell me, but I couldn't pass on anything worth knowing about it from personal experience. However, let that go"—as Wyndham visibly bristled. "What I'd like to ask you, sir, is how long you'd back yourself to stay out there alone and uncaught, given that you were sane, which Selby isn't supposed to be, and that you know your way about, which he presumably doesn't. Do you think you'd last a fortnight?"

But the Chief-constable evaded the question with a snort.

"Fellow's mad," he said. "Can't possibly tell what a madman will do."

Although they were both very hungry, when they reached their hotel they found that they could expect nothing to eat for half an hour. The *Wheat-sheaf* was anxious to please, lest its customers betake themselves across the road to the more expensive *Falcon:* but it had not yet got into its stride. That being so, they settled themselves in their communal sitting-room, which had the air of a museum for worn-out furniture and stuffed pike. Tony suggested trying to grill one of the latter in front of the gas fire, but agreed that the smell of burning varnish was unpleasant.

"Be patient," said Beale. "You'll probably get as good downstairs."

"In which case I shan't bother to unpack yet. But it makes you think, doesn't it? The hungrier I get, and it's a rapid process, the more I disbelieve in the babe-in-the-wood theory. Can anybody seriously suppose that Selby's existed on fresh air and fir cones for a solid fortnight? It's all nonsense—he's being harboured."

"And let out periodically to do a bit more damage with his little iron bar?"

"I don't know—it doesn't sound right. Do you mean he didn't do the murders at all?"

"Oh no—I'm not out to make trouble for myself, only to avoid it. I agree that it certainly looks as if he must be getting help of some kind, and the least ridiculous supposition is that every now and then he gives his caretakers the slip. What I was going to suggest to Wyndham was that Selby mightn't find it so hard as he thinks to get hold of another victim."

"Them as brings his bread and butter?"

"Exactly. Who they are—if any—we don't know yet. The likeliest choice seems to be the sister, with or without Dr. Wrench, in spite of what Peake says. They'd hardly dare take anyone else into their confidence. What's the matter now?"

He had looked up to see Tony frowning fiercely.

"Same things—hunger and incredulity. I want to know why all these supposedly sane people seem so dashed anxious to believe the impossible. Even Peake and that Superintendent fellow have come round to thinking that all's as it appears to be, and they both struck me as being a cut above Wyndham as regards nous."

"Definitely: but remember that they're the only ones who've considered the help idea at all, as far as we've heard. Anybody who's capable of thinking imaginatively couldn't be satisfied. They weren't, so they both started looking for Selby's allies, and both chose the same quarter. Peake's suspicions were lulled by his suspects' apparent straightforwardness, which is something we've got to find out about for ourselves, or at any rate form our own opinions, and Dane was put off by the murders. I don't think either of them is entirely convinced, though."

"No—Dane jumped at your suggestion about Selby's having been got away, and *then* escaping, didn't he? And maybe that's why Peake has gone all out for Mrs. Jay."

"Well, which would you rather have," asked Beale: "lunatic existing on imaginary food, lunatic given bed and board and every facility for good murdering, or melodramatic kidnappers in well-cut masks?"

Tony shook his head.

"I'd really rather have my miraculous return to sanity," he said.

"Well, don't despair—we'll pray for you. In the absence of anyone to suspect but Selby's sister and Dr. Wrench, I pin my own hopes on Matthews. He's going to see that there's a twenty-four hour watch on both of them. I don't know if country cops are any good at that sort of thing, but I dare say he'll manage. It means long hours and not much comfort, but he didn't seem to mind."

"He knew it wouldn't be a ha'porth of good minding," retorted Tony with a grin. " 'Oh sir, please sir, *do* let me orf ternight—There's Wagner on the vireless, and I *must* learn to vistle it right'."

"Then all the more reason for sending him out. I dislike people who whistle Wagner—his tunes won't stand being looked at naked. What did you make of Bellamy?"

"Nothing in particular—why?"

"Oh, I just wondered. Something about him puzzles me, but I can't quite say what."

"Can't or won't?"

"Can't, unfortunately—but it's probably nothing. I hope Donovan turns up soon—I shall begin to get worried if he doesn't."

The reporter came back at ten o'clock, surveyed the remnants of their meal, and sniffed loudly.

"Thank heaven I ate elsewhere," he said. "Is that cheese or soap?"—pointing to a perspiring yellow block on a dish.

"Either," Tony told him. "It's also useful as weed-killer, pumice-stone, or sealing-wax. In addition, there's bread to match, and the potatoes were direct descendents of Argus. Can you remember off-hand why we said we'd stop here?"

Dickie sat down and thought deeply.

"Come on," urged Beale. "There must have been a reason, only I can't work it out—not enough data."

"Oh, undoubtedly there must have been, but it eludes me. Was it because I know the cousin of the man that holds the second mortgage? No, that's another pub, in another town, far far from here. Was it the individuality of the decor—near plywood and grey paint? Or was it the magic notice in the hall—'Sandwiches adapted to visitors' requirements'? I can't be sure. I think it was probably the simple belief that we couldn't possibly be disappointed here. Ponder that well—it's double-edged. Herbert!"—to a corpse-like waiter who was shuffling in. "Is there any beer left?"

"Eh?"

"Beer."

"Ay—draught or bottle?"

"Oh, draught—one more won't matter."

" 'Ow much—pint?"

"Three pints, please."

"Three pints. That'll be two bob. Ta."

He eyed them pessimistically, pocketed the coin without interest, flicked the largest crumb on the table into Tony's lap, and slowly took himself away by the longest possible route. When they grew tired of waiting, Dickie went to fetch the beer himself.

"Have you been doing anything much?" Beale asked him presently.

"Lots. I thought I'd go and see Alfred Farmer—the bloke that Selby burgled."

"Really? That was nice of you. Any luck?"

"Oh, I saw him all right."

"Sorry—tell it your own way."

"Thanks. Then let me lead you back for a moment into the distant past, when I was a pretty young thing in sailor suits. Imagine that after much lying awake and scheming I've finally got myself taken to Madame Tussaud's. This is in the days before the fire there, of course, and I'm standing in the entrance hall fascinated by an old lady in a black bonnet and a long shapeless cloak. She's just gone up to the policeman in the corner and asked him a question, and she awaits an answer: but, although he's a very life-like policeman, he doesn't seem to have heard. She repeats her question twice, each time a little louder, and everybody stops walking about, and stands listening. There is almost complete silence as she stamps her foot, bangs on the floor with her umbrella, and draws in all her ancient breath. Then she fairly bellows at him.

" 'Which way to the 'Orrors, I'm asking you, young man—which way?' "

"And one deduces what?" requested Beale, as Dickie paused. "That Farmer's an 'Orror, or that you're an old woman? Or that I'm a stuffed policeman?" he added. "I feel a bit like one, admittedly."

"No, none of those. I was just trying to give you some idea of what I landed myself with. It couldn't have been any harder for that old woman to make her waxwork talk than it was to get anything out of Farmer tonight—he's incredibly deaf. We resorted to pencil and paper in the end, but that wasn't as good as it might have been because of our foul writing. However, I think I've got things pretty clear. He knows nothing about anything except that he wants his clothes and things back, and he'll start a one-man revolution if he doesn't get them soon. He's no interest in escaped lunatics or slaughtered policeman or missing servant girls—he wants his suit back.

"He's very tall, and very heavy, and black-haired, and he scowls all the time through glasses at least three-eighths of an inch thick. Also he smokes the vilest possible tobacco—greasy black twist that he cuts off with a rusty pen-knife. It smells like a bonfire of decayed cauliflower stalks. On the 29th ult. he was working on a novel till past 1.00 in the morning: he wanted to read me a chapter, only I said he wasn't to spoil the effect of the whole. Then he went to bed, and heard nothing unusual in the night, which I can well believe. He didn't discover his things were gone till Saturday, when he went straight to the police-station.

"He lives quite by himself, incidentally, though a woman from the nearest village comes in for an hour or two most mornings and cooks him something. By the look of things I should think he manages on about twelve and six a week—when I got there he was eating baked beans and a huge slab of bread and dripping."

"Together?" enquired Tony, with a respectful note of awe.

"Together—I had to watch him finish. He's not a scrap self-conscious, which is quite the nicest thing about him. Except for his books, perhaps—he's got a hundred or so that I wouldn't mind any day. He's also got a very old typewriter and a gold-fish named Gollancz."

"Why?"

"Because—he says—it swims steadily from right to left. A bit weak, I thought."

"Does he lock his front door at night?"

"No—he lost the key ages ago, and the bolt's as rusty as his pen-knife. But nobody would be likely to burgle a small place like that."

"Yet he *was* burgled."

"I know—I only said it wasn't likely that he would be. And anyway, Selby wasn't an ordinary burglar—he was after clothes and a razor, not silver-plate. If he had been he certainly wouldn't have gone to Farmer: no plates there at all, if eating off a cork mat shows anything."

"Not the baked beans?" cried Tony in horror. "That would be too much: it was a last week's crumpet, and you didn't recognize it."

"Not the beans, no—they came out of their tin. What it is to be a word-monger!"

"By the way," said Beale, "did you happen to ask what food was stolen when he lost his other stuff?"

"Yes—it wasn't anything much: half a loaf of bread and two cold sausages. He missed them the next day, of course, but persuaded himself he'd eaten them till he found out about the other things."

"And how much money?"

"Yes, he was a bit sick about that—the best part of ten shillings, he says, which he'd left lying on the kitchen table. There again, though, he didn't think much of it till he started looking for his suit."

"I see. Does he ever sleep away?"

"Never. He wanders off into the woods in the day-time, writing, but apparently he hasn't stayed with anyone for years. I shouldn't think he's got many friends—he seemed a lonely sort of cuss."

"Is his house visible from the woods?"

"It isn't a house, it's a three-roomed cottage. Yes, plainly—no catching me out like that; I went across specially to look, and I shivered all the way there and all the way back."

"All the way?"

"Oh, only a hundred yards of open moor, but far enough. I was expecting to be laid by the heels any minute."

"Isn't Farmer afraid?" asked Tony.

"I did raise the point, but he was quite hurt at the idea that he could possibly die before he's finished 'the' novel."

"But he's written others, hasn't he?"

"Half a dozen. This is different, though—on a bigger scale altogether. 'Instead of illuminating the life of one man, it seeks to illuminate the Life of Mankind.' That's what he wrote down about it himself. He lacks not ambition—nor talent, I believe: only he isn't everybody's meat."

"And how does he illuminate his three-roomed cottage?" enquired Beale. "That interests me more at the moment."

"With a smelly oil lamp."

"And he went to bed between 1.00 and 2.00?"

"Yes—therefore no light after that. I think you could still see the place from the woods, though, but I can't be sure because I didn't wait to look. You ought to be able to—it stands on a bit of a rise, and there's nothing behind it in the way of trees. And anyway, Selby may have gone there at dawn."

"Yes, true. Are there any other houses near?"

"A cottage about a couple of hundred yards away, but that's all for half a mile."

"Who lives in it?"

"Some woman or other—a Mrs. Muggeridge or Massingbird or some such."

"Montgomery!" exclaimed Beale and Tony simultaneously, and then looked at one another.

"And who the devil is Mrs. Montgomery, pray?" asked Dickie.

"Well, don't go romancing about it," he warned them, when he had been told. "The poor wretch has got to live somewhere."

"Oh, I shan't romance," Beale assured him. "Me, with my plain face? It's interesting, though, all the same. Nurse Spence is a friend of hers, and has presumably visited her dozens of times, which means she must almost certainly know who lives next door, and probably all about him. Moreover, Nurse Spence would talk herself hoarse if she weren't stopped. The question is, did she ever talk to Selby? If so, I don't see why he shouldn't have gathered a pretty good idea of Farmer and his habits, if he was sane enough to be interested. Anyway, it's a possibility, and it would explain a lot of things—why he apparently wasn't afraid of being caught, for one.

"That mayn't apply, though, of course—it's difficult to work out what a lunatic might have thought. Possibly the idea of being caught never occurred to him: but I doubt it, somehow. Anyway, I'll have a few more thousand words with the woman tomorrow.

"Well, Dickie, I'm very grateful to you."

"Not at all—now tell me how you've been getting on."

"Oh, I see—a *quo* to catch a *quid.*"

But the reporter denied this.

"I really do want to help," he said. "I knew Wilson, you see, and he wasn't a bad chap at all, what I saw of him."

He listened attentively, and displayed interest at the mention of Mrs. Cornelius Jay.

"So you can't say she isn't a real person any more," he remarked. "But I wonder what she's doing over here."

"She'll be real if she turns up," said Beale: "let's leave it at that."

"Oh, she's bound to turn up," declared Tony. "The whole plot demands it."

"What plot?" demanded Dickie instantly. Tony leant back and smiled largely.

"Prepare to hear wonders," he said. "My friend on the left here hinted just now that he never romances. Well, you shall judge. The question before the committee is, what conceivable connection can there be between Mrs. Jay's visit to Balmer's Court and Simon Selby's disappearance from it? The answer—in two words, as Sam Goldwyn would say—is blackmail. With the help of secret agents, identity necessarily unknown, she's kidnapped Peake's prize patient, and the ransom will be a clean bill of mental health for Thomas Love Peacock, or whatever his name is. Simple, ain't it?"

"And the murders?" queried Dickie, unimpressed. "And the missing boots?"

"Done by aforesaid agents, of course: sane men endeavouring to give convincing imitation of lunatic killer at large. If Peake doesn't pay up—'Without re-examination or any pertinent evidence I hereby unreservedly declare Thomas Bluebird to be as sane as Sophocles'—more murders transpire, more victims expire, more coppers perspire, and all the time the secret agents conspire. Inspiration comes in my department, of course—or my clever friend's."

"Yours," said Beale, yawning. "You have my permission to inspire till you're tight with air, and then stay put: never never breathe out again."

"One day I shan't," replied Tony gaily. "Nor will you. Fortunately, that time hasn't come yet. Except for poor devils like Lee and that girl hiker," he added, more soberly.

"But, to go on with the *roman policier:* if Peake threatens to tell on her, Mrs. Jay laughs nastily. 'Prove it, my friend' she hisses. 'And thundering big damages if you don't.' "

"And what about my being there tomorrow?" asked Beale. "Or perhaps I'll be drugged?"

"Probably—unless she doesn't realize you aren't. If not, nothing will happen till she and Peake are alone—or she thinks they are. You'd better arrive early and curl up inside his desk: then you'll be able to hear the whole fell business unbeknownst, and probably get made a superintendent, and I'll take half the difference in your screw for my trouble. How much would that be?"

But he agreed, when he was told, that it would be barely worth his while to press the point, and they went to bed soon afterwards in good spirits.

XIV

IT WAS NOT the fact that they could have slept more comfortably on iron gratings which caused their faces to be so sober about quarter to eleven the next morning; nor the lingering bitter taste of the *Wheatsheaf's* coffee in their mouths. It was the sight of Prudence Hill's body hideously doubled up, the flesh of her face discoloured and her eyes protruding. About the place where she lay, under a fallen branch in the thickest part of the wood, the air smelt foul, for she had been dead a week. Her clothes were sodden where her mackintosh failed to cover them—there had been heavy rain four days previously—and her straw hat with its pink ribbon, from which the dye had run, was stuffed under her right arm. Five yards away, also roughly concealed, was the bicycle she had been using on the night of her disappearance. The bell and handle-bars were streaked with bright new rust, and one tyre was burst.

Beale stared at the huddled form for some moments, then forced himself to lean over so that he could see the bare head with its limp stringy hair and its blood-crusted hole behind the ear. He looked also at the legs, observing that the left stocking was half down and the left shoe missing. Then he turned away, revolted, and walked apart from the rest as steadily as he could.

'Could a sane person do a thing like that?' he asked himself presently, when he was able to think clearly. 'Make a living girl into a twisted dead scarecrow, a damp decaying monstrosity? But of course he wouldn't know she'd look like that. Why in the world is it so damnably easy to die? It takes months and months to get born, and start the machinery going, and a fraction of a second to spike it.'

After a time Tony came up to him, but said nothing for some minutes. Then he spoke in a deliberately casual voice.

"Dr. Wrench and Miss Selby have just arrived—would you like to see them?"

Beale nodded.

"All right," he said. "Is Peake there too?"

"No—at least, I didn't notice him. Are you still going this afternoon?"

"Yes—there's one or two questions I want to ask him."

"Since last night?" said Tony, surprised.

"Ones I forgot, or hadn't thought of," Beale explained. "I lay awake for quite a bit this morning."

"So did I. Could you bear to hear an idea I thought of?"

"If it isn't fatuous."

Tony shook his head. He realized, and understood, that his friend was not in the mood for clowning, and went on quite seriously. He was not feeling particularly cheerful himself, for ever before his mind's eye lay the cold remains of Prudence Hill, and his nose unwillingly still savoured the smell of death.

"It's entirely rational, and I think there may be something in it. You remember those bars we tried yesterday? Well, I want to tackle them a different way, and compare results. I want to tie a strong rope on to one of them, or two if you like, pass it over the courtyard wall, fix it on to the car, and then drive away. If the rope doesn't break, and the back of the Bentley holds, then the bars will give way, and we can see what sort of a mess is left behind."

Beale turned to regard his friend with definite interest.

"That does sound rather brilliant," he said. "There'd be marks on top of the wall, though, wouldn't there? Where the rope had chafed, I mean. We must look before we do much else, and go carefully, too. If anything like that did happen, it seems probable that somebody in the house was concerned, and we don't want them to know we've any suspicions. I must say I like the idea, though: it would change the complexion of things if we could be sure Selby was helped to escape. Don't go talking about it."

"Of course not. I thought I'd tell you before you saw Wrench. He's very honest-looking—they both are: but you never know."

Beale studied the doctor and his companion closely during the time he was with them, and found nothing to amend in Tony's description. Both expressed horror at the latest discovery, both seemed sincere, and Lavinia Selby declared herself thankful that she had not needed to see the body. One was quite enough, she said, even if only a glimpse at that.

Wrench had made a brief examination, however, and was able to say that the cause of death was almost certainly the same as in the cases of Betty Trotter and Sergeant Lee.

"And the missing shoe, too," put in the girl. "It's simply terrible, Inspector—do please find my brother before he does any more of these vile murders. I feel I shall go mad myself soon if it doesn't stop."

"Steady dear," said Wrench in a quiet tone, and put his hand on her arm.

"All right," she answered—"sorry."

"I'm doing everything I can," Beale assured her.

"I'd like to ask you a question or two some time, if you could make it convenient."

The girl turned to him eagerly. "Of course—anything you want to know. I feel so helpless."

"Thank you: would now be too soon?"

"No—and not too late either, I hope." She smiled at him faintly as she said this, but only with her mouth: her eyes remained desperately unhappy. The doctor, Beale saw, still kept his hand on her arm, and she gave no sign of minding.

'But for her brother' he thought, 'they'd probably be married by now. And not a bad couple either, if looks count. He's handsome, except for that scar, and I wouldn't quarrel with anyone who said she could be beautiful. That poor devil Wilson was right for once.'

He had not in fact anything he especially wanted to ask, but he needed an opportunity for observing her and Wrench together, and was in no doubt that he would be able to invent some plausible questions. Over things like that he had learnt, with satisfaction though without undue pride, that he could rely on his wits to see him through: and often, he had found, the necessity for asking something had caused him to query a point which he might otherwise have overlooked to his disadvantage. It was a commonplace that an apparently insignificant detail, in detection, might make all the difference between success and failure; but every crime was so hedged about with details that it was frequently a matter of luck whether the important or the unimportant got passed over.

It had once been unkindly said of him that he asked more questions than any other three men at Scotland Yard: the implication being that two-thirds of his were unessential. He had defended himself stoutly, however. Questions in connection with criminal affairs, he had pointed out, should be put with regard not only to the information they sought to obtain, but also to the person who was to answer. For the purposes of his job the detective had to be, in his differing way, as much an actor as the criminals he hunted. He started with the admitted handicap of rarely knowing who they were, whereas his profession was no secret, and his very name would probably put them on their guard: but it was by no means an insuperable handicap. It only meant that he had to treat all persons remotely capable, in imagination, of being those he sought as if they were in fact so: but when the quarry was likely to be the amateur of crime, then the detective's attitude of mind must never be exposed.

"The difference between the amateur and the professional is

immense," he had told Tony more than once, "and the difference in the technique to be employed for catching them is immense too. The one is usually suspicious if you appear to suspect him, and the other if you don't. The amateur has hardly ever been caught doing anything wrong before, and quite often hasn't in fact done anything, criminally speaking. 'Why then' he asks himself, 'should this prod-nosed copper behave as if I were a regular at Dartmoor? He certainly knows nothing against me previously—therefore he's spotted something to do with the present business, and I'll find myself in gaol soon if I don't watch out.' A clumsy or tactless approach may mean that the black sheep's scared out of the flock before you've had a chance to see his colour—or goes and gets himself effectively white-washed. The worst thing a detective can do is to look as if he knows more than he really does: he should always appear to know less. Detectives in real life, that is, not in fiction: otherwise they'd mostly be vacuums.

"At times, naturally, clumsiness is almost as successful in some ways as skill would ultimately have been. The thief, thinking that all is discovered, flies for his life and so labels himself; or the murderer, feeling his head in the noose, sticks it inside the gas oven instead. Whether that's a good thing or a bad in the long run I don't know, but it's the result of inefficiency on somebody's part, and sooner or later that kind of inefficiency will let a clever and cool-headed amateur—and therefore a dangerous one—escape.

"But the police are on a different footing with the professional criminal. He's been caught before, probably a number of times, he's nearly always been caught for doing the same kind of job, and if he's at liberty when something in his own line is pulled off, even though he didn't do it, he certainly expects a visit. He knows his past record is good enough reason for suspecting him in the majority of cases, and if he's guilty nothing worries him more than to be left alone. Of course, it's not so important to play up to him as it is with the amateur—often it pays not to; but if he is questioned, then let it be done, in general, as if there were no possible doubt of his guilt, and that all you're waiting for to arrest him is enough evidence. Nine times out of ten he'll go away quite happy, confident you know nothing and are trying the usual stuff."

Beale turned now to Lavinia Selby with his most pleasant smile.

"When did you last see your brother?" he asked, and immediately felt like a Roundhead.

"The previous Sunday—April 25th, I think it was. I used to go over for an hour or two every weekend except when he was—ill."

"Did he give you the slightest impression of being more than usually rational?"

"No—but he *was* very rational most of the time, you know. Not a bit like the general idea of a lunatic, except that he looked so peculiar with all that hair. That's right, Charles, isn't it?"

Wrench nodded in agreement.

"You see, Inspector," he said, "not even Professor Peake could tell just what was the matter with him. After years of close observation the root of the trouble is still a mystery."

"Yes, I'd gathered that. How long had he been abnormal, by the way?"

"Just over six years," answered the girl.

"Did he have any other regular visitors but you?"

"Nobody. We haven't any relations, thank goodness."

"So the only people he ever saw"—to Wrench—"were you two, the Professor, Nurse Spence, and Bellamy?"

"Yes, for all practical purposes. Sir Digby Grant came down for a few months early last year, and every so often we had a dentist in to examine his mouth, but I think that's all."

"None of the domestic servants ever went near him, I take it?"

"Oh no, never."

"Nor the other patient?"

"No—I don't believe they ever met."

"Or knew of one another's existence?"

"Well, I wouldn't go as far as that. Nurse Spence is inclined to talk rather freely at times, so she may have mentioned Miss Vining to him."

"I see. Now, Miss Selby, did you grow up with your brother?"

"Yes—though I was always a bit behind: seven years."

"And can you remember if he was fond of climbing when he was a boy, or particularly good at it?"

"Climbing? Oh, you mean about the wall. I don't know. We lived in the country, in Kent, and he used to go up trees now and again in the holidays when he was home from school, but I don't think he was ever any better than me, and I'm sure I couldn't climb into the road from the courtyard."

"No, it isn't very easy—I tried yesterday. Did he ever strike you as being specially strong?"

"How do you mean—healthy?"

"No—muscularly strong."

"Yes, I think he was—but then he was so big, of course. He

didn't make a fuss about it, though—not go round bending pokers and things like some people do."

And here, surprisingly, she turned her head to smile suddenly at Dr. Wrench. The reference was obviously to some private joke between them, and Beale made no attempt to get it explained.

"Thank you," he said. "I think that's all, if you're absolutely sure that nobody else is likely to have an interest in him. No question of rival inheritors under a will, or anything similar?"

"None at all. Our money's all invested, and it's all our own—we've no expectations."

"And there are just one or two points for you, Doctor. Had he a good memory?"

"In general, yes, considering his state of mind."

"More particularly, had he a good visual memory? If he was in a room he knew, could he reach out for the door handle without having to look first?"

"Well, that's rather hard. You'd better ask Professor Peake, I think—I can't honestly say I ever noticed."

He spoke rather apologetically, but with evident curiosity about the purport of the question.

"I wanted to know," Beale explained "because of the marks on the wall. I wondered if he'd be able to find them again in the dark, supposing he knew where they were in the daylight."

"You mean the foot-holds that fellow Dane found? I can't say at all."

"And another thing: had he a good appetite?"

"Not very—he was a bit faddy over his food."

"Would he eat chocolate, do you know?"

"Yes, if it was plain—why?"

But Beale shook his head.

"Just an idea that occurred to me," he said. "Did he ever have any letters?"

"None that I remember."

"And finally, give me your frank opinion: did he escape by himself, or was he helped?"

At this Wrench and Lavinia Selby looked at one another queerly. It seemed to Beale, watching, that they read into the question more than its surface meaning: yet he could not bring himself to believe that either had a guilty conscience. He found their manner and appearance most convincing.

"If you don't mind," said the doctor after a pause, "I'd rather answer that another time. Quite soon, I hope."

XV

"IN WHAT CAPACITY am I here?" asked Beale with a smile. He and Hilary Peake were waiting for Mrs. Cornelius Jay in the lounge at Balmer's Court, the time was just short of three o'clock on the same afternoon, Saturday, and they had been together for only five minutes.

"Oh, that'll be all right," said Peake. "You leave it to me. If she thinks you're in the way she'll say so—and that'll be all the bigger reason for you to stay."

He was clearly preoccupied with the coming visitor, and there could be little doubt that he was disturbed by the idea of meeting her again. Windy, Tony had called him, Beale remembered, and the word seemed apt. Peake's mind, he thought suddenly, was shivering: he *was* afraid. Because an old woman had crossed the Atlantic? That reason must surely be inadequate; yet there might be sense in it. He would not condemn the man without evidence: he would look closely upon Mrs. Jay.

"Are they still hunting for Wilson?" added the Professor, changing the subject abruptly.

"Yes—searching Whiteladies' Enclosure, I believe."

"Ah. I used to like the Forest before all this happened, but I reckon I won't go there any more—it'll be haunted. Hell take this woman—why doesn't she come?"

He spoke peevishly, and glanced at the clock: then went to the window and stared gloomily out at the tulips.

At ten minutes past three she arrived, and Beale's first thought was that Dickie, in describing her as a small woman, seemed to have been misinformed: but his second admitted that after all he supposed she was small.

Her hair, where it escaped from her close-fitting felt hat, was silvery, and her plain face colourless, making her deep-set violet eyes more noticeable. They were shrewd experienced eyes, he felt, reflecting a mature and possibly ruthless spirit. Mrs. Jay would fight on, though her last weapon were taken from her and her cause already lost. So much he permitted himself to be confident about after a single steady glance.

Contrary to his expectations, she made hardly any objection to his presence. She greeted Peake coolly, though without apparent hostility, sat down, and at once asked a question.

"And who's your friend, Professor—an attorney? I guess so. Let him stay if he cares to—my business is very simple."

She looked entirely self-possessed as she pulled off her gloves: far more so than Peake, who remained silent, perched expectantly on the edge of his chair and frowning fiercely. Beale stood, since there was no other seat conveniently placed for observation.

'She doesn't look quite as if she's come to threaten' he thought, regarding her deep-lined oval face. 'And yet she's here for something definite—her whole manner shows that. If she's going to plead with him, then she's making a pretty cool start: but that would probably be like her.'

He saw that her clothes were good. She wore nothing obtrusive—just a simple grey coat of some rough material, below which was a hint of dark green. On her left hand were two rings, and one on her right, and her knuckles were inclined to be nodular.

'That's supposed to be the sign of a good mathematician' he reminded himself. 'Anyway, she isn't got up to impress. Ah, she's speaking.'

Her voice was soft but nasal: far more so than Peake's, which sounded to Beale's ears as if it had become half anglicized.

"I guess you know right well why I'm here, Professor," she began, "and it's nice of you to see me. I appreciate it."

Peake waved aside the second part of her remark a little impatiently.

"But I'm not sure I do know why you wanted to see me," he said, and Beale noticed the change of tense. It seemed to imply that whatever her reason for coming, that reason was clearly no longer valid, and he hoped that she would realize as much.

"Oh but surely!" she exclaimed. "There's only but the one thing in my life that would bring me all the way from the States, and you don't need telling what that is.

"Professor Peake, I'll be glad for you to hear me out. I haven't a lot to say, and I won't make it more than it need be, but do please understand I mean it. I wouldn't presume to waste your time or my own in trifling."

(' I fancy she is going to plead after all,' thought Beale. 'Wonder what sort of a show she'll put up—don't care for the beginning.')

"There's been some kind of an impression circulating around back home," she continued "that all we Jays are concerned about is power and position—that we like to think of ourselves as a sort of uncrowned royal family. Well, maybe in the past it wouldn't have been right out of place to talk on those lines, but that's all over and done with long since. Any pretensions we may ever have had are gone, and we know it—and I for one don't regret it. I'm getting an old woman now, I'll be seventy-seven next fall, and I don't much admire to spend my last years leading a home-made army against half the world—and the only half that counts much at that, I guess.

"To be brief, Professor, I want to strike a bargain with you."

(At this Peake's face registered strong disapproval, but Mrs. Jay continued without a pause, and to Beale's ever-growing amazement.)

"I don't reckon I'd be wrong to say that you've given up most your whole life to the study of mental disease. I know I wouldn't be wrong to say that you know more about it than any other living man. The fact that in the case of my poor grandson it was your opinion and nothing else on two occasions that settled things proves that. If you said a man was sane, in America he'd *be* sane, and if you said he was mad, so would everybody else, whether they knew anything about it or not.

"Well, I guess I am talking more than I meant to,"—and here she gave him an unexpected glittering smile, switched on and off so rapidly that Beale could not be certain, a second afterwards, that he had not imagined it.

"You know, and I know, that what I want more than any one thing else in the world is to have my grandson Thomas Jefferson back in the Jay home again, sane or mad. He was my favourite son's child, and I see his dead father in him plainer than in any of the others. You say he's out of his senses, and it's no use telling you you're wrong, because nobody would believe me if I did. Very well, he's mad: but he's still my grandson, and I love him.

"I said a while back that you'd done more towards helping people like him than any man alive—if I didn't, I meant to. And yet, what have you done? Ask yourself that question, Hilary Peake. The half of your life you've had to be earning your own keep—and how many men have you trained to take your place when you're gone? You've got one young doctor with you here, I'm told—and that's all. When Hilary Peake goes, all that'll be left is one English nobody with neither name nor standing, and a half dozen books rotting on the shelves because folk haven't the time to read them."

She paused, it seemed to Beale as if with dramatic intent. She was far more animated now than when she had begun to speak: a small woman leaning forward and showering words at them. And what words, he thought! Could she really do no better than this crude hotch-potch of contradiction and flattery and false sentiment, leaving out the actual lies? What was it all leading up to? If the end were no better than the middle, she might as well have stayed in New York.

But she had still a surprise for him. As if she had read his thoughts she turned towards him for the first time since she had miscalled him Peake's attorney.

"You look like a sensible man," she said. "Which is better, a lifetime's work that gets you a big name and stops dead when you die, or ten years' work that'll last when nobody remembers who you were even? Maybe you don't see what I mean, though, so I'll tell you—and you too, Professor. The bargain I want to make is this. I want you to come right back to New York with me, examine my grandson again, and tell the world he's sane. No, hear me out"—as Peake made an exclamation of incredulity. "There's two sides to every bargain, and I'm not trying to shirk mine. In return I'll place at your disposal five million dollars—a million pounds English money—on condition that you use it to set up a research college for psychology, or psychiatry, or whatever you call it, and undertake to train at least fifty suitable students to carry on your work.

"There, Professor: five million dollars for the treatment of insanity on the lines it deserves, on the lines you've spent your life in working out, at the price of giving me the custody of my own grandson. You know as well as I do that if you declare him sane, they'll let him out. What do you say?"

She sat watching him keenly, and as he fumbled for words she began to open her bag quietly. Beale saw Peake notice the action, and tense himself, but nothing worse came out than a slip of pink paper.

"There's the money," she said, and held it out to him. "It's good —I could write a cheque for ten times that and not have it come back."

"And what did Peake do then?" asked Tony, when his friend had related the afternoon's events up to that point. "It must have been a pretty staggering offer, and not to be sniffed at if he really is all that keen on his job. I may be congenitally dishonest, but I don't somehow fancy I'd let a few scruples stand in the way of doing what I thought was a million pounds' worth of good."

Beale smiled at this, but shook his head.

"A million pounds is certainly a lot of money," he said: "but Peake was sharper than you seem to be—he didn't let it dazzle him. He picked out the flaws in the scheme like a schoolmaster exposing a false but plausible translation. I'd rather expected he might boil over and gibber, but he did it all very calmly after the first sentence or two.

"To begin with, he pointed out that he was sixty-five, and his heart not too strong, and that he could have very little hope of living long enough even to see this proposed research college completed as a building, let alone peopled. He then went on to emphasize the more important aspect of how the transaction would affect his professional reputation. There'd be no possible hope of persuading anyone that he hadn't been bribed to say that Thomas Jefferson Jay was sane: and once that was put about he might as well try to teach the next generation to play baseball as anything he knew of mental derangement. Nobody would trust him an inch. He finished by telling her that in any event he wouldn't dream of seriously considering her offer until it had been formally made to him through some qualified firm of solicitors with a sound name, whether English or American; and he very much doubted if she'd be able to find such a firm to act for her. To try to do so, however would be in his opinion far stronger evidence of good faith than the waving of a cheque in his face. And, anyway, such an inherently questionable proposal could only be handled adequately by lawyers."

"A tall order to find any willing," agreed Tony. "No, it doesn't shine so much when you look a bit closer, does it?" '

"It does not: which worries me. Unless she's quite dumb, which I'm certain she isn't, she must have known it would be a sheer waste of time to make the offer at all, on her own like that, and consequently a waste of time and money coming to England, into the bargain. Why then do it? The only sensible explanation would be that she managed to persuade herself it was worth while because she wanted it to be: and yet I can't altogether believe that."

He paused, frowning.

"The way she led up to the offer was so tactless. There was no delicacy about it whatever, and very little impression of sincerity—it just didn't ring true. Her flattery was too primitive, and her boasting about the size of the cheque she could write and still have it honoured was quite out of place. Maybe you can explain that by saying it's the kind of woman she is: crude and self-centred and overbearing. All the same, I'm not thoroughly convinced. To put it plainly, I somehow got left with the idea that she never for a moment expected him to treat her offer seriously.

"Yes, I know that sounds ridiculous: to make a fantastic and definitely discreditable suggestion like that, believing firmly beforehand that it'll be refused. In front of a total stranger, too, without even bothering to find out who he is beyond making a wild guess. Yet the way she behaved after Peake had said his bit supports that view."

"How did she behave?" asked Tony. "Straighten her hat and say she hoped he'd reconsider his decision some day, and if he did to be sure and let her know?"

"The very opposite—being casual is the last thing I'd charge her with. No: from being a small hard-eyed old woman supposed to be pleading for her grandson's liberty, she suddenly changed into a white-haired fury. Yes, really suddenly—just like that"—and he snapped his fingers.

"I don't mean she got up and flung herself about—far from it: but what she did do was almost worse. She sat very still and spat bitterness at him. She scarcely moved in her chair at all: it was only her expression that altered, and her tone—the difference between a bumble-bee and a 'cello. I can't remember now everything she said, it came out so fast, but the general drift was to call him a clam-minded hypocrite; a kind of inverted snob who delighted in helping those who couldn't repay him, but wouldn't lift a finger for people in the Jays' position in case he got done out of his comfortable saint-like feeling. That doesn't seem to make quite such good sense now as when she said it, but at the time it was an unpleasant point of view.

"Eventually she got up and swept out—or almost out—before we could do much more than grasp the fact she was going. But she turned back at the door, and I nearly choked myself trying to swallow a very premature sigh of relief. I'd thought it was all over, and it wasn't.

"Up to that moment she hadn't so much as mentioned Selby or the murders, nor even shown she knew about them, but now she did."

"Oh, did she!" murmured Tony. "So Uncle guessed right after all."

"Uncle did not. What she said to finish with was more or less this. 'I was sorry for you when I came, Hilary Peake, but now I'm not. As well as being a so-and-so and the other as a person, you're no blamed good as a loony keeper, letting one out to kill wholesale like that. In the eyes of every decent person, whatever this creature Selby does will ultimately have been done by you, and I hope it drives you as mad as he is to know that's what the world thinks. You deserve to go mad, and then they'll take *you* away and lock you up where nobody can see or hear you screaming, and nobody cares if they do. My curse on you, Peake!' And out she went at last.

"I won't guarantee the rest of the phrases, but the last is gospel. 'My curse on you, Peake!'—as if to say 'And that'll about settle your hash!'."

" 'Whose tongue outvenoms all the worms of Nile'," said Tony. "She'll be getting carted off herself one day if she goes on talking like that. Is Peake doing anything about it?"

"Oh, he took it very well, and seems to derive some satisfaction from my being there. He thinks she won't dare organize any more brick-slinging or car-skidding now because she's given herself away in front of a stranger. He's taking the trouble to let her know exactly who I am, by the way, to make sure. I dare say she'll catch the next boat back to America, and that'll be the end of it."

"Unless she stays to see if the curse works," suggested his friend. "Not much point in uttering one if you don't believe it will, and not much fun hearing about the results at second-hand. I'm sure genuine witches always stuck close to their victims, so that they could watch them slowly shrivel.

"Did anything else happen?"

"Not with her, but I told Matthews to look at the top of the wall if he got half a chance—he was lurking about to say he hadn't found out anything so far against Wrench or Miss Selby. I also saw that terrible nurse. She may have mentioned Farmer to Selby, or again she may not, but he never seemed to take much notice of what she told him anyway, though she used to do her best to cheer him up with a nice bit of news now and again. And so on. Peake was more helpful, but I'll tell you about that later, when Dickie gets back—otherwise he'll grumble."

XVI

FIVE OF THEM settled down that evening to a discussion in their sitting-room. Beale had decided not to move across to the *Falcon* because of Mrs. Jay's presence there, and instead had tackled the *Wheatsheaf's* manageress. The result was already apparent in greatly improved service.

The fifth member of the party was Superintendent Dane, who had willingly accepted an invitation. He shared the couch with Matthews, taking a few hours off duty, and was listening with marked attention.

"One of the main problems, as I see things," said Beale, "is whether Selby escaped by himself or not. I've already told you about Tony's brilliant idea, but unfortunately it hasn't led anywhere yet. Matthews says the top of the wall shows no signs of rope fibre, nor in fact anything out of the ordinary, but that doesn't exclude the possibility altogether, of course. Perhaps some sort of protection was used, just so that the wall shouldn't show any marks; or the rain early in the week may have washed them out. At the moment, though, I don't think it's advisable to experiment directly on the remaining bars. It might be telling somebody too much."

"Then what are you going to do?" asked Dickie. "Stop at 'We could, an if we would'?"

"Temporarily. After all, an experiment wouldn't *prove* anything one way or the other. I imagine that the results would depend almost entirely on the speed of the car. Drive away slowly, with the rope already taut, and your bar will come out differently from the way it would if you had twenty or thirty feet of slack, and could get up a fair speed before it took the strain suddenly. For the time being we've got to be content with saying that there doesn't seem to be any particular reason why a car and a rope shouldn't have been used."

"And how do you know that?" persisted Dickie. Beale passed the question on to Matthews, who dealt with it satisfactorily.

"Outside the courtyard," he said "there's an asphalt run-way leading to the garage. Selby's bedroom was the only one on that side of the house used at night, and the only one from which you can hear indoors if anybody's putting a car away. Another bloke and I tried this evening."

"And how many cars are there in the garage?"

"Peake's big Sunbeam, the doctor's little M.G., and Bellamy's motor-bike. There's also a ladder, but nothing to show if it's been used lately or not. Probably not, I'd say."

"All right, thanks."

"Then I'll carry on," said Beale, who had been lighting his pipe. "The chief difficulty in believing that Selby wasn't helped to escape is the length of time that's elapsed without any sign of him as a person. I mean, the only reason we have for thinking he's still in the neighbourhood is the burglary and three known murders, and we only attribute those to him because we can't think of anybody better. We're basing the theory that he did them on probability, that is, not on direct evidence.

"Look at it in another way, just for a moment. Suppose, sir"—to Dane—"that the victims had all been tramps, whose disappearance didn't cause any comment, and suppose that we didn't know about them yet. Would you still be looking for Selby alive in the New Forest? Wouldn't you have assumed by now that he must be either dead or miles away?"

The Superintendent nodded slowly.

"I'm afraid we should," he agreed. "I see your point."

"And yet the murders do seem to show definitely that he's still nearby, which leaves us facing the problem of how he can have kept himself alive and uncaught for over a fortnight. As far as I'm concerned, it appears out of the question unless he's being sheltered; but if he is, then by whom, and how in the world did he get free to do the murders?

"As far as we know from the doctor's preliminary report, Prudence Hill was probably killed the evening she disappeared, May 7th, and Betty Trotter three days later, on the 10th. Wilson we can't be sure about, so we'll leave him out, and just hope."

At this Dickie nodded glumly, and it was plain that he expected the worst.

"And finally," continued Beale, "we come to Sergeant Lee, killed within a comparatively short distance of several people on May 13th in broad daylight. All that means that if Selby *was* being sheltered, over a period of at least six days he could get out whenever he wanted to, complete with weapon; and, quite frankly, the more I think about that idea the less I like it. There's nobody to suspect of wanting him out of Balmer's Court but his sister, and not much reason to give her. All we can say is that she'd probably have got Dr. Wrench to help her. Yet Professor Peake, starting with serious suspicions against them, has had to give up, the men put on to watch them haven't been able to find the least thing wrong with their behaviour, and Matthews here tells the same story. As well, I must say that they both impressed me favourably. That's nothing to go by for the rest of you, perhaps, but it's bound to carry a certain amount of weight with me.

"I asked Peake two more questions this afternoon, by the way: how heavily Selby slept and how he got on with the doctor. The answers were that he slept normally—anybody entering his room with a key wouldn't necessarily wake him; and that he wouldn't have been at all likely to take orders from Wrench—to 'follow me, because your sister wants to see you outside'. Nothing like that.

"Well, so far we aren't getting on very well, and when we come to the alternative theory that Selby wasn't helped we don't do much better. If you rule out Dr. Wrench and Miss Selby, as far as we know you rule out everybody, and then you get landed with the incredible idea that a lunatic who doesn't know the country has contrived to exist for a fortnight on fresh air and fir cones, as Tony puts it. And that, too, without once being caught sight of—or not by anybody who's lived to tell the tale.

"Oh, and while I remember, sir: was there anything edible in Betty Trotter's knapsack?"

"Yes, a packet of biscuits and a half-pound slab of chocolate."

"Plain chocolate?"

"Yes."

"And both unopened?"

"Yes—it's a point, isn't it?"

"But maybe Selby didn't care for plain," suggested Matthews. "I don't—hate the stuff."

"But he did care for it—I guessed the girl might have had something like that with her, and asked Dr. Wrench this morning. Why didn't Selby—if it was he who killed her—take the chocolate and eat it? Because he wasn't hungry? Because he was too mad to think of it? I certainly don't believe the first, assuming he was on his own, and I don't think much of the second. By my reckoning he must have been so starving hungry that food would have been the first thought in his mind: yet apparently all he wanted was her left shoe.

"There's another point to mention too, while I remember—one I sounded Peake about yesterday. Assume that Selby was sitting quietly in his bedroom when he suddenly felt an urgent desire to collect left shoes: so strongly that he escaped then and there in order to be able to do it. But does he have to go about killing people for their shoes? Wouldn't he be far more likely to ask them nicely first, and wouldn't nearly everybody prefer losing a shoe to being attacked by an obvious lunatic?"

Dane smiled.

"Fellow's mad, that's what," he said, in the manner of Captain Wyndham.

"And again, while he was in Farmer's place why not take the opportunity to pinch all *his* left shoes?"

"By jove, that's a good point!" exclaimed Tony. "I bet you only just thought of it."

He turned to Dickie Donovan.

"How many left shoes would Farmer be likely to possess?" he asked. The reporter grinned.

"About one odd one, by the look of him," he answered. "But as a matter of fact, now you mention it, I do remember seeing another pair besides those he had on—in a cupboard by the fire-place. That doesn't mean they were there a fortnight ago, though."

"Still, he did have two lots," said Tony; and then, in turn, grinned expansively.

"What somebody ought to do," he declared "is to test that burglary."

"How?" asked Superintendent Dane.

"By doing another one, just to see if he really would sleep through it. You know your way about there, Dickie: suppose you sneak in tonight and see if you can collar his bottom sheet."

Donovan shook his head.

"I don't suppose for a minute that he uses sheets," he answered. "All the same, it isn't a bad idea."

He regarded Beale and Dane quizzically.

"What about it, reverend sirs?" he asked; and the Superintendent smiled largely.

"You'll get no active encouragement from me," he said. "But if you were to do it without my knowledge, I couldn't very well stop you, could I? Only it'll be your job to humour him if he wakes up, and I wouldn't envy you—I've had some."

"Well, I'll tell you tomorrow if I went—that gives nothing away. But about your question, Ted—why didn't he ask people for their shoes instead of killing them? Perhaps he didn't just want shoes: perhaps he wanted only dead people's shoes."

"Perhaps," agreed Beale soberly. "With a man like that, I suppose no suggestion's too far-fetched; and it would explain his leaving Farmer's alone, of course. But not his leaving Farmer alive, though," he added, as the thought struck him.

"To go on: I've got the doctor's report here—all he can tell us at present. You've seen it, sir, of course, but the others haven't. He says neither of the girls had been interfered with, and the only thing worth mentioning, apart from what we already knew, is that Prudence Hill had received a severe blow on the back of the head just before she died. That seems to show she was stunned first—she could hardly have got it falling off her bicycle, he says; but it doesn't get us much further."

"And what about the bicycle, sir—any prints?" asked Matthews: the subject was especially his own.

"None that can't be accounted for," said Dane, "and nothing special otherwise. The thing had apparently been wheeled into the woods, puncturing the back tyre on the way, and there were a few recent dents and scratches which bear out Jenkins' story."

"How very thoughtful of a lunatic to steal a pair of woollen gloves!" murmured Dickie.

"And how very thoughtful of Farmer to have a pair waiting to be stolen!" added Tony. Matthews, however, confined his attention to the bicycle, while Beale sat thoughtfully refilling his pipe.

"You've checked all the prints on it, sir?"

"Yes, all the clear ones. They were made by the girl herself, Tom Jenkins, or the owner—the scullery-maid at Yewhurst Hall, where she worked.

"Well, Inspector, it's a confounded puzzle, and I'm afraid I'm not being much help. Is there any solution?"

"Oh yes," said Beale with a smile: "all we need is enough time, and enough luck, and enough imagination. Who's going to be brave enough to guess?"

"You," suggested Tony.

"Because of my greater experience, I suppose? No, I'm inviting someone else. Dickie?"

"No thanks, nothing doing. Or only a very feeble guess, anyway. Selby's managed to raid some village shop, and that's how he keeps alive."

"But why haven't we heard about it?"

"Oh, the person the shop belongs to is frightened to say anything in case the nasty police get the wrong idea, and start thinking he's an accomplice. Yes, I said it was feeble."

"Well, what about you, Superintendent?"

Dane looked very serious, his huge bulk reclining comfortably on the couch. Matthews had long since abandoned his attempt to get a fair share, and was squatting on the rug near the gas fire.

"No," he said at last, almost reluctantly. "I'd rather hear it from you, if you don't mind. I mean, I've a rough idea of what you're going to say—I think—but I can't imagine what the implications are."

"All right, sir. Tony?"

"No: but I'll ask the question I started yesterday in that courtyard. If Selby could climb over the wall at night in his pyjamas, why didn't he do it in the day-time when he was at exercise? It would have been much easier, and warmer, and he wouldn't have had to burst his bars asunder first."

"Well, I imagine the obvious answer is the right one: because it would have been far too dangerous. For one thing, he'd run the risk of being seen, and for another, he couldn't expect more than an hour's start, if that. He was never alone there for longer, Bellamy said."

"Yes, I suppose that's it—though he seems to get saner and saner as time goes on. Nobody's yet suggested that he escaped because he wanted to see the Coronation, but I dare say they will soon."

Beale ignored his last remark, and turned to Matthews; and, to everybody's surprise, the diminutive detective-sergeant accepted the challenge in a totally unexpected manner.

"Oh, I'm not shy," he said. "I don't believe the fir-cone idea, and that's a fact, and I don't believe Miss Selby knows anything. I had a bit of a talk with her last evening, and I just don't. No sir, not because of her looks, either"—to Tony, who was smiling. "Pretty girls don't mean much to me, not with my mug. You'll just have to take it I'd rather look elsewhere."

"For Selby's accomplices?"

"No, not really: for the bloke that's doing Selby's murders."

At this they all sat up, and Beale exchanged a significant glance with the Superintendent.

"It's been said!" remarked Dane, almost sadly. "You're a brave man, Sergeant—can you elaborate the idea?"

"I don't know, sir, but I'll have a try. In my opinion, Selby's as dead as the rest of 'em. Now, I know my opinion ain't evidence, and I won't bother with who did the murders, but I could make up a good story why Selby didn't. He was a lunatic, being looked after by this Professor Peake, and by all accounts Peake's got ideas of his own about how to treat lunatics. Suppose between them he and Dr. Wrench worked out some new wheeze to try on Selby: an operation of some kind on his brain, say. If it comes off, he'll be cured, and the doctor can marry his sister. If it doesn't, he'll croak, but they think it's worth the risk. Well, they have a go, and it doesn't come off—then what happens?"

It was Tony who answered.

"Wrench writes out a tactful death certificate all about influenza or bubonic plague or something noncriminal, and sends a large wreath."

But 'Horsey' Matthews shook his head.

"No go, sir—in England every lunatic that dies has to have an inquest."

"True," said Beale, nodding: "I hadn't remembered that."

"And once Selby's dead," continued the detective-sergeant, "there's trouble ahead for Peake and Wrench if some nosy coroner gets a look at the body, so they don't let him. Instead they pull a couple of bars out of his bedroom window, chip a couple of bricks in the wall, and say he 'escaped'."

"And this mangled body?" enquired Dane, smiling, though thoroughly interested.

"One of 'em went off by car and dumped it in the sea—or stayed at home and cut it up scientifically. I don't know, sir, but I don't think it rules the idea out."

"And the murders? I don't believe a word of all this, mind—Peake isn't that sort of man, and nor is Wrench: but it's damned ingenious."

"Thank you sir—but you've heard the best of it. The murders don't seem to fit in anywhere. I don't like thinking they're being done by Peake and Wrench to bear out the escape—make it look convincing. I'd rather have another idea. They're being done by somebody else who's taking advantage of the fact that Selby's bound to be suspected. Some queer cove, who always wanted to know what it feels like to kill, and sees his chance the minute it's given out there's a madman loose in the Forest. 'If I do a daft enough murder' he says to himself, 'they'll think it was him, and won't bother to look elsewhere.' So he does one—and then another one, and so on."

"A very queer cove," remarked Dickie. "In fact, pretty nearly another lunatic."

"Pretty nearly. Or else somebody who's interested in fancy feelings and things: psychology—you know the stuff."

He paused, and looked almost slyly across at Beale.

"They tell me," he said, as nonchalantly as possible—"they tell me that this man Farmer writes an odd sort of book. I never read any myself, but there's supposed to be one about a chap who couldn't decide whether to kill his father for beating his mother, or kill his mother for nagging his father. In the end he killed himself instead: but it's no good doing that first to find out what it feels like."

"Good lord!" exclaimed Tony. "Was that by Farmer?—I read the thing."

"Any good?" asked Matthews.

"Not bad, but a bit heavy going. A mixture of J. C. Powys and Julian Green, with a dash of early Doblin and a flavouring of Hermann Broch—you know, *The Sleep-walkers.*"

"Nonsense—don't show off," said Dickie. "Of course he doesn't know. Nor do I. Nor does anybody except you, I don't suppose."

"And I didn't mean the book, sir," added Matthews meekly. "I meant, did reading it make you think my idea was any good?"

"Not really—I find it a trifle indigestible, I'm afraid."

"And there I'm with you," agreed Dickie. "Have you seen Farmer yourself, Matthews?"

"Not to speak to, no."

"Well, I have, and I say the same as the Superintendent about the other two—he isn't that sort of man."

The detective-sergeant was in no way upset.

"I dare say you're right," he observed. "But that was what you were driving at, sir, wasn't it?"—to Beale.

"That Selby himself might be dead? Yes, though I certainly hadn't filled in such startling details. With all due respect, I don't think we can treat your suggestion very seriously without some sort of supporting evidence."

"Oh no, sir, of course not."

"All we can do is to keep our eyes open for that evidence—and not under the most favourable circumstances, either, since we start by suspecting everybody who matters at Balmer's Court. They'd all have to be in the plot: and can you imagine Peake trusting the talkative Nurse Spence with his reputation and future? I know jolly well I wouldn't."

In the pause that followed Superintendent Dane turned to Matthews, and posed a question delicately.

"Do you often make up stories like that, Sergeant?" he asked.

"No sir, not very often."

"But it doesn't hurt to let one's imagination have a day out at times," remarked Beale, who thought he detected a rebuke in Dane's tone. "It's better than waiting for people to come and confess, anyway. All the same, now that the idea of Selby's death has been put into words I can't honestly say I like it any more than the others: it leaves just as much to be explained. Just let me go through the possibilities.

"(1): Selby is alive, and Selby did the murders. Objections: how has he kept himself alive for so long without assistance? If he's been looked after, how did he manage to get out when he wanted to to kill people?

"(2): Selby is alive, but somebody else did the murders—that's a point of view we haven't considered yet. Objection: unless he's being kept prisoner, how can the murderer be sure that sooner or later we shan't find out the truth, and immediately stop suspecting Selby? If somebody else is responsible for the deaths, then there's no possible doubt that they're meant to look like Selby's work. But surely, in that case, it would be far safer to kill him too, and get rid of the body. While he's alive it's always on the cards that he'll get free, or be rescued, and that would make things very awkward.

"(3): Selby is dead, and somebody else did the murders. That's your packet of trouble, Matthews, and I can see now the real objection against Farmer. The murderer, to feel at all secure, must know two things: that Selby's out of the way, and that anybody else who knows that is going to keep quiet. (If he killed the man himself, of course, that doesn't arise.)

"If he isn't aware of the first, then presumably he just supposes that Selby's escaped—as you made Farmer do: when he runs the enormous risk of doing a murder in one enclosure at five o'clock, say, when the supposed culprit has been recaptured in another enclosure at half past three. If he doesn't know the second—that Selby's death is being concealed by those other people besides himself who're in the secret—then he's liable to be caught out at any time. Even if they don't mean to give the show away, they may still make a mistake.

"With regard to Farmer, how can he possibly know all that? He must either have killed Selby himself—caught him in the middle of the burglary, perhaps, and cracked him on the head: or he must have been told by somebody who knows the truth—almost certainly a somebody at Balmer's Court. Nurse Spence seems the most likely person, because of her long tongue. She tells Mrs. Montgomery, say, in the strictest confidence, and Mrs. Montgomery—who also chat-

chatters, according to Peake—goes straight home and passes it on to her next-door neighbour in even stricter confidence. But if that happened, doesn't Farmer run a still bigger risk? How can he be sure that people won't change their minds, explain exactly what's been done with Selby, and then say 'And Farmer was the only other person who knew'?"

"And that particular point would surely hold good for Peake and Wrench as murderers, too," said Dane. "Supposing them to know about Selby's death, I mean, whether they killed him or not. If Peake, for instance, goes out to kill the first suitable person he meets, whether to make the escape appear genuine or because he feels just like a nice murder, how's he to know that Wrench won't draw the line at a thing like that, and come straight to us? And *vice versa.*"

"A kindred spirit!" cried Tony admiringly. "You've caught the trick perfectly, Superintendent. It's a secret formula for detection, you know, invented by the cloud of smoke opposite, and it runs thus. 'With regard to any given crime P, let there be N possibilities. Discard Z of these on the slightest provocation, permutate Y of the remaining (N—Z) a few at a time, again discard the more unlikely, and equate what's left with zero. Reduce to the scale of four and a bit—that's you, Matthews, and discuss for two hours. Findings—if any—are keepings.'

"But, to be serious, in the case you've just mentioned the only safe way for Peake and Wrench to commit their murders would be hand in hand. I rather liked that idea of yours a moment ago, Ted: that Selby really did escape all alone, went to Farmer's place to burgle it, and was caught and killed. But then the man would scarcely go straight to the police and say he'd been robbed, would he? It would be just stupid to mix himself up in things. No, I'm afraid the theory of Selby's innocence puts us in a worse muddle than ever. What are you going to do next?"

Beale indicated that he was not at all sure.

"We want more direct evidence," he said; "or at any rate safer grounds for speculation. Let's take the murders briefly in order, and see if we've missed anything. Prudence Hill was presumably attacked while she was cycling home after her quarrel with young Jenkins. How then did the murderer, whoever he was, set about doing it? Was he waiting in the hedge for anybody that came along? He could hardly have been waiting specially for her. Did he rush across the road, knock her off her bicycle, kill her on the spot, and then set about disposing of the body and bike?"

He turned to Dane.

"How far is the Minchley Road from where she was found, by the most direct line?" he asked.

"Quarter of a mile, about," was the answer. "And mostly open country once you get through the first few trees, except for the last hundred yards. It's very thick there, though, as you saw for yourself, and as a matter of fact I don't mind telling you in confidence that that particular enclosure was supposed to have been searched last week under Captain Wyndham. It just shows how easy it is to miss things. There's no question that she hasn't been there all the time, of course—the doctor's positive."

Beale nodded.

"It's even possible that the same thing's happened with Wilson," he said.

"Quite. I think you're probably right about the method of attack. At least, we worked on those lines ourselves, though we concentrated more on the other side of the road—the one she'd be on if she were cycling."

"Why only cycling?" asked Tony.

"Well sir, you're supposed to walk on the off-side at night, in the country: then it's your own fault if you get knocked down."

"Oh yes, of course—long time since I did any walking. But would she know that?"

"Yes—we found out that she'd been told by the butler at Yewhurst Hall. Whether she took particular notice or not is another matter, though. Also, of course, there's nothing to show the murderer didn't cross the road with her body, just to throw us off the scent. It seems a bit risky, all the same. A fast car with strong headlights might have spoilt things."

Beale, by now, was frowning.

"Then let's suppose she wasn't cycling," he said. "Didn't Jenkins say she tore one of her stockings when they collided? And one of them was half down when you found her. I'm afraid I didn't stop to look very closely—was it the same one?"

"Yes—at least, the knee was certainly torn a bit."

"Had it been undone, or pulled down forcibly? Was she wearing suspenders?"

"Yes. As far as I remember, it wasn't torn at the top, so I suppose—yes, that's an idea, isn't it?"

Beale nodded, glad that Dane had been sharp enough to follow his thoughts.

"If she undid it herself, maybe she'd stopped to see how much damage had been done by her fall, and in that case she might well have crossed the road first. Would there be a hill anywhere near?"

"Why yes, Longman's Hill. Yes, that sounds very likely. I'll look at the stockings again the first chance I get."

"Thank you. I suppose quarter of a mile isn't too far? I mean, it's a goodish step to carry a dead body and wheel a bike at the same time. I shouldn't think you could put one on the other over that sort of ground, and I can't quite see Selby making two journeys of it, if it was he. What would she weigh, about? Seven stone?"

"Certainly not more, if that—she was a tiny little thing. If he gave her a fireman's lift he'd still have a hand free."

"But do it in the dark?" queried Tony: and was suitably apologetic upon being reminded that bicycles had lamps.

"Then it seems all right," said Beale. "Anyway, it wouldn't be a very safe deduction to say there must have been two persons in it. They'd probably have dumped her much further off the road, for one thing. All that worries me is that it seems just the least bit on the sane side for Selby. By the body was obviously the best place for the bike, but would he have realized that? But it's no good asking stupid questions, and perhaps it was the lamp that decided him to do things that way: or anyone else, for that matter.

"Next we'd better take the girl hiker, though I doubt if we'll get much there. The chief point, for what it's worth, is that her knapsack apparently hadn't been opened; or, if so, it had been carefully done up again, and the biscuits and chocolate not touched. If Selby was hungry, as I said earlier, that's hard to understand, and to give a good reason why he shouldn't have been hungry is even harder. Still, there may be one, for all that. Anything else?"

"Yes," said Dickie suddenly: he had been silent for some time. "What *was* there in her knapsack, Super?"

"Oh, all sorts of things: pyjamas, toilet and washing kit, a tin mug, a pair of shoes, a handbag with the usual contents, some note-paper and envelopes, a railway time-table, a set of underclothes, a knife and fork and a tin-opener, photographs of about fifty different film stars, all men, and a couple of Penguins."

"Dead ones, sir?" enquired Matthews, without change of face. "Oh, sorry—didn't know you meant books."

"Well?" asked Beale. He could see that the reporter had spotted something.

"I don't know—it depends on how sane that fellow Selby was. The way I look at things is this. The big difference between Betty

Trotter and the other victims is that she was the only one who could possibly have been carrying a spare pair of shoes."

Beale was on the alert immediately.

"One to you," he said—"I ought to have thought of that myself. I wonder if Selby *would* have looked? Unless of course he only wanted ones hot off a dead foot. Sorry"—as Tony grimaced at his phrasing. "Anyway, I'll ask Peake, though he probably won't be able to say—I doubt if anyone could.

"And lastly we come to the murder of Sergeant Lee. According to your report, Superintendent, it looked as if he'd either been with somebody he thought he could trust, or believed he was alone?"

"Yes, judging from the way he was lying."

"Then the first gives us a murderer who definitely wasn't Selby, and may have been one of the search-party, and the other leaves it open."

"But not necessarily his own search-party," said Dane: "there was 'C' only about a quarter of a mile away. Any normal-looking person speaking to him, or beckoning or calling him, would be taken for a member of some party, or somebody just joining up."

"But not a call," objected Matthews. "Far too dangerous, wouldn't it be? Somebody else might hear, and come tearing up a minute later. You can never be sure how far your voice'll carry outdoors—at least, that's my experience. If you want it to go a long way it gets blown back behind you, and if you want it to only go a few yards, a chap a quarter of a mile off complains of a headache."

"No, probably not a call," agreed Dane, smiling. "Personally I prefer nothing—a sudden attack while Lee was separated from the rest."

But Beale frowned at this.

"In that case your murderer's lying in wait for a chance to kill anybody who gets separated," he said. "It's possible, certainly, but it wouldn't be easy. It means he'd have to keep up with the party he was trailing continually, and yet not be seen. And it isn't even as if he'd be hiding from ordinary people, half asleep as likely as not: the ones he's dogging are especially on the watch for any strange movement, any suspicious shadow. As far as I'm concerned, it's Lee's murder almost more than anything else which makes me think the killer isn't Selby. I seem to have a picture in my mind of somebody known to Lee waiting about for an opportunity to catch his eye, quietly leading him well away from the rest, and pointing to a non-existent footprint. 'What do you make of that, Sergeant?' he asks, gets behind, trips the man up, and finishes things off before he can let out a single bellow."

"I bet I'd have time to bellow," objected Tony: but Beale disagreed.

"Perhaps you don't know," he said, "but it's possible, standing just behind anyone, to wind him with a circular punch round his body. It's only a trick, and not used much in polite society, but it's very effective when it's done properly. I was shown it years ago by a little sneak-thief called Dickins, who used to work, as he called it, only on foggy nights. He'd creep up behind people, lay them out like that, and go through their pockets or hand-bag while they were still gasping. A similar blow, and then a trip, would leave Lee helpless—but that's only guess-work again, of course."

"And how did your friend Dickens ever get caught?" asked Tony. "It sounds pretty foolproof to me."

"Oh, through bad luck—sheer bad luck. He tried his little trick on a man standing at a corner all muffled up and obviously waiting for a taxi to come along: and he couldn't possibly know the man was going to a fancy-dress dance as the Black Prince."

XVII

AT BREAKFAST the next morning, Sunday, there was no sign of Dickie Donovan.

"Probably in gaol," said Matthews cheerfully; then sighed suddenly, assuming a mournful expression.

"And for all the good I'm doing I might as well be there too," he remarked. "Have I got to go on watching the doctor and Miss Selby, sir? It's a wretched job."

"Well, as long as you see it gets done—"

Beale told him. "It's probably useless, but we'd look fools if it weren't."

"What do they do?" asked Tony.

"Nothing much, sir—out searching all yesterday, both of 'em. She was down in Burwood later, messing about at the station—railway, not police: but I don't know why."

"Has she got a car?"

"No sir, a bike, thank goodness. When they both go in his bus we use a motor-cycle, of course—otherwise we pedal-push as well."

Tony grinned.

"It's a pity they didn't have fairy-cycles when you were a little boy," he said. "You could have kept yours for when you grew up, couldn't you?"

Just as they were finishing the last of the toast, Beale was summoned to the telephone.

"Dr. Wrench," he told Tony on his return. "He wants to see me as soon as possible—will you drive over there? Thanks."

The doctor appeared somewhat excited as he showed them into his private room, closed the door with a conspiratorial air, and asked then to sit down. It was noticeable that the scar on the left side of his face stood out today as a livid weal.

"I hope I haven't interfered with your plans," he said, "only I very much wanted to see you. Remember yesterday you asked my opinion about Selby's escape—whether I thought he'd been helped or not?"

"Yes, I remember," agreed Beale. "You're ready to answer now?"

"Yes. The fact is, Lavinia and I have been doing a little detective work on our own. If we could have turned it over to your people, we would have done, but we thought we'd better not till we'd something worth giving you. Well, we have now and I'd like to put the whole matter before you."

"Good—but take it easy."

At this Wrench nodded a little self-consciously: he had been speaking very fast, but now became more articulate.

"Sorry if I was gabbling," he said. "I'm afraid I do at times. Well, to begin at the beginning, neither Miss Selby nor I have ever been satisfied that her brother's escape was what it seemed to be on the surface. I won't go into all the reasons for our thinking that, but just give you three. We don't believe Simon would have wanted to escape at all, in the first place, we don't believe he'd have done it in his pyjamas if he had wanted to, and we don't believe he could have pulled out those bars or climbed over the wall."

"Just a minute," interrupted Beale, who was paying great attention, his grey eyes steady on the doctor's. "I'll pass the second and third reasons, but just explain the first a bit more carefully, will you?"

"Certainly. As you've probably been told—at least, I know you have, because we both did yesterday morning—Selby was almost sane a good deal of the time. Also, which is exceedingly rare in a case like that, it wasn't only when he was sanest that he knew he was mad. Do you follow me?"

"Yes, I think so."

"Good. Well, when he knew he was mad he used to show the deepest gratitude for what the Professor was doing for him, and even at his worst he was calmer and more friendly with Peake than with anyone else. I've heard him say a score of times, even in the middle of an attack: 'How am I going on, Professor? You're my only hope, you know.' I don't suppose for a moment that you'll have heard that from Peake—he hates cracking himself up: but it's true, all the same. I'm sure nothing would have induced Simon to leave here."

"All right," said Beale—"thank you."

"Then I'll get on. When Lavinia and I found we both thought the same about things, we put our heads together and tried to work out what might have really happened. Now, mind you, I'm not pretending we got very far as regards any hope of finding him, but we did discover one or two queer things that nobody else seems to have noticed. At least, *we* think we did."

He broke off for a moment, apparently aware that he was again speaking quickly, smiled, offered Beale a cigarette, which was declined, suddenly remembered Tony sitting quietly in the corner, passed the box across to him, and continued.

"If you try to put yourself in our place for a moment,," he said, "and believe that Selby wouldn't willingly leave here, you'll see that there were only two possibilities to consider: murder and kidnapping. Well, we didn't waste much time on the first, because we couldn't think of one single reason why anybody should want to kill him, or hope to gain anything by it, so we concentrated on the second. Now, maybe you'll think we didn't get much of a motive there, either; but it was something, and it impressed us both more than the escape idea.

"Before I go any farther, though, I must ask you a question. Do you know anything about Professor Peake's history before he came to England in 1931?"

"Yes—all about the Jay business, anyway."

"Good: and did you know that Mrs. Cornelius Jay is in England, in Burwood, and came to see Peake yesterday?"

"Yes—I was there."

"Good lord, were you really? He didn't tell me that, but it makes things simpler. What Lavinia and I believe is that Simon was kidnapped by somebody on her behalf. She obviously couldn't have done it herself, because she only arrived in England on Monday; but she bears Peake an enormous grudge, and if everything one hears is true, or even only half true, then she isn't the sort of woman to forget it.

"Now, why she wanted to get hold of Simon—exactly how she planned to hit at Peake by getting hold of him—we can only guess. All that matters at the moment is that we started looking at things from that standpoint; and when we did that we started making discoveries. About whom, do you think? Have a shot."

"No," said Beale: "you tell me."

"All right—about Abel Bellamy, our male nurse here."

At this pronouncement, since Wrench so clearly expected it, both his listeners showed more than appropriate surprise, and begged him to go on. He did so willingly, talking fast and ever faster until he had to be periodically pulled up: when he would apologize, and go very slowly for the next three sentences. He spoke for perhaps half an hour, and succeeded in making his present point of view entirely clear.

Its sum was no less startling than Tony had hoped for, and sufficiently apposite to provoke thought. Dr. Wrench believed that Bellamy had been the person acting for Mrs. Cornelius Jay. He argued that Selby could not have been kidnapped without help from someone inside Balmer's Court, and it was patently ridiculous to suspect Peake himself. The servants, too, seemed out of the question, since none of them had keys to the patients' rooms. Nurse Spence he had eliminated on several grounds: partly because she had been with Peake five years, as against Bellamy's two; partly because she had definitely been in Balmer's Court at all material times on May 7th, 10th, and 13th; and partly because she was in his opinion one of the most transparently honest women he had ever met. ("Of her kind," he added quickly, and Beale smiled: he saw that with Wrench Lavinia Selby came first in all things good.) Bellamy alone was left, and Bellamy it must therefore have been.

The doctor believed furthermore that the male nurse had begun his acquaintance with Peake by deceiving him with his story of no food, no work, and no money; that the lurch two years ago in front of the Professor's car had been the preliminary cunning step to obtaining a post with him, where he could lay his plans according to circumstances. He believed, in addition, that the person responsible for the kidnapping—Bellamy—had also been responsible for the murders: hence his reason for acquitting Nurse Spence.

"Oh, come!" exclaimed Beale at this point. "Isn't it about time you gave us a little evidence, Doctor? Or at any rate some justification for your opinions?"

Wrench agreed readily that it was, and proceeded to do so with more care than might have been looked for.

The motive for the kidnapping, except vaguely as being on behalf of Mrs. Jay, and the precise manner of it, were still mysteries to him, he confessed, though it was worth pointing out that Bellamy had a key to Selby's bedroom, and had always got on extraordinarily well with the lunatic: better than he had ever done himself, he admitted. Similarly, why it had been necessary to kill three, and probably four, innocent persons was not clear; unless for once the obvious were true, and the victims had been disposed of to support the idea of Selby's continued presence in the New Forest.

"After all," said Wrench, "if a lunatic escapes, and you start looking for him, and you see or hear absolutely nothing for a week, you naturally begin to assume he's starved to death or gone abroad or something. But if, just as you're thinking of giving up, he apparently does a murder, you go on looking."

"But he didn't apparently do a murder at the end of a week," objected Tony. "The first body wasn't found till Wednesday."

"I know: but somebody had disappeared on the previous Friday, and when young servant girls mysteriously vanish the police would be fools if they didn't consider murder a possibility. From that it's only a short step to suspecting Selby. Do *you* see what I mean?"—to Beale.

"Yes, or partly. If the idea is to make people believe that he's still in the Forest, although in fact he isn't, a series of murders will do that very effectively—for a time: but what I don't understand is why such an idea should have to be entertained. Why must the police go on looking? What was the matter with letting the affair die down, and then carrying out the next section of the plan—blackmail, or whatever it is?"

Wrench leant forward very earnestly, brushing his black hair back so that it began to stand on end.

"Everything," he answered. "The whole business of Selby's escape had to be continually in the limelight, because the motive behind it all was the ruin of Peake. I said just now that it wasn't clear why four total strangers had to be murdered, but that isn't quite true. I think *I* can see why—though whether or not I can persuade you is a different thing.

"Peake's position is rather like that of a man who was in charge of a mad dog. So long as he keeps it under control, all right: people may think it's rather an odd choice for an occupation, but it's no concern of theirs. If it escapes, though, and bites a poacher, say, or a burglar, and then gets shot, people blame the dog's keeper for being careless, but are jolly glad it's all turned out so well, and say it probably served the poacher or the burglar right anyway. If, again, the dog bites a policeman or a bishop, they'll be more severe in their condemnation: not of the animal, mind you, but of the person supposed to be in charge of it. Finally, if—as has more or less happened—it escapes and bites the heads off half a dozen village children, then there'll be almost nothing too bad to call the kind of creature who let a thing like that take place and didn't lift a finger to stop it."

Beale nodded, staring at Wrench with interest.

"Yes, you certainly know something about human nature, Doctor," he remarked. "All right, the idea was to ruin Peake. Just one question: why not kill Selby himself to begin with? Or make it two questions: if Selby's still alive, what do you imagine is going to happen to him? Incidentally, where is he?"

"Heaven knows!" said Wrench, lighting another cigarette. "I might try the others, though, as I've had a definite invitation to guess. But then, I've been doing that for some time, haven't I? All right, I'll go on, only please don't think I fancy I'm dealing with proved facts. What I've got of those I'll come to presently.

"To begin with, I'll amend what I said a little while back," he continued, after exhaling a cloud of smoke and again rumpling his hair. "The motive wasn't solely to ruin Peake, but quite as much to put him in a position where he'd have to do what Mrs. Jay wanted with regard to her grandson.

"If you'd been living with the Professor as long as I have—three years—you'd know that at heart he's a thundering good fellow, only he doesn't go out of his way to let people know it. Take the case of our other patient, Miss Vining, for instance: she's practically penniless now, though she wasn't when she came here, but she continues to have the very best of attention in every way, and will do as long as she needs it, just as if she were still paying eight guineas a week. He's kind to people in general, too, not only to those he knows personally: that's why I think what I do about the way Bellamy got his job here. Naturally, though, in a pinch he'd probably do more for me, say, than he would for you: and I don't doubt he'd do more for Selby, in whom he was extremely interested, than he would for either of us.

"Given that he's a man like that, it seems to me that eventually Mrs. Jay will have him just where she wants him. In a month or two, when a few more murders have been done and Peake's frantic, she'll suddenly produce Selby, or unmistakable proof that he's still alive, and give him a point-blank choice.

" 'Do what I tell you about my grandson' she'll say, 'or not only will as many people as I can lay hands on get their heads poked in with an iron bar, but Simon Selby will too, and I'll send you what's left in a hat-box to prove it.'

"She could hardly fail, believe me. Peake would go to almost any lengths rather than have a child unjustly beaten, let alone another murder happen. He'd tear his reputation in shreds with his own hands, guarantee not to inform the police, and agree to uncertify Thomas Jefferson Jay."

The doctor spoke with such warmth that both his visitors were impressed.

"But how could she possibly prove Selby's existence without putting the game into Peake's hands?" asked Tony.

"Oh, that wouldn't be difficult: she'd provide proof that only Peake would accept, but that he wouldn't question. For instance, suppose she undertakes to do so on June 1st: all she's got to do is to send us a copy of a newspaper dated May 31st with a few drawings by Selby scrawled in the margin. Peake's made a special study of his drawings: they're quite individual, there'd be no question of forgery, and Selby could easily be got to do one. Only we two would be convinced, of course, but what of that? It's all she'd want."

"Well," said Beale, "you're certainly giving me something to think about. And now for any facts you can produce in relation to Bellamy."

These Tony found disappointing: but realized that he could hardly have expected otherwise, or the whole plot would long ago have been exposed. They amounted, in effect, to a detailed review of the male nurse's movements, as far as Wrench had been able to check them, during the period April 29th to May 13th, the most significant points being these.

(1): *April 29th.* Bellamy's evening out. Left Balmer's Court on motor-cycle at 8.15 p.m. (witness, housemaid, Nurse Spence). Returned 11.30 (witness, Wrench). *Suggested activities:* the making of final arrangements with persons unknown for the kidnapping. At that time he could not know whether Nurse Spence would decide to sleep in the next room or not, of course, so that the arrangements were probably dependent upon this not happening.

(2): *May 7th.* Bellamy's evening off, changed by his own request from previous day. Left Balmer's Court on motor-cycle at 7.00 p.m. (witness, Wrench). Returned 10.30 p.m. (witness, Professor Peake). *Suggested activities:* the murder of Prudence Hill. *Note:* Bellamy knows the butler at Yewhurst Hall, and may well have learnt Prudence Hill's habits from him.

(3): *May 10th.* Bellamy out from 9.00 a.m. to 4.00 p.m. 'searching for Selby'. He joined 'D' party at 9.30 a.m. (witness, Sergeant Overbury). He was not noticed by anyone in that party—all having been questioned—after 12.30 p.m. He was next seen again with 'F' party at 2.30 p.m. (witness, Professor Peake). *Suggested activities:* murder of Betty Trotter (and Wilson?).

(4): Bellamy set off early in the afternoon with Peake and Miss Selby. They joined 'C' party, but Bellamy returned to Balmer's Court unexpectedly, on foot, at 4.00 p.m. Asked why by Dr. Wrench, who had stayed behind because of Nurse Spence's sprained ankle, he said he felt unwell. There is no reliable check on his movements between 2.00 and 4.00 p.m. The distance between Balmer's Court and the place where Sergeant Lee was killed is approximately four miles across country, and there were no other search-parties operating between.

(5): *May 13th.* Bellamy took an hour off in the evening, between 9.00 and 10.00, going off on his motor-cycle. (Witness to departure, Peake, to return, Wrench.) It has not yet been possible to find out what he did in the interval, but it is suggested that he went to meet Mrs. Jay, who arrived in Burwood by the 9.25 train.

"Now," said the doctor, "please understand I'm not claiming too much for our amateur detecting. I don't say this theory's completely right, and I don't even deny the possibility that it may be completely wrong. All I do contend is that it's worth your while to look into. If you think the same, and agree to have Bellamy watched, I shall be satisfied. You'll do that sort of thing miles better than we could hope to. What do you say?"

Beale pondered before answering: he was not at all sure how much importance he ought to attach to what he had just heard. Looked at in one light, Wrench's ideas were a stupid mixture of hasty suspicions and violent imaginings, backed up by very little in the way of convincing evidence. Looked at in another, though, they could be deemed to contain at least a modicum of plausibility, in that the main premises on which they were founded were in his opinion just. Mrs. Cornelius Jay did bear Peake a grudge, and a strong one—after what had happened the previous afternoon he had no doubt of that; and that Selby had escaped unassisted was most improbable.

He decided that there could be no harm in investigating Bellamy's movements, whichever view was correct, beyond a possible waste of somebody's time: and police procedure was rarely to be controlled by such considerations. All the same, there were one or two pertinent questions he ought to ask first.

"You could hardly make the suggestions you have made unless you thought Bellamy capable of murder," he said. "Or could you?"

"Oh, I didn't invent a theory just to give him the leading part," was the answer.

"No, quite: but you wouldn't cast him for that part at all if you didn't think he might fit: Will Hay hasn't played Othello yet. What sort of man is he normally? What was your general impression of him before all this happened?"

"It's hard to say. He's always struck me as being a bit of a mystery: very reserved, generally civil, and never particularly friendly. We get on well enough, but only as strangers. All I can honestly say is that I don't know him well enough to give an opinion. I mean, I wouldn't dream of accusing him of anything on his face value; but I don't think I'd acquit him either."

"I see. And just supposing for a minute that Selby's escape was quite genuine, do you think Bellamy ought to have heard anything?"

"No, probably not. He wasn't as near the room as Nurse Spence, who's a much lighter sleeper, and I don't suppose there need have been very much to hear. And anyway, I'm quite certain the escape wasn't genuine."

Beale nodded.

"That *had* penetrated," he remarked with a smile. "Have you said anything about all this to the Professor?"

"Not directly, no—I thought I'd better not."

"But you quote him as a witness to Bellamy's movements on the 7th, the 10th, and the evening of the 13th."

"Yes, I know, but I had most of my information given me. You see, Peake scarcely ever sets a foot outside the front door after about 8.00 at night. He locks himself up in his study with a decanter of that vile wine he drinks, and slogs away till half past ten or eleven o'clock, when he goes to bed. That night, though, the 7th, he'd been out to post a letter, and nearly got run down by Bellamy coming in, so of course I heard about it. Have you two had any of his favourite beverage yet, by the way?"

"Yes—thank you for asking," said Tony.

"Like?"

"Horrible—sour grapes to me."

The doctor laughed.

"And he gets through about a pint of it every evening regular," he told them. "He says it sharpens his wits, and maybe there's something in that. I'm hanged if I can concentrate on anything much since Simon escaped, but he still does his two or three hours, and woe betide anyone who goes near. It's about the only thing that makes him ratty—that and cigarette ends. He's got a fire complex, you know."

"And the 10th and 13th?" asked Beale. The doctor was becoming garrulous—the effect, he suspected, of having safely delivered his theory into official hands.

"Well, I did have to ask about the 10th, but I knew about the other the same night because I wanted Bellamy myself for something, and couldn't find him."

"Thank you: and one more thing. Have either you or Miss Selby any personal enemies? Real ones, I mean, who wouldn't much mind what they did to hurt you?"

"Good lord no! What ever makes you ask?"

"Because you didn't seem to have considered the possibility that you were the ones aimed at, not Peake. If there were somebody who hated one of you, or both, he might think that the nastiest thing he could do would be to stop all hope of your ever marrying. Do you see what I mean now?"

"Yes, but it's right out of the question—thank God."

Beale queried a few more points without eliciting anything of value, and promised that he would at once arrange for the male nurse to be watched whenever he left Balmer's Court. He would also give the whole matter his most serious attention, he said.

Outside in the drive they met Mrs. Montgomery again. Parked next to Tony's Bentley was a big grey Delage badly in need of a wash and a new coat of paint, and while he was idly wondering whose it was, out of the house came its owner.

"Oh, good morning, Doctor!" she greeted Wrench, who was seeing his visitors off. "You'll think I'm a very early caller, won't you? I'm on my way to church, really, and just dropped in to see the dear nurse. But she's still asleep, they tell me, and a very good thing too. I brought a little present to cheer her up—nothing like a good deed in a naughty world, is there, and I know she wanted one. I saw it in Town on Thursday while I was up for the Coronation, and went straight into the shop and bought it. And the crowds! You simply never met anything like them. Monday and Tuesday were bad enough, but the great day itself was an absolute riot! I'm black and blue all over, and I can tell you I was glad enough to get back to my own little home—peace and quiet and lots of lovely flowers. And then to find poor Nurse had sprained her ankle! But I haven't told you what I brought her yet, have I? An enormous coronation mug with gold handles and lions and things on it, and pictures of the dear King and Queen. I left it with Bellamy, and I do hope he won't break it—you men are so careless sometimes!"

She showed all her teeth in a comprehensive smile, roguishly wrinkled up her left eye, the darker blue one, and then lowered her voice to a confidential whisper.

"Oh, Doctor, and do tell me something—how have you been getting on with him lately? Was he always so surly and disagreeable? Or does he think I've got my eye on him, perhaps? Ha! ha! But there now, I mustn't go talking scandal like this in front of gentlemen I don't know, must I? Be sure to give my very best regards to the dear Professor, won't you? If I'd been brave enough I'd have brought him back a mug too, but I just didn't dare. He's so terribly quiet in his tastes, isn't he?"

She gave them an extra dazzling smile, climbed into the Delage with an unnecessary display of uninteresting middle-aged leg, beamed again indiscriminately, and drove off with a crashing of gears that set Tony's teeth on edge.

"Ghastly creature!" remarked Wrench, apparently feeling that some explanation was needed. "There's no getting rid of her—she's always hanging about."

"Really—why?"

The doctor in his turn smiled suddenly.

"You'd never guess," he said—"and for heaven's sake keep mum about it! Ostensibly she's a friend of Nurse Spence's, but I think there's a deeper reason than that. I fancy she'd give quite a lot to become Mrs. Hilary Peake."

"Glory be!" exclaimed Tony. "But—but it's laughable."

"Yes, I know—but that's what I think. She's a widow, needless to say, with pots of money and absolutely nothing else to recommend her. She took a cottage fairly near about a year ago, and you've no idea how she pesters us. One week it's a great carload of her 'lovely flowers' for the dear Professor, and the next a cask of his beastly vinegar wine, and then there's invitations to bridge and theatres and the lord knows what else. She must know as well as I do by now that he never goes out in the evening—much prefers sweating away upstairs in his study: but she doesn't seem to get tired of asking. She worries us all—drops in on Lavinia and bores her stupid, and I get gushed over like you just saw. I think she hopes I'll put in a good word for her. The only one she doesn't play up to is Bellamy: she wants his job!"

"And what does the dear Professor do about it all?"

"Oh, he just puts up with it in silence now—found out long ago she's snub-proof. But I bet she won't catch him."

"The perils of being a bachelor, Tony," said Beale gravely. "Better look out."

But a moment later he wished he had not spoken, remembering that if it were not for Simon Selby's lunacy, Wrench himself would doubtless be married, and seeing by his face that the doctor too remembered.

"All the same," he went on hurriedly, extemporizing, "she's a useful woman."

"Useful?"

"Yes: if I hadn't met her I might have forgotten an important question. Have you been asking Bellamy any?"

"Questions? Well, one or two, naturally: but I was very tactful, and I'm sure he doesn't suspect anything."

XVIII

"WELL, I ONLY hope he's right," said Beale, on their way to the police-station. "But I rather doubt it. In my experience, people who talk as quickly as he does are hardly ever tactful. Not that the converse is necessarily true, of course," he added, recalling his own recent blunder. "What do you think of the Bellamy idea?"

"Hanged if I know," answered Tony, steering carefully round a cycling curate. "Wrench believes it all right, though—or if he doesn't, he's fooled me. But I find all this secret agent business a bit hard to swallow in cold weather—anyway, without something more friendly to wash it down. No, I know they aren't open yet, so don't apologize. And—to raise a purely practical point—how exactly is Selby's drugged body supposed to have been got out of that place? He simply must have been drugged, you know: people who get kidnapped always are, and you can't chuck an unconscious man over a wall that high, nor stick him on your back and crawl up like a fly."

"But you can get your outside accomplice to provide a suitable ladder."

"Yes, I suppose so. I'd rather have a small crane myself."

"But maybe they weren't as lazy as you are. I don't think the getting of him out would have been very difficult; nobody slept on that side of the house, and they needn't have made much noise, even in pulling out the bars. No, the thing that sticks in my throat is the incompatibility of the kidnapping theory with Mrs. Jay's behaviour yesterday. If she knew she'd soon have Peake where she wanted him, why make that fantastic offer? Why, in fact, show her nose anywhere near the place at all? Suppose he happened to fall for her million pounds, for instance—you can never be certain that that much money won't turn anybody dishonest. Then she'd have been responsible for four unnecessary murders and a snatch, as they call it, and I don't believe it's possible to do all that and not stand in some sort of danger. If not from sober-minded policemen like myself, then from imaginative people like Wrench. It doesn't seem to make any kind of sense at all."

"Yes, he's certainly got an imagination," agreed Tony. "I don't think he's a fool, though."

"Why should he be? What he said about the mad dog and his owner was quite penetrating, even if Mrs. Jay did more or less forestall him yesterday: judgement by results, especially if they're bad, and irrespective of whether you could help them or not. Even as things are, and whatever the truth turns out to be, I don't suppose for a moment that Peake will ever be able to live it all down. He'll be classed as incompetent: not only as a caretaker, but, because of that, as a mental expert too. 'How can he be clever if he lets his patients escape?' "

At the police-station they were met with more grave news. Mervyn Wilson's body had been found at last, doubled up and stuffed into the trunk of a hollow tree about a mile from where Lavinia Selby had almost stepped on Betty Trotter. He had been killed in the same way as the other victims, and his left shoe was equally missing.

"And it's a blasted shame!" growled Captain Wyndham, striding furiously up and down his office. "We've *got* to catch that devil. Can't you do something about it, man? That's what you're here for. I'll have to resign when it's all over, that's what."

He spoke morosely, as if the forces of law and order could receive no greater blow, and subjected the man from Scotland Yard to a hostile glare through his spectacles.

Beale paid little attention, but asked instead for Dane.

"Out," he was told. "Out *working.*"

"Oh, quite—don't let me keep you, sir. And please don't forget that I've something like a fortnight to catch up on your people, will you?"

But as he turned away he was distinctly worried. What *could* he do? Investigate Wrench's allegations? Go round asking more and still more questions, with but little idea of the answers he hoped for? He felt suddenly out of his depth, and disliked the feeling: he must not let himself be panicked by a short-tempered Chief-constable and a week-old body.

As he moved to rejoin Tony outside, after arranging for the male nurse to be watched whenever he left Balmer's Court, the desk-sergeant called to him.

"Superintendent Dane left a parcel for you, sir."

As Beale took it with a word of thanks he wondered a little at his own eagerness. Perhaps, he thought, it was due to the fact that at the moment he wanted nothing so much as some piece of tangible evidence he could worry over, instead of countless and apparently unprofitable speculations, and a parcel at least suggested tangibility.

Inside was a scribbled note.

"Dear Beale, I looked at the enclosed first thing this morning. Luckily they'd been labelled left and right, tho' the tear on the knee wd show which was which, of course. You'll be able to see for yself that neither is torn at the top. They were fairly new, I shd think, and not much worn—no darns. There's something else worth pointing out too—don't be offended if you've already noticed it. I can't find any reasonable explanation, but the feet (of the stockings) are about equally weather-stained; and of body. Now why shd that be, when one had a shoe on and the other didn't? A laced one, too, high in the instep as girls' shoes go. I apologize for not spotting it before, esp. if it's at all important. One other thing. Exp. on a dead pig (!) seems to show pretty conclusively that the weapon used *was* one of the iron window-bars. I got in touch with the man who supplied them to Peake, and he had an identical one in stock. When he sent it round at 9.00 I got hold of Dr. Erwin and went across to the butcher.

Yrs F. Dane."

Beale frowned, took the stockings in his hand, and scrutinized them with great care; but a glance was enough to make him agree that the feet were indeed about equally discoloured. The original shade of the artificial silk had probably been flesh, he judged, but exposure to the weather had darkened it. From knee to toe both stockings were streaked with stains: in such a way, in the case of the torn left one, that it was possible to see it had not been taut on the dead girl's leg, but rucked into half a dozen folds. Look as he might, however, he could see no part of either stocking which appeared to have been less exposed than any other part, except for six inches or so at the top of the untorn one.

Solemnly he called in Tony, and got him to substantiate the evidence of his own eyes, but refused to hazard an opinion about the import of this latest discovery. All he would say was, heavily, that it must almost certainly mean something, and Tony sighed: when he wished to, his friend could be unencouragingly ponderous.

Beale then turned to the sergeant.

"Please send somebody over at once to Yewhurst Hall with these stockings," he said. "I want to know if they're hers, and if possible whether they're the ones she was wearing on May 7th when she went out—somebody may remember. Telephone through to the *Wheatsheaf* as soon as you hear anything."

They had an early lunch by themselves, there being no sign of Matthews or the reporter, and after the meal retired upstairs to their sitting-room. First, though, Beale rang up Scotland Yard for exact information about when Mrs. Jay had landed in England. On his return he secured the more comfortable chair after polite argument, arranged himself so that he came in contact with only its more comfortable parts, and appeared to doze. But in reality he was very much awake; he felt confident that he held a vital clue in his hands, and he was determined to glean something from it.

'A certain dead body had two feet' he told himself. 'Those feet wore stockings, the right one up and the left one down. The right one also wore a shoe, but the other's was missing. The body, as far as anybody knows, was lying out of doors for over a week, not very well covered with a fallen branch. Theoretically, then, it should be possible to tell, solely by inspection, which of those stockings belonged to which leg. Then why in the world isn't it?

'Surely equal causes acting upon equal objects in equal circumstances are bound to produce equal effects. But is it also true to say that equal effects upon equal objects must inevitably be the result of the action of equal causes? Search me. All the same, because Prudence Hill's stockings definitely look as if they were exposed to the same amount of rain and dew and so forth, I can't help feeling I ought to conclude that they have been.

'Which means what?' he asked himself, and for some time could get no intelligible answer. But after perhaps twenty minutes there leapt into his mind a possible solution, and one so pregnant with implications as to be almost overwhelming. He sat very still, trying to consider them all without excitement; and he was glad that he had pursued his thoughts to their apparently logical end before Dickie Donovan burst unceremoniously into the room, just after two o'clock. He at once looked up.

"Was it a good fight?" he asked, and there was reason in his question. Dickie's left eye was bruised and bloodshot, his collar was prevented from falling off only by his tie, and his waistcoat lacked three buttons.

"Very good, thanks," he answered. "The heavy hand of one Alfred Farmer, as you've probably guessed."

"Matthews thought you'd probably be in jug by now," said Tony.

"Then he'll be disappointed. Am I invited to tell all about it?"

He spoke flippantly, but Beale could see that he was both tired and depressed: doubtless he had heard about the finding of Wilson's body.

"If you feel like it," he said.

"Oh, I don't mind. Of course, it's all your fault, really,"—to Tony. "You put the idea into my head. When I got upstairs last evening I made a bargain with myself. If I could manage to sleep on that creaking nightmare these people call a bed, I would: if not, I'd try to find out how easy it was to burgle Farmer. Well, needless to say I didn't sleep, me always having been that sensitive to touch, so about 4.00 I got up again and sneaked out. I had a bit of a job getting hold of the bike, but it wasn't impossible, if illegal, and I reached Crab-Tree Cottage—that's what he calls it—by quarter to five. It was still dark then, of course, and very silent everywhere, so I stopped the engine before I got near, and did the last bit on foot.

"It was easy enough to get into the place. The door certainly made a bit of a row opening, but not nearly enough to wake a man like that, and I'd have been all right if I hadn't been fool enough to forget a torch. I risked one match downstairs, but it didn't help much except to stop me knocking little Gollancz to glory, and I took ages getting up to the bedroom door."

He paused, smiling at his thoughts.

"I don't think I'll ever take up burgling professionally," he told them. "I didn't like the feeling I got standing there at all—that I was all alone in the dark in somebody else's house, even if the only other blokes in it were a deaf barbarian and a dumb goldfish."

"Well, there are other ways of earning a living," Beale pointed out. "And anyway, it's not a fair comparison. A real burglar's got something to spur him on—money or jewellery, or the desire for them. All you stood to gain was the satisfaction of knowing that you could parade round a deaf man's house without waking him."

"Well, I don't think I'll be one, all the same. I don't mind telling you I very nearly crept downstairs again and cleared off, only I thought that would have been a bit feeble: so I went on in, and got what was coming to me."

"A booby trap!" said Tony, with sudden inspiration.

"Just that—and I can assure you I made a fine booby. Down came about a couple of gallons of icy cold water all over everything—me and the floor and the bed and Farmer on it. I let out a shriek, of course, and so did he, and the next minute we were going at it tooth and nail in the dark. He's a strong brute, too, but luckily I had the sense to pretend he'd laid me out before he really did, and he got off to light his smelly oil lamp. Then, of course, the explanations started, and I must say he behaved extraordinarily well. It took about two hours to clear it all up—what I was doing there, I mean, not the water: we just left that to soak in. Then we made some tea and got quite friendly, and it was eleven o'clock or so before I left.

"And then they told me about Wilson when I got to the station," he added, his voice become quite grave, "and I've been getting the story together and phoning it through ever since."

He sighed, lit a cigarette, and stared moodily out of the window. It had just begun to rain, and the streets of Burwood were deserted: the pavements were dark and slippery, and the sky above dull grey.

"What are you two doing?" he asked presently. "No work on Sundays?"

"Only mental, not manual," answered Beale. "I've been busy with a puzzle."

He explained its nature, and asked the reporter's opinion; but Dickie shook his head.

"Her shoes leaked," he suggested. "It rained pretty heavily in the interval, you know, and a week's a long time."

"Sorry, not good enough," said Beale, shaking his head.

"All right, I'll buy it: what's the answer?"

"Oh, you must do the same as I've done—try to find one yourself. See how you get on if you can't sleep tonight—-and remember it's the implications that count. They seem to turn the whole business into something out of Bedlam."

"Which strikes me as being about the mark," said Tony. "If you're determined not to share your precious secret, for goodness' sake stop waving it at us."

"Oh, and talking about shoes," interrupted Dickie with sudden animation, "I did get one interesting bit of news out of Farmer. Don't curse because I didn't tell you before—it's only just come back to me. He's really been burgled again—hence the booby trap."

"What!" exclaimed Beale, thoroughly roused.

"Yes, burgled. You see, when that blessed jug came tumbling down, the water swamped everything near, including his shoes—his other things were all right because he'd chucked them the other side of the bed. I suggested he should put on another pair, and he said they'd been pinched."

"Shoes again, eh? You certainly ought to have mentioned this earlier. Now wait a bit, don't go too fast. How many pairs had he got?"

"Two after Selby's visit, and one now."

"And no slippers?"

"No."

"Where did he think the second pair was?"

"In a cupboard downstairs in the living-room. They were newish ones that he hadn't been using because he didn't want to spoil them. He's terribly hard up—all he's got in the world is what he makes from his books, and that isn't much, and ten shillings a week that an aunt left him. As a matter of fact, he quite often goes about barefoot, he says."

"Poor wretch!" remarked Tony; but Beale seemed strangely impatient.

"Very sad, but keep to the point please," he requested: "it may be most important."

At that Dickie stared a little, but did as he was asked; he could see that for some reason his news had created a deeper impression than he had expected. Briefly he gave the facts he knew: that to the best of Farmer's knowledge the shoes had been in the cupboard for the past week; that both had certainly been there on Friday evening, because he had seen them himself; but that they had been missing about six o'clock on Saturday.

"What made him look?" asked Beale.

"He'd been out for a tramp, and his feet ached, so he thought he'd give them a change."

A careful search of the cottage and its contents, not a long task, had convinced Farmer that they must have been stolen, though nothing else seemed to have been taken.

"And he's absolutely flaming about it," Dickie wound up.

"Doubtless—most annoying. I suppose it was only a fluke that he noticed whether the things were there or not for some time?"

"Oh yes: but you surely aren't thinking Selby went back there, are you? It'd be fantastic—much more probably a passing tramp."

"Maybe," said Beale, rising, his manner definite, as if he were at last beginning to see things clearly.

"Tramps don't usually stop at shoes, though, if they steal at all, do they? How are you getting about these days—your usual hired motor-bike?"

"Yes—mine's in town."

"Then do you mind going back to Farmer and telling him as forcibly as possible that he's to stop making a fuss? He's not to go near the police, nor to tell anybody that he's had anything taken. Can you do that, d'you think?"

Dickie supposed he could, provided he could supply a sensible reason for the command.

"Spin him any old yarn you like," he was told. "Say somebody's been caught with one of his precious shoes in each pocket, only we've got good reasons for not charging him yet, and want Farmer's co-operation. All quite impossible, of course, but it'll do if you can't think up anything better."

"But he'd expect his shoes back, wouldn't he?"

"Oh, tell him they're evidence."

"All right, I'll do what I can. Any hope of knowing what it's all about?"

Beale gave him a worried look.

"I wish I could be sure I wasn't just guessing," he said. "It may be all drivel, but I can't afford to assume that yet. And if I am right, the fewer people who know about it the better, so I'll keep quiet for the present, if you don't mind. That jug of water may turn out to be a real stroke of luck, though, even if you don't think so. Just soothe Farmer for me somehow: and stay on there with him tonight, will you, if it isn't too much to ask? In return I'll save the story for you—if there is one."

"Oh, don't bother about returns," smiled the reporter. "I know you'll play fair. If you want Farmer watched, I'll do it, though I can't imagine why."

He prepared to depart, but before he could get out of the room Beale had changed his mind: a fact which betrayed to Tony the depth of his uncertainty. Resolute one minute, and dithering the next: it wasn't like him at all.

"Sorry," he apologized, "but that won't do—staying there, I mean. When you've done what you can about quieting him, have a go at something really hard. I don't suppose a few more minutes will make any difference, so listen."

He proceeded to give a concise account of what Wrench had suggested that morning, and finished with his new request.

"See if you can discover what Bellamy was up to on the evening of May 7th," he said. "If the doctor's all wrong, it shouldn't be impossible. If the man wasn't out murdering Prudence Hill, he may have been doing something law-abiding and innocent like drinking beer in a pub or visiting friends, or even making enquiries for Selby on his own. But you mustn't ask him direct what he was doing—not on any account.

"It's a pretty tall order, and I haven't the slightest idea how you'd better set about it, but I'll be most grateful for anything you can pick up. Get Matthews on the job too, if you see him—he'll be glad of a change."

"All right, but tell me something first. Do *you* think Bellamy was out murdering Prudence Hill?"

"No," said Beale decisively. "If he was, my guess will get a pain in its inside and expire."

At ten minutes past three came a telephone call from Burwood police-station. The stockings about which he had enquired were undoubtedly the girl's own, he was told, and those she had been wearing the day she was killed.

"And us?" asked Tony, when he returned. "Whom do we trail—the sinister Mrs. Jay?"

"No—we'll go back to Balmer's Court and ask a few more questions."

"Good—nothing like it. Us for the private asylum every time, I say, privacy being everything."

XIX

IT WAS HALF past three, and the weather fine again, when they drew up at the top of the drive for the second time that day. The door was answered by Bellamy, dressed in black, his suit cut according to a bygone fashion and his boots well polished. He looked as if he had just come from or was just going to a funeral, and for a moment Tony began to think the worst; but then he remembered that it was Sunday, and the male nurse from his face clearly the sort of man who would mark the day with more than his usual solemnity.

"Yes sir, the Professor's in his study," he said, without any particular expression, in answer to Beale's conventional query. "I'll find out if it's all right for him to see you."

A few minutes later they were going up the wide staircase, Tony again remarking the ill effect of the cheap distemper on the walls, and thinking how great an improvement could be made for a few pounds, intelligently spent. He would have cheerfully undertaken himself to make the place look more like a home and less like a deserted preparatory school. Then they were shown into Peake's study, and both all but gasped: the room was bright with tulips, vividly triumphant in a dozen vases.

"The lady you met on the stairs the other day," Peake told them, anticipating their inevitable remarks. "Mrs. Montgomery—she has a large garden."

"And she's evidently studied the catalogue to some purpose," said Tony politely. "She must be very fond of you," he added; but Peake refused the bait, turning instead to Beale.

"The daily dozen?" he asked gently. "But I'm quite free, so carry on. How are things going?"

"Slowly," Beale told him. "It's a brute of a business. I'm sorry to be a nuisance again, and I won't bother you more than I can help. By the way, I hope you haven't been hurting yourself?"

As he spoke he glanced pointedly at the Professor's right hand, which was heavily bandaged, and Tony wondered. It was not like his friend to pass personal remarks of that kind; nor to go about with such a preoccupied air, as if he were thinking of other things all the time. Peake, today, seemed by far the more alert of the two, though the signs of tiredness were upon him, and the depths of worry in his eyes made Tony pity him. It must indeed be an unenviable position in which he stood: the person ultimately responsible for the escape of a homicidal maniac. If only he had put in stronger bars, he must be thinking, or given the lunatic a bedroom at the top of the house, or raised the wall to twenty feet. . . .

"Oh, it's nothing much, thanks," was the answer to Beale's query. "I burnt myself this morning making my breakfast. You see, I don't get on very well with bacon and eggs and things like that, and my cook here hasn't the vaguest notion how to make a waffle. I tried showing her, but it was hopeless, so I bought one of those electric gadgets, and when I feel I particularly want one I do it myself. I guess I was a bit clumsy today, though."

"Bad luck," said Beale in a sympathetic voice. "Can't say I ever thought of waffles for breakfast—I'll have to try them one day."

He paused, and smiled rather indecisively: and it began to be clear to Tony that he was entirely shut out of his friend's confidence. If there were questions to ask—though he could think of none himself—why not ask them? If there were none, then why this present visit? Perhaps, though, the poor old chap really was out of his depth for once, and casting about desperately for a lead: and Beale's next words seemed to confirm that view.

"Well, now I am here I'm not quite sure I know where to start. Don't think I'm too inquisitive, but what are you going to do if Selby doesn't turn up?"

Peake stared at him in surprise.

"Funny you should ask that," he said: "I'd been wondering myself. Is there anything fresh that makes you think he won't?"

"No: but it's a possibility that can't be overlooked. It's three clear days since the last murder."

"But it was eight days between his escape and the first one," the Professor reminded him sharply.

"True—it's all very puzzling. Would you consider going back to America?"

"Not unless I were deported. By choice I wouldn't even live in the same continent as Mrs. Jay after yesterday."

"No, and I don't much blame you. She was very violent."

"She's a devil!" said Peake, with sudden warmth. "I heard from her again this morning."

"Really? A letter?" Beale spoke casually enough, but did not deceive Tony: apparently the man was waking up at last.

"Yes, in answer to mine yesterday telling her about you."

He took a sheet of paper from a pigeon-hole in his desk, and held it out.

"I can't imagine why you bothered to tell me the person with you yesterday was a policeman," it began curtly. "Why should I care what he is? All I'm concerned about is my poor grandson and the monstrous injustice being done him. Every time I think of Thomas shut away in Perryville I boil, and it's your fault, you narrow-minded bigot. Men like you are a disgrace to America, no wonder you had to quit. The way you behave towards our family, you might be mad yourself, I often think. What harm did we ever do you? But one day I'll read that *you've* been taken off to be locked up, and I shall just laugh and laugh. Poor Thomas denied the only thing that would give him back his full powers—my love and care, and all because of nobody but you, Hilary Peake. There's no charity in you, no feeling for others, nothing but your miserable pride and your stupid reputation—a cold-blooded machine for labelling lunatics. You can let the dangerous ones escape, too, but not harmless unfortunates like Thomas. But God won't let you off. Thomas will haunt you, and I when I'm dead of my sorrow—I pray it. Caroline Jay."

Beale folded the letter up again and handed it back.

"Now I should have said that whoever wrote that was hysterical," he observed.

"Undoubtedly."

"But nothing—more?"

"Oh no—she's as sane as I am, though I hope I'm not quite so vindictive."

"Shall you answer it?"

"I have done. It came by hand about midday, and I sent Bellamy down with a reply within the hour. A fool thing to do, maybe, but I guess I boiled too."

"I hope you weren't too eloquent—it generally doesn't pay with people like that."

"No—when I'm cross I snap."

He smiled as he said this, and looked for a moment less desperately tired.

"I took a copy, as a matter of fact, to be on the safe side," he added, and passed across a second sheet of paper. On this were three lines in a fine poised writing.

"Mrs. C. Jay, Falcon Hotel, Burwood.

"Madam, Kindly do not communicate with me again except through my lawyers, Exeham & Trink, Grays Inn Road, London, W.C. Hilary Peake."

"And what effect do you think that will have?" asked Tony. It seemed to him a feeble retort, though the kind of thing, he admitted, that a man will derive satisfaction from penning in the heat of anger.

"I can't say, sir, but it makes my position clear—puts it on a legal footing, as it were. If anything else should come direct I shall pass it on to Trink—he'll tell me what to do."

"Yes, very wise," agreed Beale. "He knows the whole position?"

"Everything prior to today—or he will tomorrow morning, when he gets the letter I sent him yester-day."

"Good. And now I've one or two routine questions I ought to have asked you before. When I saw you first, you told me you'd given up suspecting Dr. Wrench and Miss Selby of knowing more than they ought to. Do you still hold to that opinion?"

"Yes," said the Professor simply; but it seemed to Tony that his manner had become more cautious.

"Then, supposing the idea of an assisted escape had to be entertained, which would you sooner suspect, Bellamy or Nurse Spence? It would have to be one of them, you know—unless you feel inclined to go for the domestic servants."

"Oh no—how could they have done anything without a key? Must I answer?"

"You aren't compelled to, of course—but please do."

"Very well, if you insist. But I don't like it, and remember I'm only guessing just to please you. If I had to choose, I think I'd go for Nurse."

"And why?"

"Because it was up to her whether she slept next to Selby or not, and she didn't."

"You mean you think she ought to have done?"

"No, no—nothing of the sort. I haven't the slightest doubt, if I'd seen Selby myself at half past ten, I wouldn't have expected her to. I wish I had now, of course, but it can't be helped."

Beale was frowning by now.

"I'm sorry, but I don't quite follow," he said: "why you'd suspect her before Bellamy, I mean."

"No? Look at it this way: it was up to her where she slept, not Bellamy. How could he possibly lay any plans till he knew one way or the other what she'd do? And how could he know till well after she'd done it? He was out that evening, and didn't come in till about half past eleven, Charles says: and how could he make any plans at that time of night?"

"Yes, I see what you mean now—thanks. But you don't really believe that either of them had a hand in anything?"

"Now now, Inspector! Don't try to tie me up in knots. I don't suspect anybody, and I don't know what happened but that Selby escaped—disappeared. If you can find out the rest, then I might go as far as saying I guessed it all along; but I shouldn't believe me if I were you."

He spoke a little bitterly, as if still grieved about his own failures of observation.

'Frog-marching himself again!' thought Tony. 'How he keeps going at all beats me—he doesn't look as if he's had any sleep for a month.'

Meanwhile Beale was fumbling in his pockets abstractedly. Then, with his hand on the pipe he sought, he paused.

"Do you mind if I smoke?" he asked.

"Of course not—I should have asked you to. I don't myself, though, and I never remember. But you'll be careful of your matches, won't you? Fire's the one thing I'm really terrified of. Charles thinks I'm an awful coward, but I can't help it. When I was a child in New Orleans I only just missed being burnt to a cinder—had to jump out of a third-floor window into a blanket, so I guess that's why."

"And presumably you jumped straight," smiled Beale. "I wonder you have an upstairs room for a study, though. What would you do if you had a fire here?"

"Run for my life!" said Peake without hesitation. "Oh, I would too"—as Tony laughed. "I chose this room partly because I'd be out of everybody's way, and partly because it'd give me two chances. There's another staircase as well as the one you came up—a narrow little thing that leads down to the garden through a door behind that screen"—nodding over his shoulder towards the grinning dragon.

"And if I couldn't get down either way I'd tackle the drain-pipe outside, old as I am—I'd rather break my neck than be cooked any day. The old house is stone built, though, and there isn't much danger. Even I admit that."

"And while I think of it," said Beale, "here's a point that I've had at the back of my mind. You've probably guessed long ago that it's one of those awkward ones that wants to know all about everything. This has got no practical importance, but I'm still curious: how many of your rooms have peep-holes?"

"Ten, all downstairs—I used to have four or five patients at one time, you know. In fact, only the dining-room and the kitchens haven't got them—and the visitors' lounge, of course. Why do you ask?"

"I was just wondering about Bellamy and Miss Vining—is that her name? Presumably the peepholes are to peep through?"

"Yes—it saves disturbing the patients unnecessarily. But Bellamy isn't that sort of man, and anyway he's strictly forbidden to go anywhere near Miss Vining's rooms alone."

"I see—thank you. One more probably irrelevant point, and then we'll stop worrying you. Was there any reason in particular why you didn't tell Dr. Wrench that I was present yesterday afternoon when you interviewed Mrs. Jay?"

At this Peake expressed impatience—and justifiably, Tony thought.

"Because I didn't want him to think I'm a bigger baby than he does already, if you must have it," he said. "He needn't know I'm afraid of old women as well as lighted candles."

"I'm sorry—forgive me for asking. Well, we'll be going now. You've been told about Wilson, I suppose?"

"Yes, Wyndham rang me up. He's properly upset, and I don't much fancy he's specially taken with you, Inspector, somehow. Anyway, I got that impression, though maybe I oughtn't to say so."

"Oh, I'd guessed that—but I've got used to being expected to work miracles where other people can't even do a plain conjuring trick."

Peake looked at him shrewdly.

"So you aren't getting anywhere?" he asked abruptly.

"Not at present—I'm in as big a fog as anybody, though not necessarily the same one. No, please don't bother to come down with us—I'd like to inflict myself on the doctor again before I go, and I know the way. Good-bye for now, and many thanks for your patience. Will you be in this evening, if anything else crops up?"

"Yes, I'm always here at night—it's then I do my real work."

A discreet tap at Wrench's door produced no answer, and after another slightly louder one Beale quietly entered, beckoning Tony to do the same. Inside, he looked round swiftly, surveying the half-dozen shelves of books, the photographs of various cricket and football teams on the walls, the stamp-collecting album and equipment lying on the table, until finally he saw what he wanted. On a small table by the window stood a typewriter, a standard model of a familiar make, uncovered and without paper in it. He walked over, but made no attempt to use it; instead, to his friend's amazement, he copied down the number of the machine in his note-book. That done he gazed round for another few seconds, saw nothing else to interest him, and led the way out.

"And what was all that about, pray?" grumbled Tony. "You're getting beastly mysterious all of a sudden, Ted—been reading low fiction?"

"No—and I'd hoped I was at least being unobtrusive."

"Oh, sorry—sorry. I blenches."

"You needn't. If I'm on the right track I ought to know pretty soon, and I'm beginning to fancy I may be. Let's go into the courtyard for a moment and look at those marks on the wall again. If your rope was put over it, the bars would either drag along the ground and bust up the flowers, or go bashing into the brickwork. The flowers seemed all right to me the other day, so perhaps what we thought were foot-holds weren't meant to be at all: or the newer one wasn't."

XX

AS SOON AS he opened the glass door at the end of the passage near Selby's bedroom, however, he became aware of two things: that the sun now shone and that the courtyard was occupied. Sitting in a deck-chair at the far corner, wrapped in shawls and a rug and apparently asleep, was Nurse Spence. She was recognizable because of her cap, and her injured leg supported on a stool, and even at a distance of thirty yards it was possible to see plainly that her mouth was open and her head sunk into her chest. Near her, in another chair, was a girl whom he had not met before, and it was only when she rose to approach, and began at once to address them in a deep expressive voice, that either realized her identity.

"I'm so glad you've come," she said: and the words could hardly have been uttered more sincerely, nor the accompanying smile have been more full of welcome. "We must all work together—yes, indeed we must. I know we haven't been introduced, but that doesn't matter—things are so urgent."

She looked at them gravely then, expectantly, as if hoping that they would immediately agree; but for once Beale was completely at a loss. He had a very limited experience of lunatics, and he had never imagined that one could look so sane as Mary Vining—so entirely normal and attractive. He was able to do nothing better than smile at her uncomfortably, and hope that Nurse Spence would soon awake, and it was Tony who dealt with the situation.

"Come over here and tell me about it," he invited without a trace of artificiality in his manner. He might have come there to visit her in the quiet walled garden solely for the purpose he suggested.

"You see, my friend doesn't speak English on Sundays," he added, with equal seriousness: "but I'll help if I can."

"Oh, thank you—because it is very important. The mouth of strange women is a deep pit—that's why *she* can't really understand."

As the girl spoke she nodded towards the still-sleeping nurse, smiled at them both with sudden nervousness, and then, as naturally as possible, took Tony's hand in hers.

"Wickedness, wickedness everywhere," Beale heard her say, as they began to walk slowly away from him: a tall girl in a brown dress and a taller man in blue whose back seemed strangely unfamiliar. "But a wise king scattereth the wicked, and bringeth the wheel over them. I've been searching—"

He watched them go with a deep pity in his heart, and a sudden sense of his own futility. He could do nothing whatever to help her.

"It's a shame," said Tony dejectedly half an hour later, as they drove again towards the police-station. "She'd be such a nice person if she weren't wrong in the head—in fact, she still is nice, in spite of it, but she's in a terrible muddle. I couldn't make out what, exactly—something to do with being responsible for other people's sins, and having to find ways of making them better, and feeling desperately wicked herself. And anybody who looked more harmless I never saw—poor kid."

"She's alleged to be in good hands, anyway," said Beale.

"Yes, that's one consolation, I suppose. But I'm sure I don't know how anybody can stick much of it—Wrench, and the nurses, and even Peake himself. He's had forty years, didn't he say? I'm afraid forty days would find me in the same state. How did you get on with the wall?"

"I can't tell yet. If Dane's in I want to try an experiment."

The Superintendent readily agreed, and produced for them the iron bar with which he had that morning attacked the butcher's dead pig.

"And now a brick wall, please," said Beale.

"Well, you'd better come round the back. Even in Burwood on a Sunday evening I don't imagine you could throw things at the front of the police-station for very long without somebody noticing."

The results of Beale's experiment were satisfactory. He succeeded in making a mark sufficiently like the one in the courtyard to render it possible that the latter had been caused by the use of a car and a rope, and Dane agreed.

"And I quite forgot to say in my note this morning that you needn't worry any more about the bicycle," the Superintendent continued. "I got my daughter to sham dead—she's only twelve, but a bit of a podge, and I dare say she weighs quite as much as Prudence Hill. I found I could easily lug her about and wheel a bike at the same time—as a matter of fact, even my wife could, and I can give her a few stone."

"Good," said Beale, referring to Dane's conclusion, not the size of his wife. "I hope your daughter didn't mind?"

"Not unduly—it only cost me sixpence. What did you make of those stockings?"

"I'm not sure, but it set me thinking all right. Have you got her shoe here?"

"Yes, inside."

"Has it been examined for fingerprints?"

"Yes, of course, but there was nothing to show."

"Really? All the same, I'd like my sergeant to look at it some time."

"Well, he's inside too, going over her bike again."

'Horsey' Matthews readily undertook to examine the shoe, and after twenty minutes bore out Dane's statement that it was free of prints.

"And I can tell you why," he added, thus justifying his presence in Hampshire. "This thing's obviously been exposed to the weather for some days—no doubt of that. By the position her foot was in, though, the left side didn't get the same exposure as the right, 'cos it was facing the ground. That means that if there'd been any prints on it to begin with, they'd still be there now, even if the ones on the other side weren't. Well, there aren't any, like I said, and the reason's because somebody wiped it clean."

"That's just what I was hoping you'd say," remarked Beale, pleased. "You're sure it was wiped? Not just handled with gloves?"

"No sir, wiped—you won't catch me out over a thing like that. Shoes were what I used to practise on when I first went to the Yard."

"And what does that mean?" asked Dane: but Beale declined to answer.

"You set me a riddle this morning. Now I'm setting you one—does it mean anything? If so, what? If not, why not? Kindly illustrate with a sketch-map where possible. Do you bet, Superintendent?"

"Not scientifically."

"Does Captain Wyndham?"

"Well—I think he would if he fancied he was bound to win."

"Then see if you can't get him to wager you five pounds he won't be able to sleep out in the Forest for a week and have nothing happen to him. Even if you lost, you wouldn't have to pay."

Dane laughed.

"Nobody gets on with him for the first six months," he said. "But are you trying to say there won't be any more murders?"

"Not in so many words: but I don't expect any more at the moment."

Tony good-humouredly but pointedly refrained from asking further questions on their way back to the hotel, but Matthews was not so reticent.

"And why won't there be any more murders, sir, please?"

"Because—I think—it wouldn't be any good doing any more at present."

"Well, if you say so—That means you've stopped suspecting Selby?"

"Yes, I'm afraid it does, though not definitely and finally. If he were to leap out of that shop over there now, roaring and brandishing his iron bar, I wouldn't feel he'd made a complete fool of me."

"No sir—I reckon you'd be too busy making sure he didn't make a dead one of you."

And then, realizing by Tony's manner that his words were capable of misconstruction, he hastily changed the subject.

"Nice fellow, Dane," he remarked.

"Yes, a long way better than the average of his kind."

"And not afraid to think on his own—away from the copy-book."

"No. His chief trouble is probably that he's just a bit slow, and perhaps not quite bold enough. He got as far as disbelieving in the Selby idea, but he wouldn't put forward the alternative idea himself."

"I didn't notice you were specially eager to yourself," Tony reminded him.

"Oh, I was prepared to, I assure you, only I thought I'd give the rest of you a chance."

"Why?" persisted his friend. "You don't usually."

"I see. You're pulling faces because I wouldn't let you look at my pretty picture-book. All right, put it that for once I remembered to be considerate."

"And probably Dane was doing the same."

"Oh, why stop at probably? We're both models of modesty."

"Charming thought! One plain-clothes dog-violet wagging its tail and begging for a biscuit. But it's more likely to be a tercuit, if I know my *Wheatsheaf.*"

"A tercuit consisting of what, exactly?"

"That which has been thrice cooked, of course."

At quarter past six Dickie returned. He reported the successful soothing of Alfred Farmer, and the freeing of Bellamy from any suspicion of having murdered Prudence Hill; but Tony still made little comment. Doubtless the whole confused business would be explained in due course, but for once he felt too far behind for it to be worth trying to catch up.

"That's absolutely reliable?" Dickie was asked.

"Absolutely: on May 7th Bellamy spent the evening at the *Spotted Dog* in Pendlebury, ten miles away on the other side from Minchley. He got there at a quarter past eight, when the girl was still at her grandmother's, and he was playing skittles till 11.00 with the landlord and half a dozen others. It was a private match, and no question of him sneaking out for half an hour, or anything like that. Whoever polished off Prudence, he didn't, which puts the lid on Wrench's fancy-work: which leaves us what?"

"Our native intelligence, if any," said Beale unhelpfully. "How did you find out? I always like to compare other people's methods."

"The usual way—by spouting all the biggest lies I could think of. You told me the butler at Yewhurst Hall was a pal of his, so off I went. I'd been commissioned to buy Bellamy's story—you know, *Life in a Private Asylum,* by *Male Nurse:* but I simply couldn't get the man to open his mouth. If only I could find some common ground of interest, perhaps I'd do better, so please Mr. Butler, can you possibly give me some idea of what he does in his spare time? Photography? Cycling? Butterflies? The Cinema? Oh, really, skittles? That's splendid—I *do* know something about that. And so on."

"What it is to be born with a silver tongue in one's mouth!" observed Tony to Matthews.

"And how tragic to have to pawn it for a penny farthing a word and insufficient expenses," added the reporter. "I simply must write more words, that's all."

After their evening meal they returned upstairs, Beale silent and preoccupied. Once or twice the others looked at him curiously, but received no encouragement to talk. For perhaps twenty minutes he remained still, sucking a half-empty pipe. Then he was called away to the telephone, returned with the news that Mrs. Jay had indubitably been on the high seas until the evening of the 10th, sat down again, and almost at once rose with a gesture of impatience.

"It's no good—I must go and find out," he said, as if he expected them to know what he was talking about. "Sorry to bother you, Tony, but I ought to see the doctor again. Will you take me over, or lend me the car, if you'd rather?"

"Oh, I don't mind coming, but you can drive if you like."

At the door Beale turned back to Dickie and Matthews.

"Take a chance?" he suggested; and it said something for their belief in him that without hesitation they accepted.

Only he and Tony went in when they reached Balmer's Court: the other two were advised to wait in the car. The time was twenty minutes to eight, and they entered without notifying their presence, since the front door was unlocked.

They found Dr. Wrench in his private room deep in talk with Lavinia Selby, whose pale Grecian face still fell infinitesimally short of its full beauty because of her anxious look. Both appeared surprised to see them, and Beale's opening words did nothing to make things clearer.

"Is anybody who lives in this house left-handed, Doctor?" he asked.

"Nobody," he was told.

"But what a peculiar question!" exclaimed Lavinia, regarding him with interest.

"Yes, isn't it? Please forgive me if I don't explain—my friend her will tell you I've got a bad attack of secrecy."

He looked round the room, and was at once struck by the fact that the typewriter had been moved. Previously on the small table by the window, it now stood on the floor. He bent down, picked it up, and turned to Wrench.

"Yours?" he queried.

"Peake's—but I use it a good bit."

"Does he?"

"Oh yes, we both do."

"When does he use it?"

"In the evenings, mostly. It'd be upstairs tonight, only he's hurt his hand, so he told Bellamy to bring it down again in case I wanted it."

"Hurt his hand?" echoed Beale, doing his best to nudge Tony unseen. "Badly?"

"*I* don't know," answered Wrench, shortly. "You see," he added, "he rather snapped my head off when I offered to have a look at it. A burn, he said."

"Thank you."

As he reached for his note-book he was telling himself that he was probably wasting his time: there was no apparent difference, once the cover was off, between the machine confronting him and the one he had seen that afternoon. But he was wrong: the number he had written down, 172432, failed to correspond with the one stamped on the steel of the undercarriage, 173411.

He faced the doctor again with a very grave expression.

"Give me something you typed at least a month ago," he requested.

Wrench, manifestly puzzled, began fumbling among the papers on his desk, and soon produced a report on Mary Vining's health, dated March 27th. Meanwhile Lavinia was staring at Beale with increasing astonishment: and Tony was staring at Lavinia, whom he considered worth it.

"And a sheet of plain paper, please," continued Beale. "Sorry to be such a howling nuisance."

Except for the tapping of the typewriter, the room was silent as he satisfied himself that machine No. 173411 was indubitably Peake's own. Then he looked at his wrist watch: the time was just eight o'clock.

"But I thought the Professor didn't settle down till about now," he said to Wrench. "That's what you told me this morning, wasn't it? Then how did he come to send the typewriter down in case you wanted it?"

"Oh, he always starts work an hour earlier on Sun—what the devil's up *now?*"

But there was no answer, for Beale was already out of the room in a furious rush.

INTERLUDE

Why has Chief-Inspector Beale rushed out? Where is he going? What does he think he may find when he gets there? The mind of the reader who can fully answer these questions will have worked along the same lines as the detective's. He will know the true motives for the murders, and, knowing that, be aware who did them. In fact, he could probably write most of the next chapter but one for himself. Nevertheless, it is put in for those who may need it.

XXI

"DEAD?" they echoed, in tones of varied horror and amazement. A full five minutes had elapsed before Beale's return, and he was now delivering his news.

"Yes," he said, "quite dead."

"But how?" demanded the doctor incredulously. "Let me see him."

He made to go past, but Beale blocked the way.

"I'm sorry—not now."

"But how do you know he's dead? You're not a doctor."

"But you are," was the pointed answer, accompanied by a very square look. "I know what I'm doing all right—and that's why you'll please stay here."

Wrench coloured furiously with anger, but before he could find words in which to protest, Lavinia Selby interposed a question.

"Do you mean murdered, Inspector?"

"No, Miss Selby—suicide almost for certain."

"What? Who?" came in a hoarse whisper from the door, and Bellamy entered unbidden. He was dressed in a green baize apron, and he still held a duster in his hand—he had been cleaning silver, judging by the faint smell of metal polish he brought with him. His manner was agitated, and after Beale had explained he turned away for a moment, his bushy eyebrows contracting.

"God rest him," he muttered at last. "He was one of the best, just the same."

"But *how* did he die?" persisted Wrench. "You're being very high-handed all of a sudden, Inspector."

Again Beale turned to face him.

"The occasion demands it, Doctor, I'm afraid," he said. "You see, he clearly took poison, and there'll naturally be questions about where or whom he got it from. You understand, I hope? There's no possible doubt that he's been dead for half an hour or more, unfortunately."

"Could I—could I see him again?" asked Bellamy brokenly.

"Presently, old chap—but he doesn't look the same as when you knew him. Poison isn't always an easy way out, you know."

Lavinia shuddered, her face as pale as alabaster.

"It's horrible," she said. "And why? He was always so—so happy till this happened. Till my brother escaped, I mean. Was that what made him do it?"

"I couldn't say, Miss Selby."

"Then he didn't leave any message?" asked Tony.

"No—at least, there's nothing in his room."

But almost before he had finished speaking Bellamy wheeled round.

"Message!" he repeated. "Here, I forgot—he give me a letter to you to post earlier."

He raised his apron, fumbled in his waistcoat pocket, and produced a stout envelope addressed in typescript to Inspector Beale, c/o Police-Station, Burwood. Gravely Beale opened it, and stood silent for some minutes reading. Then he sighed, shaking his head.

"Well?" asked Lavinia breathlessly, voicing the general curiosity.

"Bad," he said. "Where was his bedroom?"

"Next to his study," Wrench told him—"why?"

"I think we'd better go up there. This can't possibly be hushed up, so in fairness to everybody you may as well know about it straight away."

He led the way up the stairs, and the rest followed close behind, no one speaking. It was on the landing outside Peake's study—now locked, and the key in his pocket—that he remembered Matthews and Dickie outside in the car. He called to Tony to fetch them, opened the bedroom door, switched on the light, and looked in. Then he entered, apologizing with a gesture to the girl for preceding her.

The room was cold and barely furnished—single bed, wardrobe, chest of drawers, and small table—and the distempered walls and shabby linoleum gave it a desolate effect. It seemed obvious that Peake had had either no money or no inclination to surround himself with personal comforts. Once inside, Beale looked round quickly, consulted the letter again, bent down, and peered under the bed. He saw what he expected to see, a large wooden box: it was old and dirty, bound at the corners with rusty iron, and fastened with a padlock. This he had just pulled out by the handle when Tony returned with the other two. He could tell by their faces that they already knew what had happened, and so wasted no time in further explanation. Instead he turned to Wrench.

"Have you ever seen this before?" he asked, indicating the box.

"Yes, I think so—not lately, though. Look here, is it absolutely necessary for Miss Selby to stay? I'm hanged if I can see the point of it."

Beale regarded him a little more mildly.

"Of course not, if she doesn't want to. I thought perhaps you might all prefer to learn the truth now, and as it affects her in a way—"

"Me?" exclaimed the girl. "Don't be silly, Charles—I'm all right. Please go on, Inspector."

He nodded, and spoke next to Bellamy.

"And do you know this box by sight?"

"Yes sir—it used to be in the lumber room."

"Ah—when did you last see it there?"

"I couldn't say, off-hand. A month or two back."

"Oh well, it doesn't much matter now."

He stared round thoughtfully at the circle of attentive faces, and attempted a weary smile.

"I'm going to read you his letter," he said. "It explains a lot of things, so please listen carefully."

"But why up here?" expostulated Wrench.

"Oh, do shut up for a bit, Doctor," said Beale, as if addressing a troublesome child. "The letter concerns what's in the box, and the box can't be moved till the Chief-constable gets here—I know the regulations, even if you don't. Do please keep quiet and let me do the talking."

"Yes," agreed Lavinia, unexpectedly supporting him. "Be good, Charles."

"It's sent to me," Beale went on, "and undated.

> " 'Dear Inspector, I didn't like the look in your eye last time I saw you, not one bit. But I don't greatly care now—don't know when I last had a decent night's sleep. Sleep, sleep, there isn't any more, no more, it's all gone, dried up, taken away away and only they stay standing and staring. My head is aching, terribly much, but don't run away with the wrong impression now. I'm not ill, but I have something very particular to tell you. Nobody else knows, except those who can't talk—and can you guess *why* they can't talk? That's what I'm going to tell you, so read very carefully, because I must put it all down quickly, because I shan't sleep any more till I do, night after night lying awake and seeing them all standing around the bed staring and peeping at me and not saying anything, but going on staring and then all

lifting up their feet to show me, and asking for their shoes back—' "

At this point Lavinia Selby uttered a little cry, and he paused; but she recovered almost at once, and motioned to him to continue. The others were raptly intent on what he was saying: the doctor's eyes full of unbelieving horror, Bellamy sunk into profound dejection, as if he listened unwillingly, but could not stop his ears.

"Sit down," suggested Beale, stepping aside to let her pass. "On the bed—yes, you'd better."

" 'And asking for their shoes back'," he repeated—" 'the fat policeman, and the little girl on the bicycle, and the young man in the green sweater, and that other girl with the white bare legs. And he is there too—poor Simon, poor poor Simon, that I almost loved. But he had to die, and the first, because I couldn't any longer stand not being able to cure him. Oh but I tried, I did try, all night long sometimes I sat up thinking and worrying and planning a new line of treatment, yet he was still the same whatever I did, except a little better when I let his beard grow. But that was a long time ago, and nothing fresh for years. I couldn't bear having him look at me any more with his sad eyes and saying how am I Professor? And now he is always looking at me, at night.

" 'Yes, I killed him—I killed them all. Only, why did I kill the others? I don't know, I can't remember. If only my head would keep still. It all seems as if it happened to somebody else, and it won't come back clear. I crept down in the night and killed poor Simon, at half after one—I reckoned it would be a nice time for him to die. I opened the door very quietly with my key, and over to the bed, and just one hit with a hammer as he slept. Yes, I do begin to recall it all afresh now. I am waking up as I woke up then, to find him a body and beyond all cures, and if I were caught they would hang me, they do that over here. And I won't say I did it when I was mad, because I am not—not. I know what mad people are like, I have lived with them all my life and I know I am not the same. So there he was lying still, and I had to do something before anyone came, and think quickly. I went round quietly and got a ladder and put it into the courtyard over the wall and then fetched the car and pulled out the bars with a rope to make it look as if he had escaped, and stood listening a long time, in case I had been heard, but nobody came. My head was aching too, then, like it is now, it has done most days since. It is all very funny, really, and I would laugh if I could forget the look in the eyes of that man who came here asking questions. But I know he has seen too much. I can feel it, and I don't make mistakes over what people notice. He will be too sharp for me, but only because of my buzzing head. If it would stop for just a few minutes, I should be too clever for him, and if they would go away at night and leave me alone, not stand round with their eyes on me never letting me sleep.

" 'What I did with poor Simon I won't tell anybody, I was fond of him and I would not like people to see him dead and laugh at his hair. Poor Simon. I pretended he had run away, and they all believed it, and even that gabbling nurse was useful for once. Something woke her and she was the one to find him gone. Maybe it was when I put the car away again I guess, that was about half after three because I had been very quick. And to think she might have come before and caught me. And then after a week I began to see they would not go on believing he had escaped, although I had taken clothes and things from a man who lives all alone and is deaf, that Nurse told me about once, near that fat woman who gives me wine and flowers. So I went out down my own stairs one night when everybody thought I was working and walked a long way until I saw a light coming, and I hid in the bank, and a girl on a bicycle came along, and I was waiting to jump out when she stopped, just as if God was making it easy. She stood with one foot on the bank and started taking her stocking down, I don't know why, I couldn't stop to ask. I just ran across and hit her and held her face in the road and jabbed the bar into her head, it was a way of killing I had read about somewhere and it was very quick, not even a scream out of her. It was very hard work carrying her and the bicycle into the woods even though she was small, but I managed it, and then I walked home, and Bellamy nearly ran me down at the gate. He gave me a terrible shock, I didn't know what to do at all, I said I had been posting a letter, and I don't think he suspected me. I am almost sure he did not, but you never know with Bellamy what he thinks, he is so silent, he frightens me at times now.

" 'And then I did it again, and I will now tell a very great secret, that nobody could ever guess unless I did. I enjoyed killing the little girl on the bicycle, and being smart enough to take her shoe off so they would all think Simon had done it. Poor poor Simon, forgive me. The others were easy—that girl in the woods leaning against a tree reading a letter, an ugly creature. I hit her too, and took the letter away, and a shoe. And then the boy in the green sweater—he was asleep. Then I went back to my search-party and pretended to go on looking, and nobody suspected anything because I had been so simple and so cunning and remembered to wear gloves. Then a few days later I went out searching again with Simon's sister and Bellamy and sneaked away when no one was looking and made a policeman come over and got him to bend down to look at a foot-mark and I gave him a push and hit him too—just a downward stab with the iron bar out of poor Simon's window. I was glad I had kept one, the other I threw into the river with him, poor Simon in his sack and heavy stones. You are better off dead, I could not cure you and it is very unhappy to be mad, it must be I mean, if I ever felt I was going to be I would want to die too.

And then that man started coming here asking questions and staring at me with his grey eyes. I didn't mind the tall ugly one, Purdon, but the other frightened me, Beale, yes, and I could not sleep any more after killing that policeman, suddenly they all started coming at night and showing me their feet, and all the time their shoes were safe in my box under the bed, but when I offered, they wouldn't take them and go and leave me to sleep but just stood looking. I think in my heart they were waiting for me to go with them.

" 'I am beginning to be very sorry about it all now, and more frightened. I have tried to fool that man, but it is my head. There was that woman Jay too—she made me afraid, saying I was mad and I know I am not, I would rather die. Then I could tell Simon I am sorry I could not find out how to make him better. He has been here again today and I know he doesn't believe me any more, I was sure the bandage was clever, but he kept staring at it. I must keep cool and remember to send this letter because I would like the girl to know what happened, and Charles. Good-bye Charles, I think I am going with them, they have started coming in the daylight, they want me, don't let people say I was mad, you know I am not. Good-bye. Just one drink of my sharp red wine and I will be safe and sleep. Hilary Peake.' "

"My God!" exclaimed Wrench in a low voice, as Beale ceased reading. He was sitting on the bed now, his arm round Lavinia, who was softly crying. Matthews and Dickie stood motionless by the door, Tony against the wall, and Bellamy at the window. It was to him that Beale spoke next, gently. .

"You'd guessed, hadn't you?" he asked. "Wasn't that what you meant by 'Just the same'?"

For a moment the male nurse stared at him dully, then suddenly nodded.

"But I *couldn't* say anything," he whispered: "not whatever happened."

"You *knew?*" gasped Wrench, and again Bellamy nodded miserably.

"Ay. That day I came back early, Doctor—said I was ill and you give me a dose. I just had to come back—I'd seen him kill that sergeant with my own eyes. It was awful."

In the silence that followed he turned despairingly to Beale.

"But I couldn't have told on him, sir—not if he'd gone on killing and killing, I don't believe. He was always so good to me."

"I understand. I think you were wrong, mind—I'm sure you were: but it must have been a hard choice."

He stood silent for a moment, then walked across to the box, while everyone moved closer.

"I wonder," he said, half to himself, felt in his pockets, took out a bunch of keys, and undid the padlock at the second attempt.

"Where did you get them from?" asked Wrench sharply. "His?"

"Yes—keys are always the first thing to look for on a body. Yes, there they all are."

As he spoke he moved away, having lifted the lid, so that all could see the contents of the box: four odd shoes, two men's and two women's, a letter, a hammer, the clothes taken from Alfred Farmer's cottage, a second pair of thick woollen gloves, the shaving outfit, a letter addressed to Betty Trotter, and Simon Selby's watch. Lavinia identified this last with a sob of misery.

"Oh, but why?" she asked piteously. "Why?"

"Can't be any doubt," said Wrench, holding her closer. "He was mad himself—must have been."

Beale nodded.

"I'm afraid so," he agreed. "And to think that nobody ever guessed."

He sighed, and then looked again towards the male nurse.

"You'd better tell me now if there's anything else you know. I'll do my best not to pass on any thing you've said, of course, but I can't promise definitely."

"No sir."

"But that letter ought to satisfy any coroner. Did you suspect before you actually saw him kill Sergeant Lee?"

"No sir—oh no, sir. That's why it came as such a terrible shock. I happened to look round and noticed somebody away in the distance moving a bit stealthy, and I thought maybe there was something wrong, so I went a good deal closer, and then I saw it all, and I simply couldn't move."

"And afterwards?"

Again Bellamy hesitated.

"No good hiding it," he said at last. "I guessed what he was going to do when he told me to take the typewriter away tonight. 'I shan't want it any more, Bellamy' he said, 'no more. Post this letter for me, please, and—and stick to water.' That's what he said, 'stick to water'."

Once more Beale nodded, and when he spoke his voice was just perceptibly louder.

"You can come out now," he remarked.

About what immediately followed, and how much of it he actually witnessed, Tony has never been quite sure. He believes he was looking at the wardrobe when its door opened and Professor Peake stepped out, blinking as his eyes met the unaccustomed light. He believes also that he directed his attention to Bellamy in time to notice the change in the man's expression, from the apparent depths of sorrow to terror-stricken incredulity. He then—he says—turned to Lavinia at her sharp cry, but away again at the sound of Peake's voice saying, 'You durned liar, Bellamy!' so that he missed the girl's collapse in a faint. He maintains stoutly, however, that with his own eyes he saw the male nurse clutch suddenly at his head, sway a little, croak something unintelligible, put one hand tentatively towards his heart, and pitch forward with a crash. But only Matthews saw Beale's rueful expression as he surveyed the body, or heard his quiet comment: 'Damn! I never thought of that'.

XXII

IT WAS THE NEXT afternoon before Beale found time to explain, as the others had made him promise to do the previous night. He had made his apologies to Lavinia Selby and Dr. Wrench far earlier, though, for the deception he had been forced to practise on them, and to his great relief both had taken the matter with the utmost good will.

"To begin with," he said now, "I could never quite bring myself to believe seriously in the burglary at Farmer's place, not even in London, when I first heard about the escape: though it's worth pointing out that I was never meant to, in the long run. Everything was just a little too good to be true—that an escaped lunatic should so conveniently strike on a lonely cottage whose owner wasn't only deaf, but also possessed exactly the clothes he required in approximately the correct sizes, and all discoverable in the dark. Even had Selby been told about Farmer by Nurse Spence, there was still the question of the razor. We were supposed to accept that all Selby was armed with, to remove three years' growth of hair, was a safety and the usual brush and soap: no mirror, no scissors, not even a towel. As well, there was every reason to think that he had an absolute horror of being shaved, and certainly wouldn't have attempted to barber himself.

"Again, I disbelieved in Selby's ability to remove those bars, even though it was always possible that the missing ones hadn't been so firmly fixed as the others. I also disbelieved profoundly that he could have hidden himself for so long in the neighbourhood and still remained alive: but we dealt with those points the other day. Incidentally, Doctor, that last was one of the two big flaws in your theory. The police were to go on searching happily for another month before Mrs. Jay produced her proof of Selby's continued existence, but I'm sure that ages beforehand even Captain Wyndham would have begun to think that somebody else was doing the murdering.

"On and off I must have spent some considerable time over the whole problem of Selby's escape, and its possible connection with the series of murders that began just over a week later. The main conclusions permissible seemed to be these. (1), Selby alone was responsible for both; or, (2), Selby for the escape and somebody else for the killing; or, (3), somebody else for the escape and Selby for the killing; or, (4), somebody else for both.

"Now the first, as I've already said, I couldn't credit, the second didn't make much sense in view of the doubtful burglary, and the third, which I suggested to the Superintendent earlier, hadn't got us far. In any case, the more murders that happened, the more unlikely it was. I therefore concentrated on the fourth.

"I assumed, I think quite fairly, two things: that there were almost certainly at least two persons responsible for the 'escape ', and that these persons were also responsible for the murders. The reason for the first assumption was the enormous difficulty of anybody outside Balmer's Court being able to get Selby away without help from inside, and the corresponding difficulty of anybody from inside being able to do it without help from outside. In both cases he must have been either drugged or killed, which meant that his body was inert, which meant two persons to do the job with any ease. The second point is equally clear. Provided Selby didn't do the murders himself, then somebody must have been deliberately leading us to suppose he did. The police were meant to label him as the killer, and exclude everybody else, and as I said the other evening, the only persons in a suitable position to mislead us like that were those who knew where Selby really was.

"An additional reason for thinking that one was a resident at Balmer's Court, by the way, was the extensive knowledge shown of the man and his habits. Since the burglary was now a fake, whoever did it must have been familiar with his size in clothes and shoes, and his growth of hair, and his fondness for collecting improbable things, and also his attachment to the watch his sister gave him.

"Now, it could be stated definitely—if perhaps too obviously to need statement at all—that these unknowns were either both mad or both sane: one of each would be simply incredible. To suppose them mad, however, involved a number of difficulties and contradictions. For one thing, they must be very sanely mad, since they so thoughtfully provided a scapegoat before doing their murders. For another, I wasn't prepared to consider these as the work of insanity unless their author was Selby himself as mad shoe-collector: their nature was against the supposition.

"In general, and allowing for any possible contradiction in terms, mad motives for killing consist of a grudge against either the whole of humanity, or only a particular section of it. The first is sometimes synonymous with, or easily degenerates into, slaughter for the sheer love of slaughter—fortunately that isn't very common; and occasionally the second, as I believe was so with Neill Cream. Nearly always, though, there's a sexual basis for this love, or lust, and one which is self-evident in the results. There was nothing remotely like that in the present instance; and I defy anybody, however demented, to find much in common to a domestic servant, a reporter, a girl hiker, and a country policeman, as types. In any case, there were several other objections to the idea of madness. Why wait a week before killing? Why let the easiest victim of all escape—Farmer? Why none of the usual accompaniments of such murders—mutilation, or at least a multiplicity of wounds? I came to the conclusion that if Selby were ruled out, then the killer was sane.

"I say 'killer' advisedly, because in spite of everything I've said I wasn't yet contemplating seriously the possibility of two actual sane murderers, both doing the same kind of crimes deliberately, so that all would seem to be the work of one man. Why that should be so I can't say: a somewhat unusual reluctance to be imaginative, I suppose.

"Well, I was faced now with the necessity of finding an adequate sane motive, and again the same point about the victims held good: nobody could conceivably have personal reasons for destroying them all, especially as two were strangers to the district. Accordingly it seemed not unreasonable to go a step farther, and suggest there mightn't have been any personal reason at all—that any other four victims would have done as well. What the murderer had set out to do was not to kill named individuals, but convenient ones, and this idea was borne out by the probability that three of the four—all but Sergeant Lee—were quite isolated at the time of their death.

"But there I stuck for a bit. The one sane motive I could think of at present was that, in some way, the murders were designed to hit at Professor Peake. He was the only person connected with the affair who was known to have a bitter personal enemy. It did occur to me vaguely at one stage that perhaps Dr. Wrench and Miss Selby might have been aimed at: with her brother's insanity beyond doubt for ever, they could hardly hope to marry. I gave up considering that, though, on the doctor's assurance that they had no such enemies.

"I didn't draw any definite conclusions yet: I merely noted what I've just said about the Professor as a possibility, with the addition that if it were true, then the ultimate author of the murders was undoubtedly Mrs. Jay.

"Now, let me go back for a bit to the problem of Selby's disappearance: who in Balmer's Court could have had a hand in it?

Just now, by the way, I ought to have said that it was always remotely on the cards for there to have been two conspirators inside, and none out. As a beginning I excluded the servants. Although three persons, Superintendent Dane, the Professor, and Dr. Wrench, had separately decided at one time or another that Selby was got out, instead of getting himself out, not one of them had even suggested suspecting the domestic staff. As well, they would appear to have had no means of access to his room, or experience in dealing with him if he happened to wake up before they could silence him. I felt that the people to study were the people with keys and capabilities.

"In the case of Professor Peake, however, the only imaginable motive for either 'escape' or murders was madness, which I'd already almost washed out. I decided I needn't bother about him unless everybody else failed. He could have had no sane reason for wanting Selby removed from his asylum which he couldn't have satisfied legitimately, excluding such things as Matthews' rather fantastic suggestions the other night.

"Nurse Spence, for the time being, I left open as regards the escape. As you said the other day, Professor, she was certainly in the best position to have achieved it because she alone knew whether she was going to sleep next door or not. The one point in her favour seemed to be that it was she who gave the alarm. If she'd been concerned, I thought, she probably wouldn't have done. I felt justified in disqualifying her for the murders, however, on the strength of what Dr. Wrench said about her being in Balmer's Court at all material times. If he were guilty, I argued, then she wasn't, since I couldn't imagine that he'd choose a chatterbox like her for an accomplice. It did strike me once that she might be playing a part, but then I remembered that she'd been with Peake two years before the doctor came along, and she couldn't have suddenly put on a new character without rousing suspicion. But if Dr. Wrench were innocent, then there was no reason to doubt his conclusion that she was too. He'd been in a very good position to find out about her movements, and the way he fastened on to Bellamy's showed that he wasn't to be put off lightly. Also, of course, there could be almost no question of her acting for Mrs. Jay: but I'll come to that in a minute.

"The doctor himself I likewise excluded from the murders. He couldn't be working for Mrs. Jay either, since her plans must involve at least Selby's kidnapping, and probably his death. If the first, then it would be ridiculous for him to give me the clue himself; if the second, he could have no possible regard for Miss Selby, and I was convinced that he had. Nor could I see how it would help to suppose that she was in it too, after serious thought. That would mean finding another murderer, as I didn't believe either of them capable of killing four quite innocent persons in cold blood just to cover up the fact that they'd unlawfully removed Selby from Professor Peake's charge. I leave out the slur they'd be deliberately casting on her family name, since they too would have to be putting over the idea of a lunatic killer.

"For the escape, however, I left him as a remote possibility, in case he might have had some motive I hadn't thought of. The strongest point in his favour was that he didn't try to make people believe the escape was genuine; and also, of course, neither he nor Miss Selby had done anything suspicious for the last ten days.

"I then came to the fourth choice, Bellamy, and all I could say with any confidence about him was that he must definitely be sane—which holds good for Nurse Spence and the doctor too, of course. There was no evidence that he'd be likely to work for Mrs. Jay, but equally none that he wouldn't, bar the Professor's testimonial. If he should be, though, I had to bear in mind that his outside accomplice couldn't be her, since on April 29th she wasn't in England. I'm talking now about the escape, of course.

"The chief item against him was the doctor's yesterday: there was nobody else in Balmer's Court who'd really do. As well, there was another consideration—the one on account of which I ruled out Nurse Spence just now as Mrs. Jay's agent. If the latter had anything at all to do with the business, her plans must necessarily have been laid *after* the Professor's visit to America in 1934: until he'd given his second decision about her grandson's sanity she couldn't know that she'd still have a grudge against him. Therefore any agent of hers in Balmer's Court must have been introduced there since that time, and the only recruit was Bellamy. It was extremely unlikely that she would have tried squaring Dr. Wrench or the nurse: a false move would have spoilt everything. In support of the idea that Bellamy might be in her employ, though, was the possibly suspicious way in which he'd got his post: your point again, Doctor. To lurch in front of a car driven by a notoriously kind-hearted man, and then say you're destitute and desperate for work, is at least a good first step to obtaining a job with him.

"At the moment, then, the alternatives before me were these. For the escape, Nurse Spence—highly improbable if Mrs. Jay were involved, because of the time-factor I've just mentioned, and there was no hint of any other motive in her case; Dr. Wrench, presumably acting for Miss Selby—also most improbable, on the whole; and Bellamy, assumed to be acting for Mrs. Jay. The last was the one most worth consideration. For the murders, Bellamy again before everybody, so I decided that I'd go for him: what's even only semi-probable ought always to be investigated before what isn't.

"After due thought I put down two possible suspicious things against him. One of them I'd already noticed for myself, though it took me some little time to realize what it was that bothered me. Although he was described by the Professor as so reserved and hard to get anything out of, that wasn't quite the way he behaved when Tony and I first saw him. If anything, he was inclined to be conversational: he certainly didn't answer us in one-word sentences. The second point was that Nurse Spence, in her monologue last Friday, distinctly said that if she couldn't get Selby to have his temperature taken, she used to get Bellamy's help. That sounded rather as if he had some influence with Selby, and might therefore be favourably situated for entering his room at night: if the man did wake up, he'd stand some chance of being able to calm him. Later, Dr. Wrench said much the same thing.

"As far as I could see after the doctor had put his theory before us yesterday morning, there was nothing serious against the idea that Bellamy had a hand both in the escape and in all four murders, given two things. The first was that he could have told more or less by inspection whether or not Nurse Spence was sleeping next to Selby on the night of the 29th, and the second that he had no alibi for the evening of May 7th. And then, before I could do much towards checking those points, I was faced with a fresh problem altogether: that of why Prudence Hill's stockings had apparently been equally exposed to the weather over a period of eight days, although the foot of one was supposed to have been covered with a shoe all that time.

"There seemed to me to be only one possible answer: that they had in fact been so exposed. Now, that could have happened in a number of ways. One or both of the stockings she was wearing when her body was found were not the ones she'd been killed in; or, immediately after her death, both shoes had been removed, and the right one put back just in time for us to find it; or—by far the most likely—the right shoe was first taken, and later, approximately half-way between death and discovery, it was exchanged for the left one. The first possibility was ruled out by getting the stockings identified, and the obvious objection to the second one was the condition of the shoe itself. Matthews was positive that it had been not only wiped but also exposed, and the exposure was far more likely to have happened on her foot than off it. The wiping, however, definitely supported the idea of an exchange.

"I set myself to find a plausible reason for such a procedure, and the most sensible seemed to be that whoever killed her had made a mistake, and gone off with the wrong shoe. But Prudence Hill's murder was the first we knew about, and I could hardly believe that if the person who did it had also killed Wilson and Betty Trotter, he'd have forgotten it was the *right* shoes he must take. Therefore it began to look as if there might be two murderers—two sane ones; and that when they compared notes afterwards it was discovered that one of them had made a mistake, which accordingly had to be rectified. The whole intention in taking any shoes at all, of course, on this reasoning, was to make it look as if Selby were responsible. An atmosphere of madness was aimed at, and to take only one was infinitely madder than to take both: and yet, because of Selby's rigid if self-imposed limitations with regard to the eligibility of what he collected, it must be the same one each time. The reason for effecting the exchange on the body of Prudence Hill, and not on the others, is also obvious. Betty Trotter's feet were stocking-less, and as the murderers couldn't possibly tell when she'd be found, it would be very dangerous to risk having that happen when her covered foot was dirty and her exposed one clean.

"After lunch yesterday the position was this. I was disposed to consider Bellamy and an unknown as the murderers, and—as I told Dickie—quite ready to learn that Bellamy had an alibi for May 7th. Also, if ever I found out who the other person was, I shouldn't be surprised to hear that in turn he had an alibi for some or all of the other murders. In this way, they would reason, they'd be secure against all suspicion. Definite acquittal from any one murder would serve for the lot, since all were to bear so strongly the trade-mark of the same hand.

"Then Dickie came back with the news that Farmer had lost another complete pair of shoes. That I ever did hear about that was a sheer fluke, and I ought to make it clear that I've been most extraordinarily fortunate all the way along: at least two other huge slices of luck. This fresh burglary seemed too significant to be ignored. Farmer was already connected with things once, and here he was being dragged in again. In the light of what I was already thinking, there was one explanation that stuck out a mile: somebody was preparing to murder the man, and had got hold of his shoes beforehand. This, incidentally, made me more inclined to believe that perhaps the other missing shoes were being kept for some specific purpose, which fitted in very well later.

"We'll probably never know the details of the plot against Farmer, but there can't be any doubt there was one. In many ways he was an ideal victim, and there was also a possible reason why another murder should be desirable. The doctor had been questioning Bellamy, and, with all due regard, I don't suppose for a minute that he was as tactful as he imagined. The man was getting a bit frightened, very likely, and thinking that his alibi for May 7th was hardly enough safeguard. A fifth death when he was clearly otherwise engaged would be just the thing to free him from suspicion.

"As for why it should be necessary to take Farmer's shoes *before* killing him, Dickie supplied the answer to that a few moments later, and luckily I heard what he said. With that particular man, it's not certain that at any given time he won't be bare-foot; but to make his death seem one of the series, he'd have to have a right shoe on. He's also a careless sort of creature, and unlikely to notice whether anything's been taken or not; but all the same, it looked to me—if there was anything at all in the idea—as if I'd better hurry. My first thought was to ensure him protection by getting Dickie to watch him; but I decided that it might give too much away. That may sound a bit callous, but I can't help it. I did definitely intend to put Matthews on to looking after him later. Then something cropped up—I'll come to it in a minute—to make me think he was quite safe after all: and when after that I ought to have realized he wasn't, I was too busy with other things to remember him at all. More luck, I suppose!

"I'm not sure now when I fathomed the whole business. I think daylight must have begun to show on the way to Balmer's Court after sending Dickie off to check Bellamy's movements. These things happen in far less time than it takes to explain them. I was really considering the possible methods by which Professor Peake was to be hit at through the murders, and I could think of three. First, on Dr. Wrench's mad-dog theory, they were intended only to disgrace him, but I ruled that out because I couldn't see the necessity for more than one murder, and it's never safe to make one's hypothetical criminals run absurd risks for no special reason. Secondly, again on the doctor's theory, he was to be blackmailed: but that wasn't fool-proof by a long way—the other big flaw in it. Peake might have decided to go straight to the police, thinking it the best thing he could do in Selby's interests. As well, the idea didn't fit in with Mrs. Jay's outburst on Saturday afternoon. Then I thought of the third one, and immediately liked the look of it: the plot was to land Peake with the murders.

"Put baldly like that, it probably sounds ridiculous, but there were adequate grounds for not passing it over: the shadow of the truth waiting just round the corner. Such a project would clearly work only if Peake too were dead, and couldn't contradict the suggestion that he was a murderer, or prove he wasn't: therefore he must die as well. Also, I'd already decided that nobody could suppose him guilty without first assuming him to be mad: and then came sunshine. The *real* motive—Mrs. Jay's—*was* to make Professor Peake appear to have been mad, and the whole business of murdering had no other object.

"Why? Because only by that means could she hope to get his verdict on her grandson revised. There can't be any question that Thomas Jefferson Jay's insane: and equally none that Peake would ever agree to say he wasn't. If the Professor were to die normally, too, there'd never be any reason for doubting that he knew what he was talking about while he was alive. The only way to do that was by making him die in the guise of an undoubted madman himself: nothing else would be a quarter so likely to invalidate every judgement he'd ever made.

"In addition, I could now see the true reason for Mrs. Jay's presence. As I'd felt at the time, she never for a moment expected her breath-taking offer of a million pounds to be accepted. She made it only so that she would seem to have a credible reason for coming to Burwood, and to cover the fact that she was really here to direct the final operations. Also, I fancy, she had another purpose in view: while the Professor was still alive she wanted to start the idea that he wasn't all there. She hinted as much on Saturday, and did so again in the letter she sent up yesterday.

"I now faced the question of Bellamy's possible accomplice. The qualifications needed were these. X must have come to the neighbourhood *after* Professor Peake's return from America in 1934, and must preferably have access to Balmer's Court, in order to keep in touch with Bellamy. Writing mightn't be very safe because of post-marks, and the man wasn't entirely master of his own movements. As well, X mustn't appear to be friendly with Bellamy; must have an alibi for some or all of the murders subsequent to Prudence Hill's; must have a car, or the use of one, to dispose of Selby on the night he disappeared and to pull out the bars; and, as well as being able to have done the burglaries at Farmer's place, must be likely to know that sometimes Farmer wore no shoes.

"I then discovered that—again through sheer luck—I already knew of just such a person: Mrs. Montgomery.

"The main thing likely to be against the idea was her being a woman: but she was a big one, and could have made quite as good a job of carrying Prudence Hill's body about as Professor Peake; and what the Superintendent said yesterday about his wife was significant. Still more luck. Another smaller point to get over was her apparently deep friendship with Nurse Spence: but upon consideration I decided that voluble good-natured women like the Nurse are just the sort to be imposed upon by affable and amicable strangers.

"In favour were a number of details: her readiness, for instance, to point out what she'd been doing between May 10th and 13th. Whether she really did go to London for the Coronation is beside the mark: she went out of her way to tell me she did. I thought at the time that her gush to the doctor yesterday morning was just the least bit forced—as also her unfriendly reference to Bellamy. Again, she was in an ideal position to study Farmer's habits and movements, living only a couple of hundred yards or so away; and she was also able to have conveyed his shoe to Balmer's Court—perhaps with that coronation mug she talked so much about. If she bought the thing for Nurse Spence in particular, why not bring it when she came to see her last Friday, the day we first met her? Why tell us in the drive, in almost the same breath, that she knew the Nurse wanted one and that she'd brought it along to cheer her up—presumably out of the despair occasioned by her sprained ankle? Small points, those, admittedly, but not without interest: nor the fact that she'd have had ample opportunity, if she did go to Town, for telling Mrs. Jay just how things stood.

"And now, not before it was time, I passed on to the problem of how the Professor was to be killed, and yet 'confess'. An alleged self-acknowledgment of his guilt was essential, and it must be a written one. A mere verbal message delivered, say, by Bellamy, wouldn't have been nearly convincing enough. There'd be only his word for its validity, and suspicion might be roused.

"The obvious solution was a fake suicide and a fake letter, and lots of corroborative evidence in the way of shoes and iron bars and stolen razors. But the only way to forge such a lengthy document as his 'confession' must necessarily be was by typing it; and on his own machine at that, because the discovery that some other had been used would blow the lid off everything. Therefore, I told myself—partly while babbling away to the Professor yesterday afternoon, Tony—there must be a second machine in Balmer's Court, for his and Wrench's use while the real one was booked. Whether it would actually be there yet I didn't know. All I hoped was that it hadn't come and gone, which would mean that the Professor was due to be killed at any minute.

"I did have several genuine points to enquire about in visiting him, though: whether Bellamy could have known if the room next to Selby's had been vacant, for one, and whether Peake suspected Bellamy, for another. The fact that all the relevant downstairs rooms had peep-holes in the doors cleared up the first—the judicious use of a torch would have told him all he wanted to know. The second didn't get me very far, though I had the impression that the Professor was a good deal more suspicious than he admitted.

"My principal reason for thinking that was his bandage. I don't quite know why, but the moment I saw the thing I suspected that he hadn't really burnt his hand at all, and that view was soon confirmed. If you had hurt yourself," he explained, turning to Peake, "you could hardly have taken a written copy of your answering note to Mrs. Jay. Unless, of course, you were left-handed, or you didn't have your breakfast till after midday. I afterwards satisfied myself about the first, and I can't say I bothered about the other.

"I'm still not certain why you put the bandage on, but if I had to guess, I'd say you'd somehow jumped to the conclusion that there was a plot against you to make you appear responsible for the murders. If you did your hand up, you argued, there wouldn't be any more killings for a bit: nobody would dare do one that couldn't be ascribed to you."

Peake nodded.

"I reckoned I was being the daftest fool on God's earth to imagine such a thing," he said. "All the same, I took what I thought was a good precaution—I had Mrs. Jay up against me, and I wouldn't put anything past her. What actually started the idea in my head was what you just pointed out—her continued mention of my 'madness'. That and her presence here at all."

"Well," Beale went on, to Lavinia's amazement without marked signs of hoarseness, "when I'd roughly worked things out so far I began to enquire whether the Professor could have left his study unobserved: in order—so the confession would run—to murder Prudence Hill. I already knew that he was out searching in the Forest the day Wilson and Betty Trotter died, since it was he who gave Dr. Wrench the time for Bellamy's reappearance at 2.30 p.m., and I also knew that he was in the same party as Bellamy when Sergeant Lee was killed. Luckily, with the help of what he himself and the doctor had told me about his horror of fire, I was able to learn about his private staircase; and then his dislike of being disturbed in the evenings, and his habit of locking himself in, would all fit into the plot. I'll say one thing for Bellamy: he made good use of his material. He even noticed the colour of my eyes.

"Later, when I got back to our pub, I realized I ought to have made sure whose the typewriter was that I'd seen in the doctor's room. That was after Dickie had backed up my theory by supplying Bellamy with a good alibi for May 7th. Good, that is, in the sense that he certainly couldn't have killed Prudence Hill, but not quite so good in that to play skittles in the circumstances, with Selby still missing and the Professor worried to death, wasn't altogether in keeping with his character of devoted and self-appointed factotum.

"As you all know, I returned to Balmer's Court, found out that Peake wasn't left-handed, and so presumably hadn't hurt himself, and then realized in a flash, actually while I was apologizing to Miss Selby for not explaining my question, that the bandage wouldn't afford any protection at all, since Bellamy too must have spotted it was a fake. I was unpardonably slow there. Then I examined the typewriter, found it was a different one, and began to get really worried.

"I'd already guessed that the 'suicide' would be committed by means of poison in the red wine: Bellamy could make his own opportunity for putting it in, and heaven knows the stuff's pungent enough to cover a lot of additional flavours. The Professor drinks it regularly, and if he were really committing suicide, it wouldn't be an unlikely way.

"Things, I decided, were undoubtedly coming to a head: and then I suddenly learnt that he didn't start work on Sundays at eight o'clock, as Wrench had inadvertently led me to believe in the morning, but an hour earlier—before I'd even got to Balmer's Court. For all I could tell, he was stone dead already.

"I think I tore up those stairs quicker than I've ever moved in my life before: and had my last and greatest stroke of luck. Professor Peake had been sharp enough to suspect everything and everybody, and hadn't touched his fatal dose. In fact, though I'd never have guessed it, he'd been waiting for it to be poisoned for days—though putting the anticipatory blame on Mrs. Montgomery, who insisted on providing him with the stuff."

He turned to Peake, and smiled suddenly.

"I simply can't say how grateful I am to you," he declared earnestly. "Your wine's got nothing on you, if that's good American."

The Professor indulged in an answering grin.

"You can't be half as glad about it as I am," he said, "so let's call it quits. If you had the luck, you were the only man jack of us who could use it."

"Thank you. Well, once you were found to be alive I had to think hard, and quickly too, because somehow Bellamy must be made to incriminate himself. We decided to let him believe everything had gone off all right, and the trick worked, though I honestly didn't dream for a moment that he'd crack up and die of shock. If that had occurred to me I'd have been very chary of carrying on with the scheme at all: suppose Miss Selby had done the same, for instance, or even old Tony."

"The significance of that 'even' breaks my heart," said his friend gravely, and bowed.

"And doctors and sergeants don't count," observed Matthews with a smile.

"Oh yes—if I'd thought of one I'd have thought of everybody," demurred Beale. "Including reporters"—with a glance at Dickie." But I quite expected you were going to ruin everything at one stage, Doctor, by asking too many awkward questions. Luckily my nonsense about regulations shut you up, though, and didn't seem to upset Bellamy.

"That we did manage to trap him wasn't altogether a matter of chance. Admittedly we were fortunate in choosing the right room, the bedroom: but then, it was the only possible one, with the wardrobe the only possible hiding-place. The study obviously couldn't be on view, since there was no body to bear out the story.

"I think the decision to finish things up yesterday evening was taken as soon as Mrs. Jay heard about the bandage—almost certainly when Bellamy delivered the answer to her letter. She suspected—rightly—that the Professor was beginning to piece the plot together, and felt that it was high time to get rid of him. And that's what saved Farmer's life, of course: there just wasn't time to kill him first.

"I don't doubt that Bellamy had to bustle round a bit yesterday afternoon. There was the box to put under the bed, once the necessary evidence was in it, the confession to finish, the typewriter to replace, and the poison to get ready. I was a little surprised, as a matter of fact, at there being no 'last message' in the study—placed there beforehand, naturally: but it was probably wisest for there not to be, in case the plan miscarried. Bellamy would produce it—as he did—with apparent honesty at a suitable moment. I rather fancy he wanted to make quite sure first that the Professor really was dead, though, and that that's why he asked if he might have a final look. My manner seemed to convince him that there was nothing to worry about, however, and Tony's very timely question made things easy for him.

"The rest you know. Mrs. Jay and Mrs. Montgomery were arrested last night, Bellamy's room was searched, and we found there the second typewriter, which he hadn't had time to dispose of, and one of Farmer's shoes. Mrs. Montgomery's cottage produced the other, and also a bloodstained iron bar; a bad mistake, since it was supposed to be in the river.

"The details of the actual murders we can only guess at, of course. Selby was probably stunned in his room, and killed outside, and the body bundled over the wall with the help of a ladder. Incidentally, that must have been a hard job, but not impossible for two people, and I don't suppose for a moment that they used the one in the garage. Its presence would be enough to bear out Peake's 'confession', though. Then Mrs. Montgomery would drive off with him, after pulling out the bars: the fact that we couldn't find any traces of rope fibre doesn't mean much, since some sort of protection, such as a leather coat, would be an obvious precaution to take. But they probably couldn't prevent the bars from crashing against the brickwork, and that's how the new 'hand-hold' was made.

"Prudence Hill was murdered by Mrs. Montgomery, without doubt. The doctor's suggestion about previous knowledge of the girl's habits is probably sound: she was waited for, while Bellamy played skittles. His turn came with Wilson and Betty Trotter—there was a gap in his movements that Dr. Wrench couldn't explain: and later he accounted for Sergeant Lee. It was essential, with regard to all the deaths, that nobody should be able to turn up afterwards to clear Peake's name, and that part went off very satisfactorily. To my way of thinking, the two big mistakes in the whole complicated plan were the presence and behaviour of Mrs. Jay, and the method employed to eliminate the Professor. It was the first, in point of fact, that defeated the second: if she hadn't roused his suspicions he'd probably have drunk his poisoned wine, and we'd all be execrating his memory now."

"But suppose I *had* agreed to her suggestion?" queried Peake. "Wouldn't that have spoilt everything."

"No—why should it have done? Naturally the murders would have stopped, and their authors have escaped as quickly as possible, but Mrs. Jay would have achieved her object.

"From the point of view of detection, the most interesting feature of the case is the way it was possible to build up so complete a hypothetical solution to the mystery almost solely from consideration of Mrs. Jay's presence, history, and character. And then, when the time for checking came, the details fitted: a changed typewriter, a bandaged hand, a game of skittles, a dead girl's stocking that wasn't quite as it should have been. There were half a dozen things that would have baulked me, though: not knowing about Peake's movements on the 7th and 10th from Dr. Wrench; never hearing that Mrs. Montgomery 'disliked' Bellamy, or that Farmer's second pair of shoes were gone, or that he sometimes didn't wear any; not being present at Mrs. Jay's visit.

"There'll be a good case against both the women, I think: it oughtn't to be impossible to establish some financial connection between them. We haven't yet succeeded in locating poor Selby's body, but doubtless it *is* in the river. And I hope," he added, turning to Wrench and Lavinia "that when it is found you'll have a post-mortem done. Mayn't there have been some physiological basis for his trouble—a tumour of the brain or something?"

The girl smiled at him gratefully.

"It's nice of you to think of us like that," she said. "You were going to have that done anyway, though, weren't you, Professor? And Charles knows how much I hope we'll be able to marry. I'd like to be taken somewhere right away for a long time."

"So that's the whole story," remarked Superintendent Dane presently. "It's a marvellous bit of work, Inspector—you make me feel like a Bow-Street runner with flat feet."

"Nonsense: I tell you, I was lucky. I'd like to add a final word about motive, though. All the way through I've spoken of it as affecting Mrs. Jay alone, but of course Bellamy and the other wretch had theirs too: money. To be able to do a deliberate murder at all you've got to have a certain kind of mind, or outlook on life, and there's no doubt that some people do have it. I should imagine that the sort of bribe Mrs. Jay would be likely to offer, anything up to half a million, say, would swamp quite a lot of scruples.

"We'll probably find that both of them have bad records, and heaven only knows how the old woman got in touch with either. There's nothing intrinsically unlikely in the idea that she *could* have done, though. There are all manner of bad eggs going about that most people wouldn't credit unless they met them. I could give you the name and address of a gentleman who lives down the Fulham Road way who follows the same trade to a lesser degree. Unless he's put his price up since his last spell in gaol, for three pounds he'll willingly undertake to knock out any specified person with a knuckle-duster, kick him where it does most damage, and slash his face with a razor-blade if you say the word. If such swine can flourish, what devil couldn't you buy for even twenty thousand?

"The plan, of course, was Mrs. Jay's—and not half bad at that, except for a fatal touch of over-cleverness. She had to butt in herself, and that spoilt everything. The 'confession', though, was quite good enough to take in the average coroner, I think, and even the signature worked out well. There was the Professor's bandage to account for any noticeable difference from the normal. Also, in my opinion, the motive attributed to him was brilliant. He killed Selby because he couldn't cure him: because he suffered from the same complaint."

"Yes," agreed Wrench: "nine times out of ten it *would* have come off, but this was the tenth, with you to stop it."

"But not alone, as I keep saying. You did a great deal of useful work yourself, Doctor, and chance played a far bigger part than I care to think about as far as my reputation goes. This time"—with a look at Dickie "I've definitely been a lucky policeman, if not perhaps quite so talkative as usual."

And, after speaking almost uninterrupted for one hour eleven minutes, he wondered why they all laughed.

THE END

RAMBLE HOUSE's
HARRY STEPHEN KEELER WEBWORK MYSTERIES

(RH) indicates the title is available ONLY in the **RAMBLE HOUSE** edition

The Ace of Spades Murder
The Affair of the Bottled Deuce (RH)
The Amazing Web
The Barking Clock
Behind That Mask
The Book with the Orange Leaves
The Bottle with the Green Wax Seal
The Box from Japan
The Case of the Canny Killer
The Case of the Crazy Corpse (RH)
The Case of the Flying Hands (RH)
The Case of the Ivory Arrow
The Case of the Jeweled Ragpicker
The Case of the Lavender Gripsack
The Case of the Mysterious Moll
The Case of the 16 Beans
The Case of the Transparent Nude (RH)
The Case of the Transposed Legs
The Case of the Two-Headed Idiot (RH)
The Case of the Two Strange Ladies
The Circus Stealers (RH)
Cleopatra's Tears
A Copy of Beowulf (RH)
The Crimson Cube (RH)
The Face of the Man From Saturn
Find the Clock
The Five Silver Buddhas
The 4th King
The Gallows Waits, My Lord! (RH)
The Green Jade Hand
Finger! Finger!
Hangman's Nights (RH)
I, Chameleon (RH)
I Killed Lincoln at 10:13! (RH)
The Iron Ring
The Man Who Changed His Skin (RH)
The Man with the Crimson Box
The Man with the Magic Eardrums
The Man with the Wooden Spectacles
The Marceau Case
The Matilda Hunter Murder
The Monocled Monster
The Murder of London Lew
The Murdered Mathematician
The Mysterious Card (RH)
The Mysterious Ivory Ball of Wong Shing Li (RH)
The Mystery of the Fiddling Cracksman
The Peacock Fan

The Photo of Lady X (RH)
The Portrait of Jirjohn Cobb
Report on Vanessa Hewstone (RH)
Riddle of the Travelling Skull
Riddle of the Wooden Parrakeet (RH)
The Scarlet Mummy (RH)
The Search for X-Y-Z
The Sharkskin Book
Sing Sing Nights
The Six From Nowhere (RH)
The Skull of the Waltzing Clown
The Spectacles of Mr. Cagliostro
Stand By—London Calling!
The Steeltown Strangler
The Stolen Gravestone (RH)
Strange Journey (RH)
The Strange Will
The Straw Hat Murders (RH)
The Street of 1000 Eyes (RH)
Thieves' Nights
Three Novellos (RH)
The Tiger Snake
The Trap (RH)
Vagabond Nights (Defrauded Yeggman)
Vagabond Nights 2 (10 Hours)
The Vanishing Gold Truck
The Voice of the Seven Sparrows
The Washington Square Enigma
When Thief Meets Thief
The White Circle (RH)
The Wonderful Scheme of Mr. Christopher Thorne
X. Jones—of Scotland Yard
Y. Cheung, Business Detective

Keeler Related Works

A To Izzard: A Harry Stephen Keeler Companion by Fender Tucker — Articles and stories about Harry, by Harry, and in his style. Included is a compleat Keeler bibliography.

Wild About Harry: Reviews of Keeler Novels — Edited by Richard Polt & Fender Tucker — 22 reviews of works by Harry Stephen Keeler from *Keeler News.* A perfect introduction to the author.

The Keeler Keyhole Collection: Annotated newsletter rants from Harry Stephen Keeler, edited by Francis M. Nevins

Fakealoo — Pastiches of the style of Harry Stephen Keeler by selected demented members of the HSK Society.

RAMBLE HOUSE's OTHER LOONS

Slammer Days — Two full-length prison memoirs: *Men into Beasts* (1952) by George Sylvester Viereck and *Home Away From Home* (1962) by Jack Woodford

The Organ Reader — A huge compilation of just about everything published in the 1971-1972 radical bay-area newspaper, THE ORGAN.

Old Times' Sake — Short stories by James Reasoner from Mike Shayne Magazine

Beat Books #1 — Two beatnik classics, *A Sea of Thighs* by Ray Kainen and *Village Hipster* by J.X. Williams

Invaders from the Dark — Classic werewolf tale from Greye La Spina

Fatal Accident — Murder by automobile, a 1936 mystery by Cecil M. Wills

The Devil Drives — A prison and lost treasure novel by Virgil Markham

Dr. Odin — Douglas Newton's 1933 potboiler comes back to life.

The Chinese Jar Mystery — Murder in the manor by John Stephen Strange, 1934

The Julius Caesar Murder Case — A classic 1935 re-telling of the assassination by Wallace Irwin

The Contested Earth and Other SF Stories — A never-before published space opera and seven short stories by Jim Harmon.

Freaks and Fantasies — Eerie tales by Tod Robbins, collaborator of Tod Browning on the film FREAKS.

Vixen Scandal — Two sleaze masterpieces from the 60s by Jim Harmon: *Vixen Hollow* and *Celluloid Scandal.*

Maniac Siren — Two more sleaze marvels by Jim Harmon: *The Man Who Made Maniacs* and *Silent Siren*

West Texas War and Other Western Stories — by Gary Lovisi

Marblehead: A Novel of H.P. Lovecraft — A long-lost masterpiece from Richard A. Lupoff. Published for the first time!

The Secret Adventures of Sherlock Holmes — Three Sherlockian pastiches by the Brooklyn author/publisher, Gary Lovisi.

The Universal Holmes — Richard A. Lupoff's 2007 collection of five Holmesian pastiches and a recipe for giant rat stew.

Tales of the Macabre and Ordinary — Modern twisted horror by Chris Mikul, author of the *Bizarrism* series.

The Gold Star Line — Seaboard adventure from L.T. Reade and Robert Eustace.

The Werewolf vs the Vampire Woman — Hard to believe ultraviolence by either Arthur M. Scarm or Arthur M. Scram.

Black Hogan Strikes Again — Australia's Peter Renwick pens a tale of the outback.

Four Joel Townsley Rogers Novels — By the author of *The Red Right Hand: Once In a Red Moon, Lady With the Dice, The Stopped Clock, Never Leave My Bed*

Killing Time — New collection of short novels by Joel Townsley Rogers

Night of Horror — A short story collection of Joel Townsley Rogers

Twenty Norman Berrow Novels — *The Bishop's Sword, Ghost House, Don't Go Out After Dark, Claws of the Cougar, The Smokers of Hashish, The Secret Dancer, Don't Jump Mr. Boland!, The Footprints of Satan, Fingers for Ransom, The Three Tiers of Fantasy, The Spaniard's Thumb, The Eleventh Plague, Words Have Wings, One Thrilling Night, The Lady's in Danger, It Howls at Night, The Terror in the Fog, Oil Under the Window, Murder in the Melody, The Singing Room*

The N. R. De Mexico Novels — Robert Bragg presents *Marijuana Girl, Madman on a Drum, Private Chauffeur* in one volume.

Two Hake Talbot Novels — *Rim of the Pit, The Hangman's Handyman.* Classic locked room mysteries.

Two Alexander Laing Novels — *The Motives of Nicholas Holtz* and *Dr. Scarlett,* stories of medical mayhem and intrigue from the 30s.

Two Wade Wright Novels (and counting) — *Echo of Fear* and *Death At Nostalgia Street*, with more to come!

Four Rupert Penny Novels — *Policeman's Holiday, Policeman's Evidence, Lucky Policeman* and *Sealed Room Murder,* classic impossible mysteries.

Five Jack Mann Novels — Strange murder in the English countryside. *Gees' First Case, Nightmare Farm, Grey Shapes, The Ninth Life, The Glass Too Many.*

Four Max Afford Novels — *Owl of Darkness, Death's Mannikins, Blood on His Hands* and *The Dead Are Blind* by One of Australia's finest novelists.

Five Joseph Shallit Novels — *The Case of the Billion Dollar Body, Lady Don't Die on My Doorstep, Kiss the Killer, Yell Bloody Murder, Take Your Last Look.* One of America's best 50's authors.

The Best of 10-Story Book — edited by Chris Mikul, over 35 stories from the literary magazine Harry Stephen Keeler edited.

A Young Man's Heart — A forgotten early classic by Cornell Woolrich

The Anthony Boucher Chronicles — edited by Francis M. Nevins
Book reviews by Anthony Boucher written for the *San Francisco Chronicle,* 1942 - 1947. Essential and fascinating reading.

Muddled Mind: Complete Works of Ed Wood, Jr. — David Hayes and Hayden Davis deconstruct the life and works of a mad genius.

My First Time: The One Experience You Never Forget — Michael Birchwood — 64 true first-person narratives of how they lost it.

The Incredible Adventures of Rowland Hern — Rousing 1928 impossible crimes by Nicholas Olde.

Don Diablo: Book of a Lost Film — Two-volume treatment of a western by Paul Landres, with diagrams. Intro by Francis M. Nevins.

The Charlie Chaplin Murder Mystery — Movie hijinks by Wes D. Gehring

The Koky Comics — A collection of all of the 1978-1981 Sunday and daily comic strips by Richard O'Brien and Mort Gerberg, in two volumes.

Suzy — Another collection of comic strips from Richard O'Brien and Bob Vojtko

Gamefinger — Incredible 1966 sado-sleaze from Clyde Allison (William Knoles).

Dime Novels: Ramble House's 10-Cent Books — *Knife in the Dark* by Robert Leslie Bellem, *Hot Lead* and *Song of Death* by Ed Earl Repp, *A Hashish House in New York* by H.H. Kane, and five more.

Stakeout on Millennium Drive — Indianapolis Noir — Ian Woollen.

Dope Tales #1 — Two dope-riddled classics; *Dope Runners* by Gerald Grantham and *Death Takes the Joystick* by Phillip Condé.

Dope Tales #2 — Two more narco-classics; *The Invisible Hand* by Rex Dark and *The Smokers of Hashish* by Norman Berrow.

Dope Tales #3 — Two enchanting novels of opium by the master, Sax Rohmer. *Dope* and *The Yellow Claw.*

Tenebrae — Ernest G. Henham's 1898 horror tale brought back.

The Singular Problem of the Stygian House-Boat — Two classic tales by John Kendrick Bangs about the denizens of Hades.

The One After Snelling — Kickass modern noir from Richard O'Brien.

The Sign of the Scorpion — 1935 Edmund Snell tale of oriental evil.

The House of the Vampire — 1907 poetic thriller by George S. Viereck.

An Angel in the Street — Modern hardboiled noir by Peter Genovese.

The Devil's Mistress — Scottish gothic tale by J. W. Brodie-Innes.

The Lord of Terror — 1925 mystery with master-criminal, Fantômas.

The Lady of the Terraces — 1925 adventure by E. Charles Vivian.

My Deadly Angel — 1955 Cold War drama by John Chelton

Prose Bowl — Futuristic satire — Bill Pronzini & Barry N. Malzberg .

Satan's Den Exposed — True crime in Truth or Consequences New Mexico — Award-winning journalism by the Desert Journal.

The Amorous Intrigues & Adventures of Aaron Burr — by Anonymous — Hot historical action.

I Stole $16,000,000 — A true story by cracksman Herbert E. Wilson.

The Black Dark Murders — Vintage 50s college murder yarn by Milt Ozaki, writing as Robert O. Saber.

Sex Slave — Potboiler of lust in the days of Cleopatra — Dion Leclerq.

You'll Die Laughing — Bruce Elliott's 1945 novel of murder at a practical joker's English countryside manor.

The Private Journal & Diary of John H. Surratt — The memoirs of the man who conspired to assassinate President Lincoln.

Dead Man Talks Too Much — Hollywood boozer by Weed Dickenson

Red Light — History of legal prostitution in Shreveport Louisiana by Eric Brock. Includes wonderful photos of the houses and the ladies.

Gadsby — A lipogram (a novel without the letter E). Ernest Vincent Wright's last work, published in 1939 right before his death.

A Snark Selection — Lewis Carroll's *The Hunting of the Snark* with two Snarkian chapters by Harry Stephen Keeler — Illustrated by Gavin L. O'Keefe.

Ripped from the Headlines! — The Jack the Ripper story as told in the newspaper articles in the *New York* and *London Times.*

Geronimo — S. M. Barrett's 1905 autobiography of a noble American.

The Compleat Calhoon — All of Fender Tucker's works: Includes *The Totah Trilogy, Weed, Women and Song* and *Tales from the Tower,* plus a CD of all of his songs.

The Naked Trocar with **The Best Revenge** — Two misdemeanors by Fender Tucker from 2007

Printed in Great Britain
by Amazon

24324404R00118